THE BASEMENT

A GRIPPING PSYCHOLOGICAL THRILLER

ALAN PETERSEN

JOIN ME

Want to be the first to get exclusive insights into my books, hear the latest news, and enjoy sneak peeks and more? Join my newsletter!

It's easy! Just sign up at www.alanpetersen.com/signup

ONE
JANE

THE STEPS CREAKED AS I MADE MY WAY DOWN TO THE basement in the regular spots. But this time, they sounded more menacing than I remembered. Then again, I had been drinking for several hours, so it might have been the vodka messing with my head.

My hand gripped the weathered wooden railing. Its surface felt rough and splintered beneath my fingers as I tried to steady myself. I stopped halfway down and stood there, feeling woozy, and looking down into the darkness below. One thought flitted across my mind as I waited there: *let go*. I tried to ignore the dark whisper of tempting fate.

My survival instinct, however faint, held me back from giving in to my dark thoughts. Besides, it might not have been enough, anyway. With my luck, I'd end up with a feeding tube in some convalescent home, so I continued down the steps and into the basement where the air was cold and thick with the scent of damp and neglect, the atmosphere which clung to your skin and settled in your lungs.

I flicked on the light switch. Fluorescent lighting flickered for a moment until it finally bathed the basement in an off-white weak light over a lifetime of memories stuffed in cardboard and plastic storage boxes that cluttered the floor. My heart drummed a frantic rhythm, a stark contrast to the eerie stillness that enveloped me down there.

"What do you want?" The words slipped out, barely a whisper, as if speaking them louder might conjure something sinister from the shadows. Only silence greeted me, a heavy, suffocating blanket that seemed almost tangible in its presence.

I made my way towards the utility room, navigating through the cluttered floor. The door to the room was ajar. I stepped inside. Amidst the mundane—the root cellar door, the hum of the chest freezer, the drip of a leaky faucet—sat an anomaly. A blue accordion folder. I had placed it on top of the dryer days ago, but I couldn't go through it. It sat there watching me, casting its judgment.

I glanced at the meat freezer next to it. "What do you want from me?" I asked, but there was no response. With trembling hands, I reached for the box, its contents a Pandora's box of pain and regret. I grabbed the folder and sat down on the floor with my legs crossed.

I carefully spread it open. A face from the past confronted me. A stack of missing child flyers, each one a testament to a moment frozen in time, to a pain that had never dulled. They were all the same boy. His face tilted to the left, an awkward crooked smile, and wide brown eyes stared back at me, the boy frozen in time. Each flyer was from a different year. One for each year since he had gone missing. A stack of fifteen flyers, with slightly different verbiage, but the same picture of the same boy looked back at me as I shuffled through them. Tears broke free, tracing paths down my cheeks as I cradled the flyers close to my chest.

This basement, this house, had borne witness to too much. The weight of the past, of decisions made and lives altered, bore down on me with a force I could no longer withstand.

"No more," I whispered into the void. A vow to do what I should have done long ago. To make this right.

"The lies end tonight," I said out loud to myself. With a resolve I hadn't felt in years, I rose, the flyers in hand, a plan forming in my mind. A plan to end the cycle, to break free from the chains of the past. I placed the flyers back in their pouch.

As I turned to leave, I heard a sound. A soft, nearly imperceptible shuffle froze me in my tracks. My breath hitched. My heart stalled. In the room's corner, just beyond the reach of the flickering light, something moved.

TWO
CASSIE

Three Days Later

There I was, stranded in the purgatory of airport delays, surrounded by a sea of disgruntled faces, each absorbed in their private world of glowing screens and fleeting distractions. I squeezed between an indifferent youth wearing chunky wireless headphones lost in his digital bubble and a middle-aged woman engrossed in her e-reader, their ignorance of my presence a small mercy in this crowded space. The last thing I wanted to do was chat with strangers.

The incessant jingle of slot machines, a bizarre symphony that's become the backdrop of my life in Las Vegas, failed to distract me from the gnawing sense that I shouldn't be taking this trip.

I ignored it, and I sat there for a while, waiting for an update from the airline.

The sounds of slot machines at the airport were still surreal, even though I'd been living in Las Vegas for almost two years.

If there was one thing Las Vegas did well, it was making it easy to gamble, no matter where you are. Slot machines at

the airport? Check. The convenience store? Check. Gas station? Check. They made it easy to churn through your hard-earned money in Las Vegas.

The crackle of the intercom broke through my reverie. They were starting to board, a call to action that propelled me towards the gate, only to be reminded of my place at the end of the boarding queue. Resigned, I returned to the embrace of the airport's unforgiving seats. I tried to find the sweet spot, but I couldn't find it. You would have thought since, more than likely, passengers would spend a lot of time on those chairs, the powers that be at the airport would try to make them a little more bearable to sit on, waiting for delayed flights.

I shouldn't complain. At least I would be flying on a decent airline for a change. On my budget, I would have to fly on one of those discount airlines or take the Greyhound Bus.

But on this trip, I was flying Delta. Comfort Plus, no less. So, I'd have a bit more legroom. I couldn't afford the pricey ticket on my phone. I sure as hell couldn't afford more legroom. It was a gift from my brother, Brent Walsh.

When he offered it to me last night, I hesitated. I didn't have the best relationship with my older brother.

It was why I hadn't been back home in eight years. Come to think of it, since I left Big Plaine at seventeen, I'd only been back three times in those thirteen years. I basically wrote off my brother and mother long ago. I sure wasn't planning to visit my hometown anytime soon, if ever. But Mother died. I should be there for her funeral. At least that's what Brent kept telling me. He wants me there.

The timing was good. Sounds cold, since Mother had just died, but I'd just gotten fired from my latest server job a few days before.

Note to self: next job, don't hit the restaurant's booze supply hard, especially not during a shift. Management didn't take too kindly to that.

Before the call from Brent, I was in the midst of my newfound jobless freedom. I sought solace in the company of my steadfast companions, Jack Daniels and Diet Coke.

I tried to ignore my need for a job with a brief break. A staycation before hitting the strip in search of work.

I couldn't take too much time off, since without a steady paycheck, I couldn't afford my JD and coke. And I sure as hell wouldn't be able to afford rent.

So, my self-imposed sabbatical had only lasted two days. I woke up the day before hung over, but I cleaned up, and then I hit the Strip, looking for a new waitressing or bartending job.

I preferred bartending because I dealt with fewer asshole customers behind the bar, but serving paid much better, especially if I dolled up and put on that push-up bra. It was obnoxious, but I had to play the hand I'd been dealt and doing that would double, even triple my tips.

After two hours walking the strip, I had filled out three job applications when my phone rang. I excitedly looked at the caller ID, thinking I had already nailed a new job but was surprised to see the 612 area code flashing back at me. It was my brother. I let it go to voicemail. Instantly he called again, and once again I let it ring out to voicemail. A minute later a text message from him:

> Pick up, please.

> Have to tell you something.

> Very important.

> Serious!

I ignored his string of text messages as well. I leaned back on the railing in front of the Bellagio water fountain. The water works were between shows, so there wasn't much interest from the tourists meandering down the sidewalk. Two faux showgirls in skimpy outfits were walking in unison, trying to lure tourists to pose for a picture with them, to then hit them up for payment for the privilege of that photograph, to the dismay of tourists. Hey, those girls have to make a living and there was nothing free in Las Vegas.

I was halfway thinking I should ask the showgirls about a job, in case things get desperate, when my phone buzzed. Another text from Brent. Okay, now he had my full attention. What the hell was going on?

I looked at the text, and it was just a website link. I could see from the phone preview that it was a link to an obituary.

I clicked on it, and it was an obituary. Mother's obit.

I must admit, that took me aback. I wasn't expecting it. My mother wasn't that old. Sixty-two. It wasn't until you're well into your mid-seventies that people didn't act as surprised when you die. At sixty-two years, many folks would say it was too soon.

Mother didn't have any illness that I knew about. Not that we were close enough for me to know if she'd been sick this past year.

We had only talked a few times a year over the phone. Brief calls. Proof of life. I guess that's a moot point now.

I wasn't sure how to process her death right there on the Strip.

I didn't break down in tears. In all honesty, I didn't really like my mother. I know it was a terrible thing to say about the woman that gave birth to me. But it was how I felt.

There was more to being a mother than giving birth. Sure, it hurts like hell, but that was the simple part. Raising kids was the toughest part.

It wasn't always bad between us, but when it turned bad, it went to shit, fast.

It was why I left home days after graduating high school. I didn't play sports, and I didn't have the grades or money for college, so I joined the military. Happy to give them years of my life to get me far away from Minnesota and more importantly, my family.

I thought back to the last time I saw her. Four or five years ago. That's right. I was living in San Francisco then. Mother came out for a visit. Not that I asked her to come. She just did. And I think the main reason she came out was because she always wanted to visit California.

Mother's visit didn't change things between us. But she had a great time visiting Alcatraz, The Wharf, riding the cable car up Powell, and walking down Lombard Street.

I hadn't seen her since, and now she was dead. How the hell did she die? I read the obit.

Jane Walsh, 62, of Big Plaine, Minnesota passed away on April 16, 2019, at her home.

Mass of Christian Burial will be Saturday, April 20, 2019 at 10:30 a.m. at St. Agnes Catholic Church in Big Plaine. Friends may greet the family from 4-7 p.m. at St. Agnes Catholic Church on Friday, April 19, 2019, with a parish rosary being recited at 4 p.m. and continue one hour prior to the funeral liturgy.

Burial will be at Holy Cross Catholic Cemetery, Big Plaine.

Jane was born Feb. 3, 1957, in Wadena,

Minnesota. She moved to Big Plaine with her parents when she was five years old. She graduated from Big Plaine High School in 1975. She received a degree in education from Winona State University, then returned to Big Plaine, where she worked in education at the Big Plaine high School for over twenty years.

Jane was preceded in death by her parents and husband. She is survived by her children, Dr. Brent (Jillian) Walsh, MD, Minnetonka, and Cassie Walsh, Las Vegas, Nevada. And her three beloved grandchildren.

Memorials may be directed to St. Agnes Catholic Church in Big Plaine.

There wasn't much information on there about what happened to her. Just that she was dead and here is the information on the funeral.

I stayed there in front of the Bellagio until the fountain show came to life with streams of water dancing around elegantly, synchronized to a Frank Sinatra tune as folks stopped in their track to watch the spectacle.

My job search would be on hold for a bit longer. I made my way back to my tiny studio apartment, two miles off the strip, and I sank into my couch, finishing the last of my Jack Daniels as I doom-scrolled Netflix. My neighbors were arguing again. It was the same argument as usual. Either she was accusing him of cheating or he was accusing her of the same. I wonder if they switch it around. Monday, Wednesdays, and Saturdays, you accuse me of cheating. Tuesdays, Thursdays, and Fridays, it was my turn. Sunday was their day of rest.

I went back to my phone, and I read the obit again. Nothing changed, of course. What was I expecting? One of those living books from Harry Potter?

"Fuck it," I said out loud. It was just me in my apartment, even though the thin walls made it feel like my neighbors were my roommates.

I hit the button to call my brother back. He picked up after the first ring.

———

THAT WAS THE DAY BEFORE. By the next morning, he had my ticket and had sent my boarding pass to my Apple wallet. I still couldn't believe it. Mother was gone, and I was going back to Minnesota for the first time in eight years for her funeral.

I wouldn't be going if it weren't for my brother paying for my airfare. I wasn't a leech. He was always offering to help me, financially, but I turned him down. I didn't want his pity-money, even though it would come in handy. But this was different. I should be there, no matter how badly I wanted to skip it.

And I couldn't help thinking about Mother's estate. She wasn't rich like my brother. There was no such thing as a rich public school teacher, unless they were born rich or married rich, and felt guilty about it, so what better way to give back than teach at some broke ass public school with dreams of being Michelle Pfeiffer in Dangerous Minds.

But there was the house, and she must have had a little something squirreled away in the bank. She didn't need it anymore. I sure as hell did. I was two months away from not having rent for my crappy studio apartment. So, if I could go back with my inheritance — I laughed at calling it that,

but that was what it would be — maybe it would be enough to give me some breathing room until I find my next waitressing job.

I asked Brent how Mother died. And I was shocked.

"She killed herself," he told me over the phone.

I never thought she would do that. Especially since she had become reacquainted with God and the Catholic Church for the last few years — another reason for us drifting even further apart. The last thing I wanted to hear was her talking to me about religion, after what she had done back when I was a kid.

I was rusty on my religious studies, but as I recall, taking yourself deep was a big no-no with the powers that be at the Vatican. Yet, my brother somehow finagled to get her a full Catholic funeral and burial. Well, he was rich, so, as usual, the rules that apply to the rest of us could be waved bye-bye by his ilk: rich, white, and male.

I was so lost in thought that by the time I looked around me, I noticed just about everyone had boarded the plane.

Shit. I got up and ran up to the check-in person at the counter. He smiled at me as I waved my cell phone with my boarding pass at the scanner, and it beeped.

"Welcome aboard, Ms. Walsh," he said, all friendly. I gave him a half smile as I blew hair strands out of my face, and I went down that long metal tube into the plane.

My seat was in the aisle. My brother tried hard to win me back. He remembered how I got all panicky in the middle seat or by the window. I didn't think I was truly claustrophobic, but then again, I'd never discussed it with a doctor. But when I was shoved into a tight space, I felt like a cornered wild animal ready to claw myself to freedom in the form of a panic attack.

I settled in. There was some preppy douche sitting next to me. He smiled widely at me with ultra-white teeth.

Not a chance, bro, I thought as I shoved my earbuds in and listened to some music. I got into a Minnesota state of mind with a mix of The Replacement, The Suburbs, Soul Asylum, and Prince. As the music kicked in, the plane pulled away from the tarmac. I figured it wouldn't be long before I could order a drink. I needed it.

THREE
BRENT

I was anxious. Cassie was returning. I was aware she wanted no contact with me, just as she desired no contact with our mother before her passing. However, she was my sister. I couldn't let her just cut me out of her life. I didn't know how things became so strained. Well, that's not really true, I did know, but it'd been a long time since we were kids. How could she continue to harbor such resentment and animosity? What's past is past. What's been done could not be undone. So why bother devoting even a second thinking about the past? I glanced at the flight tracking app on my phone. The plane was finally up in the air after the delay.

"She's en route," I informed my spouse, Jillian, who merely gazed at me and sulked. She despised my sister. And I got it. She only perceived matters from my perspective. I was the one attempting to connect with Cassie through text messages, emails, via social media private messages, and she disregarded them all. I mailed her our family's holiday card, which was a feat since she relocated frequently. And Cassie did nothing to reciprocate. She never phoned or texted me.

She had essentially cut herself off from me, and Mom, for the past several years. We were the only family she had, and now, it was just me. So, I had to reach out to her to let her know about Mom's passing and to let her know she should be there for the funeral, regardless of the past.

But Jillian didn't understand. Cassie had endured a challenging existence and barely scraped by. I had not. I lived in a multi-million-dollar home on Lake Minnetonka, and I had a prosperous medical practice. If I could assist my sister in her chaotic life, why not? My wife, bless her, was unaware of what Cassie experienced when she was younger. If she was, perhaps she would be more understanding when it came to Cassie. But all I got from Jillian was a scowl.

"Come on, babe. She's my sister. I can't just let her cut me out of her life without putting up a fight. I'm just surprised she agreed to come home."

"I'm not," Jillian said coldly. "You paid for her damn ticket. She's likely eager to see what funds she can squeeze from your mother's estate."

Estate? That caused me to chuckle aloud. "What estate? A dilapidated old house in Big Plaine. What's that worth? Fifty thousand? If that. I wouldn't be surprised if Mom's bank account and pension fund have less than twenty grand."

"That would be a windfall for your sister. It would keep her nice and drunk for months."

I exhaled. "Maybe it can help her finally get her life together," I said, even though, deep inside, I knew that was a long shot.

"Doubtful," Jillian said. The contempt in her tone for my sister was sharp and bitter.

Apart from when it pertained to my sister, my wife truly was a darling. At nineteen, she was a Princess Kay of the Milky Way for Le Sueur County. Recognized with a famous butter sculpture of her image and the whole nine yards at the State Fair. She was compassionate with a generous spirit. Very involved in several charities. Even volunteered at the food shelter in Minneapolis during the holidays. But she had no room for charity anymore for Cassie. Too many bridges burned between them. And she knew the effect Cassie's self-imposed estrangement from the family had on me. So, I understood. Jillian disliked seeing me get hurt like that. But still. I wish she would make a bit more effort to get along on the infrequent occasions we saw her.

It wasn't as if my sister was always there or hitting me up for money —I'd offered to assist her financially, repeatedly. But she always declined. She simply didn't want to be a part of my life, which I won't accept. We went through a great deal together when we were children.

But for now, I couldn't fret about Jillian and Cassie's relationship. I had to first reestablish my relationship with my sister. And I knew this would be a formidable task. I only had a few days to bury my mother, sort out her estate, and reconnect with my sister, and I knew she was going to make it difficult. Like refusing to stay at my house. I had a charming mother-in-law cottage out back. I know it would be more spacious than any of the dingy studio apartments she usually rented. So, I suggested the only hotel in Big Plaine.

"I can get you a room at the Festival Express."

"No, that's fine."

"Where are you going to stay, then?"

"I'll just stay at Mother's."

Well, that shocked me. I knew how much Cassie loathed our childhood home. All those horrific memories.

"Really?"

"Is that an issue?" she said, sounding defensive.

"No, of course not. It's your place now, as much as mine."

"I'm all set then."

"You can also use Mom's car. It's a brand-new Subaru Forester. I purchased it for her last year, and she hardly drove it."

"Aren't you the prodigal son?" Cassie said. Her voice was sharp and acerbic. Boy, my sister despises me. But I didn't let it faze me. It was like an abused animal. It will not trust you and might even bite you. But that was just because life had not been kind to it. And God knows life hadn't been kind to Cassie.

"I'm just saying. You'll have a car to get around is all. Not much to do in Big Plaine, as I'm sure you recall. So, you can head up to the Twin Cities if you get bored."

"Swell. Look, I have to go," Cassie said.

"Okay. See you..." She hung up before I could complete my sentence. I looked at the phone and exhaled.

"I don't know why you try so hard with her," Jillian said, startling me. I did not know she was behind me, listening in.

"She's my sister," I said, sounding like a broken record.

The way she talked to me and hung up did hurt me. I was just trying to help her. But didn't want Jillian to see that. So, I smiled, and gave her a kiss.

I did find our situation interesting. I knew what happened to her. I was there. It happened to me too. But I could move on with my life. Even after what occurred, I had a blast in high school playing football, hockey, and baseball. I was Prom King. Dated the most attractive girls in school.

Had even more fun when I moved out of Big Plaine with a full-ride scholarship to the University of Chicago. Then it was off to the School of Medicine at Johns Hopkins University. After putting my time in General Surgery residency training, followed by Plastic Surgery residency. I returned to Minnesota and now had a thriving private practice. I was able to move on from what happened when we were kids. Why couldn't Cassie?

That question had fascinated me for many years now. So maybe now I could figure out why I rose to the top of life, while she sank to the bottom.

FOUR
CASSIE

THE PLANE TOUCHED DOWN AT THE MINNEAPOLIS-ST. Paul airport, a misnomer as it wasn't actually in either city. But that didn't matter. I had arrived. I felt nervous butterflies fluttering in my stomach, which I could also attribute to the four Jack and Cokes I drank during the three-hour flight. The flight attendant's disapproving look when I requested a fourth drink made me think he was worried I'd cause trouble. That I would end up like one of those unruly passengers making a fool of themselves in a viral video on social media.

But he didn't have to worry about me. I had no intention of returning to jail. Once was more than enough, thank you very much. And I had no plans on becoming fodder for netizens.

The judgmental flight attendant and even the preppy creep next to me, from whom I rejected several attempts to start a conversation, shot me doubtful looks, seeing a scrawny five-foot-five-inch, 110-pound blond woman drinking those drinks, but they didn't know about the tolerance I had developed over the past few years. Those four drinks didn't affect me much. If anything, they took the edge off, calmed me down.

The plane landed without incident. I filed off the aircraft. I was sandwiched between fellow passengers. Memories of the chow line in the army and prison flooded my mind. The concerned flight attendant bid us farewell with a wave. I offered him a smile, as to say, see, I wasn't trouble, but he scowled back at me. Oh, well.

My brother insisted on picking me up and driving me to Big Plaine. I had hesitated at the idea, but as usual, money was tight, especially now that I was unemployed. An Uber from the airport to Big Plaine would set me back over fifty bucks. A steep price I really couldn't afford. How had my life come to this? At thirty years old, a fifty-dollar Uber ride was enough to throw my fragile financial situation into full meltdown mode, considering that the rent for my small studio apartment would be due soon.

I desperately hoped I could leave Big Plaine with some funds in my bank account. While Mother wasn't wealthy by any means, she must have paid off her house long ago. She was always frugal. Unless she had turned into a degenerate gambler frequenting the nearby Native American-owned casinos or fell for some Nigerian email scam, that house had to be debt-free. Brent and his wife wouldn't want it, and I certainly had no interest in living there or in keeping it. A quick sale was what I was hoping for. If the new owner demolished it, I might even show up to witness its destruction and celebrate. It held all the charm of *The Amityville Horror* house to me. But if I could walk away from it with $20,000 in my bank account, I would be thrilled. Some compensation for the pain and suffering I endured there.

Anyway, Brent lived close to the airport in the ritzy neighborhood of Minnetonka. Near or on the lake. I couldn't remember. I'd never been to his place, even though he invites me every Fourth of July, Thanksgiving, and Christmas. He offered to drive me down to Mother's house, a forty-mile journey from the airport. Considering my financial predicament, I reluctantly accepted.

Of course, he tried to convince me to stay with him and his picture-perfect family, mentioning the mother-in-law cottage he had built in his backyard. "You'll have complete privacy," he insisted. But how much privacy could I truly have when the damn cottage was in his backyard? Sure, his property was probably enormous. Despite that, I declined.

He persisted, attempting to sway me with tales of how my two nephews hardly knew me. I thought I was doing those kids a favor by staying out of their lives. Besides, getting along with his wife was like a confrontation between a honey badger and a snake. The always impeccably groomed former beauty queen could turn nasty at the slightest provocation, and I seemed to provoke her simply by existing. I chuckled to myself, picturing the scenario: Jillian was the honey badger—cute and harmless on the surface, but capable of tearing into a venomous snake for a meal without hesitation. And I would be the snake. It seemed fitting.

I took a deep breath as I prepared myself for what lay ahead beyond the passenger section of the airport. My rich brother and then Big Plaine and all the awful memories that conjured.

I traveled light. All I had with me was my backpack and small carry-on suitcase, so it didn't take me long to make it on to the terminal. I stopped to pee and brush my teeth. Brent knew I was a drunk, but I didn't want him to smell the Jack on me. I looked at my face in the mirror. Something I'd tried to avoid doing these past few years. My strawberry blond hair was down to my shoulders. It looked rough. Straggly. Like I just woke up. I looked pale. I'd always been fair-skinned — I was a Minnesotan with all Irish heritage, after all. But I looked paler than usual. Sickly. I lived out in the desert, but I was usually indoors, working or drinking in a bar somewhere in Vegas. I was probably dealing with some sort of sunshine deficiency even though in the last few years I'd been living in California and Nevada. The girl in the mirror told me I looked like shit. What have you done with your life? I told her to fuck off. I added some blush to my cheeks to give them some color. And I added some mascara. And applied lip balm to my dry lips. I tried to brush my hair, but it was too painful to deal with the tangles. I was a mess, so I gave up.

I took a life lesson from that modern philosopher, Popeye, who said: *I Yam What I Yam.*

I shoved a few Tic Tacs into my mouth, spritzed some perfume on me, and headed back to the terminal.

I walked out to the arrival area where non-passengers are allowed to wait for the arriving passengers. And I saw him standing there. He smiled. Perfect white teeth. He also had strawberry blond hair, but it was darker than mine. I wondered if he dyed it. Whatever. He dressed impeccably. That hadn't changed since the last time I saw him.

Even though he was born and raised in the same Podunk town as I was, he exuded an air of money and privilege. His high-society, frat-boy style was clear in his crisp white button-up shirt under a periwinkle and gray sweater, dark blazer, and khaki pants. I doubted the posh social circle he ran in now knew that he came from humble beginnings in the small, rural town of Big Plaine. I couldn't help but wonder if he had left his past behind or if it was still a part of him, lurking just beneath the surface. Affecting him like it did me. If what happened that night all those years ago affected him like it had me, he did not show an iota of concern.

We made eye contact, and he waved at me. What he was wearing was probably worth more than everything I had shoved into my suitcase, which was most of the clothing I owned.

I saw the shiny big watch on his wrist. Looks fancy. Probably a Rolex or a Patek Philippe which cost more than what I'd made in the past five years waitressing. Rich guys seem to be into expensive watches. See it all the time in Las Vegas.

How could he have soared so high and I had sunk so low? We both went through the same shitty childhood in that house. Going through what happened in that basement. I let that consume me. Looks like he used it to propel him forward. He lived in an enormous house on the lake. I was weeks away from being homeless. I couldn't help but feel bitterness as my good-looking, perfectly coiffed brother walked toward me. He knew better than to hug me. So, we awkwardly said hello.

"Looking good, sis," he said.

I pursed my lips. *What a fucking liar.*

FIVE

BRENT

I WAS NERVOUS AND EXCITED TO SEE MY SISTER. IT'D been four years since I last saw her in person. She had just moved down to Las Vegas from San Francisco. I was there for a conference. I was staying in the Waldorf Astoria, and we met in the lobby. She declined my invite for dinner as I knew she would. I offered to stay for a few days after the conference so we could catch up properly. She basically told me not to bother. I hadn't seen her since, and we had hardly talked since then, either.

I realized, as I waited for her to pop out of the passenger area of the terminal, that I'd probably spent about ten days with my sister since I went off to college at age eighteen. She was sixteen then. The next year, when she turned seventeen, she wanted to join the army. Being under eighteen, she needed parental consent. Dad had long been dead. Mom asked me about it. I told her not to sign. Have her wait another year until she was eighteen when she no longer needed Mom's permission. I hoped by then she would pull herself together and stop with the teen angst, the rabble rousing and military talk. Even with her terrible grades and many detention slips and suspensions from High School, she could probably still get into a community college somewhere, so she could work on her grades in order to transfer to one of the state colleges like in Winona, Mankato, or St. Cloud, some place like that. But Cassie said she would run away from home until she was of age to sign. So, Mom gave in and signed the papers. "Maybe the army will do her some good," Mom had told me. Fine and dandy during peacetime, but with wars raging in Afghanistan and Iraq, I worried about my little sister ending up there. But off she went to basic training.

I was pleasantly surprised that she seemed to do well in the army. All that structure and being told what to do, what to wear, where to stand, was good for her. She stopped partying nonstop. She ended up in Iraq during the troop surge of 2007, but luckily, she made it back stateside unhurt, physically, at least. There was a ban on women in combat, which made her angry, as she had the same training as any male soldier. I agreed in principle, but I was relieved that my sister was banned from combat. By the time the army lifted that ban in 2015, Cassie had been out of the army for years.

By then, Cassie had cut me and Mom from her life. To that day, I didn't know what Cassie did in the army. Just that it was in logistics and that she ended her enlistment with the rank of sergeant, which seemed impressive for a twenty-one-year-old. I wondered if she left the army on her own or if she was forced out, so I paid fifty bucks to use one of those sites to snoop through people's public records. And to my surprise and pride, I discovered that she had been honorably discharged. And that her job in the army was a Medical Logistics Specialist. That sounded good. I was hopeful she could parlay that into an administrator type job in a civilian hospital. But nothing came out of it. She was now a thirty-year-old waitress who seemed to move from place to place just about every other year. Atlanta, Austin, Los Angeles, San Francisco, and now Las Vegas. There might have been another location in between that I didn't know about. I know she did time at the women's prison in Chowchilla, California. Not that she shared any of that with me. Once again, I had to snoop around online to see how my sister was doing, since she never picked up when I called and rarely replied to my text messages and emails. And for being part of the Millennial Generation, she barely had a social media presence. No Facebook, Insta, or Twitter. It was as if she just wanted to disappear into thin air.

I offered her financial help many times, much to my wife's chagrin. Even offered to pay to send her to medical assistant school where I would have a job for her waiting at my practice, but she turned that down too. That really set off Jillian. But let's be honest, I was in a no-win situation when I made Cassie that offer. Jillian would have been furious at me for spending all that money on my sister, who wouldn't even be grateful — Jillian assumed — had Cassie accepted my offer. Or, like what actually happened, she rebuffed me, rudely. Jillian was angry that my sister turned me down without even much of a thank you for offering or even explaining why she didn't want my help. She said, "not interested," and then ghosted me even harder than before.

"She just wants nothing to do with you," Jillian kept reminding me. My wife thought she was just an ungrateful alcoholic, lost soul. It was what she was. "She's probably a meth head," Jillian had said on more than one occasion.

I didn't know if Cassie had a drug addiction, but I knew she drank. A lot. She started hitting the booze hard at sixteen. Soon after that day down in Mom's basement. My jaunt down memory lane was interrupted when I saw Cassie, looking haggard and with disheveled hair, walking toward me. I forced a smile. All the way from back there, I could tell she looked awful. But I smiled wider and started waving toward her as she made her way out of the restricted area of the terminal. She gave me a half shrug and a head bob. She shuffled toward me. And damn, she looked like shit. Like a transient.

She was beautiful, but no one else around her paid attention to the woman with the pale face and unkempt appearance walking toward them.

She was dressed in this chaotic, uncoordinated outfit that screamed second-hand and I've given up on life. I mean, seriously. A white novelty T-shirt emblazoned with Las Vegas. Not even a tourist would wear that, and she lived there. Purple track pants with brown stripes down the side. And white platform sandals with thick soles.

Where did she ever find such an abomination of eclectic crap to wear? Must have been at the discount bin in a Goodwill store.

And yet, I saw her look at me with such contempt. Or was it hate? I didn't know, but then again, I also looked at her with judgment. I suddenly felt stupid for wearing my $50,000 Patek Philippe watch to pick up my barely not homeless sister.

As we got close enough to hug, I thought about embracing her, but I knew she'd pull away. So, we sort of stood there looking at each other awkwardly, like I was a limo driver holding up a sign to drive a stranger to their hotel.

"Looking good, sis," I told her. *I am such a fucking liar.*

SIX
CASSIE

THE DRIVE DOWN TO BIG PLAINE FROM THE AIRPORT was painfully awkward. Now that Mother was gone, he was my only family member. And the only person left on this crappy planet to know what happened in the basement.

I felt a panic attack coming on, but I looked out the window and did my breathing exercise as quietly as possible.

I looked around Brent's car. It was a Mercedes Benz G-CLASS SUV. Clean and shiny. Meticulously clean. Freakishly clean, in my opinion. Even as a young kid, Brent was always a clean freak. OCD for real, that boy. It amazed me that someone so neat, so obsessed with cleanliness made a living tucking tummies, sucking out fat, slicing noses, and shoving silicon bags into women's chests. The thought of it made me feel queasy. Then again, in my line of work, I dealt with dirty dishes, filthy tables, and slimeball customers. I swear the people visiting Las Vegas were the worst. Like pigs at the trough when they're down there.

I couldn't count the times I'd had sticky soda, hot coffee, and plates of mushy food spilled on me during my waitressing career. And customers had sneezed, coughed, and vomited on me. Not on purpose, but still. And then the creeps leering at me. Licking their lips like I was a bowl of hot chili waiting to be slurped down. Customers had asked me out. And I'd had my ass grabbed more times than I could count. And I drove an eleven-year-old Toyota Corolla and lived in a studio apartment I could barely afford. I looked around my brother's luxury car. It was hard to believe we were related.

"Nice car, Brent. How much does it cost?" I knew it was a rude and personal question, but hey, as he always said, we're family.

I saw him blush.

"A lot," he said.

"Just tell me. I'll google it later, anyway."

"Why? You think of buying one?"

"This baby is like a thousand times out of my barely running junker price range."

"I wish you would let me help you, Cassie."

There he goes. As usual. So hell-bent on trying to save me. His own personal charity case.

"I told you. No thanks. Don't need your handouts, big brother."

"It's not a handout, Cass. Just a brother helping his sister out. I can afford it."

"I'm sure you can. Besides. You've done plenty for me already. Remember?" I felt the bile bubbling in my throat when I said that. Thinking back to that basement. It was mean. He was just offering to help me financially. And he sure as hell could afford it. But I refused to be even more in debt to him.

He said nothing. He knew what I meant. After about

five minutes of silence between us, Brent spoke up: "One hundred and eighty thousand dollars."

I looked at him, confused. "Huh?"

"That's how much this car cost. And my watch you were looking at. It cost about fifty grand. The clothing I'm wearing – around two thousand dollars when you add it all up. My underwear are two-hundred-dollar Balenciaga boxer briefs."

I looked at him and whistled. "Glad things have worked out for you, Brent." I even kind of meant it. I let what happened in the basement ruin my life. Why begrudge it didn't do the same to him? No need for my actions to bring us both down.

We actually shared a laugh after that.

I looked out the window as the urban landscape of the Twin Cities melted away and gave way to the rural vastness of Nyborg County. It felt surreal being back in Minnesota. At least it was late April, so I wouldn't be freezing my ass off. If Mother would have died in January, I wouldn't have come. I was done with days of sub-zero temperatures. Thank you very much. I thought of Mother. I still couldn't believe she was dead. I changed the subject.

"How did she do it?"

Brent looked at me.

"Mom?"

I nodded. A strand of frizzled hair fell into my face, reminding me I needed to wash my hair, not only to deal with the tangle mess atop my head, but I had caught a whiff of my hair smelling bad and since it smelled bad to me, I could only imagine what my Paco Rabanne smelling brother must have thought. I used my right hand to tuck it behind my ear. Brent had told me she killed herself, but not how.

"She hanged herself."

"No shit?"

Brent nodded.

The thought of ending things that way had crept into my head plenty of times over the years. Especially when I'd been hammered off my gourd. Luckily, I usually passed out before I could do something stupid that I couldn't take back. My life was shitty, but I guess I was in no rush to cut it short. I never thought Mother would do that, especially not that way. Pills or carbon monoxide, maybe. But that? I cringed. But I supposed dead is dead, and it didn't matter how in the end.

"Where?"

"In the basement," Brent said.

That made me feel ill. Like my blood pressure dropped. It probably did. Of course, she would do it down there. I felt a chill. I could tell Brent was looking over at me. He was alternating between looking at the road and back at me as I wrapped my arms around my stomach and looked out the window as we kept heading down Highway 169.

After a few minutes of me staring out the window in silence, Brent spoke once again.

"What do you think about what I told you? About Mom ending things in the basement?"

"It doesn't matter what I think," I said without turning my head around, still looking out the window. I'd forgotten how flat Minnesota was. Like a freaking pancake.

"Why do you think she did it?" I asked Brent since he was mister fifty questions with me all the time.

Brent drove, shrugging.

"Maybe she felt guilty," I said when he didn't answer my question.

Brent shook his head. "Mom had nothing to feel guilty about," he said, sounding angry.

"Oh, really?" I said, laying the sarcasm thick.

"Yes, really. Neither do I or you, since I'm sure you do."

We had made a pact to never talk about what happened in the basement. This was as close as we'd come to breaking our pact without getting into the specifics in fifteen years.

"About three-quarters of suicides occur in the home. Basement and garages are popular choices if you're going to hang yourself," Brent said, sounding clinical, like the detached doctor he was.

"Jesus, Brent."

"You asked."

He was right. I did. And I suppose it makes sense. In Minnesota, every house had a basement, unlike Nevada and California, where basements were a rarity. I was no shrink, but maybe that's why I gravitated out west. No damn basements.

"Look, Cass, they diagnosed Mom with Parkinson's last year."

"Why didn't you guys tell me?" I said, actually feeling hurt for not being told about this.

"You would have cared?"

Ouch. But I guess I deserved that.

"Sorry, Cass. Look, you're way out west. Nothing you could do about it."

"Were her symptoms getting worse?"

"Yes. Things were deteriorating fast for these past few months. She was having problems with balance, walking, and swallowing, which is why she probably did what she did," Brent said.

"She never mentioned it to me. And she didn't sound like she was struggling the last time we spoke on the phone."

"You come to that conclusion after what? A handful of two-minute calls you've had with her the past couple of years?"

I said nothing. Because again, he was right. What the hell did I know about anything there anymore? I just wanted to get through the funeral, go through the estate stuff as fast as possible, and hopefully I'd be back in Las Vegas in a few days.

From the highway, I saw the one and only exit sign for Big Plaine. One thing was for sure. Once this was over, I'd certainly never be coming back to this fucking town.

SEVEN
CASSIE

Brent exited off the highway. The town of Big Plaine sat about a mile from the exit ramp. I looked around. As much as I dreaded being back there, I felt this oddly comforting feeling about coming back. I mostly only had terrible memories of my time growing up there, but they were not all bad. Where you grew up stays deep inside you, even if you hate it and tried to run away from it, your hometown still clung to you. So, I couldn't help but feel a little nostalgic about the familiarity of it all.

Big Plaine rested in the fertile flat farmlands of southern Minnesota. A green metal sign with Big Plaine in large white letters greeted us. The sign showed a population of slightly over three thousand residents in the town. I thought the population had actually gone down since I used to live there. Not too surprising, I suppose. It wasn't as if the town offered a lot of opportunities to its populace. There used to be an enormous factory that manufactured pacemaker leads for a medical device company up in the Twin Cities. But those manufacturing facilities moved abroad where labor was cheaper and the corporate tax breaks bigger. The dwindling but steadfast source of income in these parts had always been agriculture. Farming had never been an easy way to make a living, so fewer and fewer of the younger generation pursued it after seeing their parents' struggles. The few farm kids that chose to carry on the family business had a hard slog of making a go at it. So, most Big Plaine kids ended up moving away.

I had been eager to leave Big Plaine. Get away from my mother and that house. I wasn't an athlete and my grades cratered after what happened in the basement, so I didn't have many options to escape but the army. I considered the navy, but being out at sea for months didn't seem appealing.

I enlisted as a goth girl, who was on a heavy Bauhaus kick and had a disdain for authority. My classmates thought I was nuts. You? In the army? But off I went. I wondered what happened to my childhood friends. I would catch a glimpse of their lives on Facebook.

They ended up marrying each other and settling down with kids. Some took over the family farms, but most worked in other jobs: insurance, accounting, and blue-collar work. I stopped accepting friend requests long ago, feeling self-conscious about how my life had turned out. Single. Alone. Hopping from one serving job to the next.

As scared as I was about joining the army, I actually enjoyed it, and I did well in its strict structure I had to live in.

I saw a bit of the world I would never have seen on my own, even though I was terrified about driving over an IED or getting ambushed on some deserted road in Iraq. The army kept me focused, busy, and sober. Sure, I got hammered plenty on leave, but so did many of my fellow soldiers. I had it under control back then. Perhaps I should have stayed in the army. Right now, I would have been about seven years short of that twenty-year retirement juncture with a pension for life coming my way with E7 or maybe even E8 rank. I would have continued doing interesting work, traveling the world instead of serving food and drinks to obnoxious Vegas tourists and drinking myself into a stupor just about every day.

I saw Brent succeed and thought maybe I could, too. If he put everything we went through behind him, why not me? So, I left the army, thinking I would use the GI Bill for college. But I couldn't move on. And with my time left for me to figure out, I drank more and more. I flunked out of Portland State University after just two quarters. And my life had been one pile of steaming shit since then. An array of dead-end jobs, hooking up with losers and criminals. And almost two years in prison for the cherry on top. All these memories fluttered in my head as I stared out the window.

"Memories?" Brent said, snapping me from my thoughts. He made me flinch. It was as if he could read my mind.

"Not good ones," I said, being honest.

Mother's house was on the other end of town, so we had to drive through all of Big Plaine — not that it would take too long — so I got the entire tour of our hometown.

There was only one major thoroughfare, appropriately named Main Street.

Small shops and two restaurants littered the street. I noticed the True Value hardware store was still there. As was Nan's bakery. Nan was a grump, but her baked goods were out of this world. There was also Murph's Diner. That'd been around forever, it seemed. I could practically smell the grease from there and I felt hungry. There was a coffee shop. That was new. It wasn't a Starbucks. Aside from a Hardees and a Subway, there weren't any big-name fast-food restaurants in town.

There was also a post office, a library, and a community center with a gym and a pool. The local high school was a source of pride for the town, with strong athletics and academics. I saw it off to my right, looking the same as when I attended classes there. And it was also where Mother worked for over twenty years. I turned my head away, looking down the road toward the vast expanses of farmland on the outskirts of town where farmers grew corn, alfalfa, and soybeans.

A few minutes later, we arrived at Mother's house. It was smaller than I remembered.

As Brent's fancy SUV pulled into the driveway, I felt a shiver run down my spine. It had been almost a decade since I had last set foot inside, and the memories of my childhood flooded back to me. Most of them were bad.

I gazed upwards at the house. Despite its small size, it felt imposing and significant, weighing on me as I sought refuge behind Brent's car.

Brent shut off the engine. He turned to look at me and asked, "Are you sure about this, Cass? I can take you to the hotel."

I wasn't sure. But I wasn't letting a damn house scare me. I did a tour in Iraq. Mother was gone. I wasn't letting what happened in that basement way back when, or what happened there a few days ago with Mother to scare me off or let it continue to eat away at me. Especially not in front of Brent.

"Cass?" Brent asked.

I'd been so lost in thought, I'd forgotten to reply to his question. Was I sure about this? Hell no. But I was there now.

"Yeah. No sweat, Brent. Just a place to hang while I'm in town."

He looked at me askance.

I managed a thin smile. "I'm fine. It's not a big deal." I was such a liar.

I stepped out of the car and approached the front door, feeling a sense of trepidation wash over me. Compared to many other houses we drove by, this one was in tiptop shape. The front yard showed signs of being neatly trimmed. And it had received a fresh coat of paint recently. There was no way Mother could have afforded to keep it this nice on her own, so I figured Brent had paid for and took care of the house's upkeep. It shouldn't have surprised me. He was too meticulous to let Mother's house go to shit. I half-expected the house to be creepy, haunted, and dilapidated-looking, but I'll be damned. It looked great which should increase its sale value.

"The house looks good. Newly painted?" I asked.

Brent nodded and smiled proudly, admiring his handiwork. I doubted he'd actually painted it. Despite that, whomever he'd hired did a good job.

"You bet. Just last year. I brought down a great crew from the Cities. I also had a new roof put on two years ago. And a new deck out back, three years ago."

I smiled, thinking of padding up the original figure I was hoping to walk away with from there.

From the driveway, the window peered subtly into the basement, partially obscured by the earthen swell of the house's foundation. It was an old, rectangular pane, wood-framed that hinted at decades of witnessing the ebb and flow of the extreme Minnesota seasons — frigid winters and scorching humid summers.

The top half of the window exposed a glimpse into the

shadowy basement below. I could see dust motes dancing in the stale late morning air. It was like an eye, half-open, holding secrets of the underground space it guarded as it glared at me with an accusatory look.

"You okay?" Brent asked me again. He noticed where I was looking.

"I'm fine, Brent. You don't have to ask me every ten seconds," I snapped back at him as I got my things from the car.

He said nothing. I knew I was being a bitch, but I couldn't help it. I shouldn't have gone back.

Brent opened the door and stepped aside to let me in.

I tiptoed inside. The old hardwood floor creaked.

As I walked through the house, I was expecting to see Mother there, but there was no one. Aside from Brent, who was hanging back, giving me space. I heard nothing but the sound of my breathing as I stepped further into the house, but I swear I heard it say "Welcome back, Cassie."

EIGHT
BRENT

CASSIE SAID SHE WAS FINE. FINE WITH HER LIFE. FINE staying at Mom's house, alone. Yet, her body language suggested otherwise. She was so stubborn. However, I decided not to push her anymore about staying at my place or the hotel. I also reminded myself to stop asking if she was okay. I couldn't help it though; she looked... so weak. It was actually pathetic, and I felt bad for her.

I had to tread lightly around my sister. It was like trying to corral a frightened, abused animal. You didn't want to make too many sudden moves, or you'd scare it off.

What the hell had happened to her? She used to be strong-willed, fearless. Now, she was just a shell of her former self. The blame couldn't lie solely on what had happened there all those years ago. Could it? Yes, she had struggled in high school after the incident. She started hanging out with the stoner crowd, the metal heads, and the Goths. Mom had kept telling me she was out of control with her drinking and drugs. Then Mom found a used condom in her bed. She said she tried to get Cassie to come around, but none of the usual punishments seemed to work on her. They never worked as well on Cassie as they did on me.

She shuffled around, walking like a zombie from *The Walking Dead*. Maybe, inside, she had already died. I didn't know how to reach her, how to help her.

By the time I was packing for college, Cassie and Mom were constantly arguing. Mother-daughter relationships could be tricky. First, the daughter loves her mommy, then there's a long period of friction, varying degrees of the daughter loathing her mother. Until eventually, like a comet coming around its orbit, the daughter once again loves and appreciates her mother. That full circle never happened between Cassie and Mom. And now it would never happen.

When we got out of the car, I tried to unload her suitcase, but she snapped at me.

"I got it."

So, I backed away from the trunk with both hands in the air.

It was a small carryon. And I was pretty sure just about everything she owned was inside it and in her tattered backpack. She was such a hot mess. It was hard to believe we were related.

Then I saw her staring down the basement window for a while. When I asked if she was alright, she once again bit my head off.

Why was she so angry? She lived her life thousands of miles away. I never asked her for anything. I was the one who had been looking after Mom, paying all her bills, making the drive down there every Sunday. She would also go up to Minnetonka and stay in the guest cottage. I would take her with us to our condo in Fort Myers, Florida, in the winter. So, for me, walking into Mom's house felt normal. It was a little weird now, of course, since I expected her to come to the door. Instead, I was greeted with silence and dead air, and Cassie's labored breathing. She didn't know it, but I knew she was trying to fend off a panic attack. *Poor thing.*

I looked around. It was pretty much as Mom had left it. I already had a cleaning crew lined up. Everything inside had to go.

I glanced at my watch. The appointment with Mom's estate lawyer was soon. There was so much to do. But getting this house ready wouldn't take long. I had never experienced sentimental attachments to inanimate objects like my mom's dresser or her so-called antiques. It was just junk to me. Just get rid of it all. I wanted to sell it as soon as possible to get it out of my hands. I doubted Cassie wanted the house. She wanted nothing to do with the family and Big Plaine. She would probably be more than happy to sell it. Get some money.

As Cassie shuffled through the house, I looked around our childhood home. It was a small house, especially compared to where I live now. The guest cottage out back was probably just as big. But people should seek after it as it was a decent starter home down there. The suicide might cool people's jets. I made a note to myself to ask the broker if that had to be disclosed.

But all that would come later. For now, I watched Cassie taking it in. I followed her into the kitchen. Off to the side was a closed door. She stopped short, staring at it as if it was on fire. It was the door that led to the basement stairs.

I wanted to grab her by the shoulders and shake her. Tell her to snap out of it à la Cher in *Moonstruck.*

But I held back. I stood by her as she kept staring at the basement door.

"Should we talk about it?" I asked.

We had promised Mom we would never talk about it, but she was gone now. Maybe that wasn't such a good idea the way it seemed to gnaw at Cassie.

She shivered when I asked her that question. She said nothing, just shook her head as she backed away from the door and meandered off toward her old bedroom.

"Mom's car is in the garage. I made sure it has a full tank for you," I said as she disappeared into her old room. She didn't reply. It was that aloofness and ungratefulness that ticked off Jillian so much. Would it kill her to say thank you just once?

I looked at my watch again. I didn't have time for this bullshit. Needed to meet with the lawyer. Check in with the funeral home. Make sure the cleaners and junk haulers would be there on time. Then head back to the Twin Cities.

"Cass. I need to head out," I yelled down the corridor that led from the dining room to the bedrooms at the back of the house.

No reply, so I walked down to her room. The floor creaked with every step I took. The door was open, so I stood at the edge.

She was sitting on her old bed, looking through a box.

"What did you find?"

She finally looked up at me, acknowledging my existence.

"Old books. A yearbook. Odds and ends of my childhood," she said.

I really didn't have time for this. "Gotta run. I have a couple of errands in town, then I'm heading back to the Cities. I left the keys to the house and the car on the table by the front door. Need anything before I go?"

"I'm fine, really," she said.

"Alright, well, call me if you need anything. I'll be back in the morning so we can go over the details of Mom's wake and funeral. And then the estate stuff. We have a lot to discuss," I told her as her attention drifted back to the damned box.

"Cass. Seriously, I'll be down here at nine in the morning. So, be sharp, alert, okay?" It was a subtle way I could tell her not to get drunk tonight.

"Yeah, I got it," she snapped at me. Like she was Ms. Dependable.

I had said my piece. So, I headed back to my car, leaving my sister in her almost catatonic state. I got in my car and started it. And looked at the house. I hoped she could keep it together until after the funeral. I was regretting pushing her to come back.

NINE
CASSIE

BRENT FINALLY LEFT. EVEN THOUGH I WAS FEELING squeamish about staying at Mother's house, I wanted to be alone. I opened my backpack and riffled inside it for a few seconds until I found what I was looking for: a mini airplane bottle of Jack Daniels. No cola, but it didn't matter; I slammed the booze like doing a shot at a bar. I'd been wanting to do that from the second I saw Brent standing there at the airport, smiling and waving at me like he was Mr. Roarke, welcoming me to Fantasy Island. The shot warmed my insides. That would keep the dogs at bay for a little bit.

I walked around the house. All of Mother's stuff was just there, not knowing she was never coming back.

I remembered my last night there. I got very little sleep, staring at the one-way Greyhound bus ticket to Minneapolis that the army recruiter had given me. The departure time was 9:15 am. I couldn't believe I remembered the exact time when the bus was scheduled to depart from Big Plaine. Then again, I remembered that day well.

THE BUS STOPPED a few times between Big Plaine and Minneapolis. There were a few more small towns along the way. Then Shakopee, which was a much bigger town than I was used to. Then a stop at the Mall of America. I had visited it once before when a bunch of us hicks went up there to hang out all day. I'd never seen so many types of retail stores ever, especially in one spot. So many food choices from places I doubted I would ever go, Italy, Greece, China, India. Small town kids like me didn't have many choices about what to eat. We ate a steady diet of ham and cheese sandwiches, burgers, tuna and Hamburger Helper, mac and cheese, and spaghetti with watery marinara sauce.

I wanted to drop out of high school. Figuring a GED would be in my future. But I ended up scraping by with grades that allowed me to graduate with the rest of my class.

I recall sitting on that bus, watching the passengers getting off at the Mall of America with envy. But I signed up for four years with the army. I wasn't getting off to spend the day loitering at the mall. So, the bus drove away and headed back onto the highway with me and a few other nervous recruits in it.

The last stop was the bus depot station on the edge of downtown Minneapolis. It was not the best part of town. But I knew the drill. The army had already sent me up to the Twin Cities before to the MEPS station downtown Minneapolis where all new recruits completed a medical questionnaire and underwent a vigorous evaluation that included height and weight measurements, hearing and vision exams, urine and blood tests, and drug and alcohol tests. I knew they would check for drugs, so I laid off even pot for a couple of weeks, and I passed with flying colors. I probably would fail now. God, even the army would reject thirty-year-old me. That's depressing.

———————

I FORCED myself back to the present. I wandered around the house. So odd not to see and hear Mother around. I looked into her bedroom from the door. Looked the same. I got a Norman Bates Mother vibe and I laughed.

I went into the kitchen, and I stood in front of the closed door to the basement.

I'd never talked to anyone about what happened there. And no one, besides my brother and Mother knew about it, and we swore to never speak of it again. And we honored that. Never talked about it. Blows my mind. Not a friend, a lover, a therapist, or a priest. I'd had no one to cry about it except for Jack Daniels, and that was the most toxic relationship I'd ever had, and I'd had plenty of those, too. I knew the booze was going to kill me if I didn't get a handle on it. But it helped me. I wasn't stupid. I knew it wasn't healthy to drink as much as I did, but it had got a hold of me, and I needed it.

Speaking of needing it. I grabbed the keys to the car and to the attached garage. It was a nice car, much newer than my twelve-year-old Corolla. I backed out of the driveway. I was tempted to head one town over to avoid the possibility of running into anyone I know, but said screw it, and I drove into town.

Luckily, a disinterested young man in his early twenties manned the liquor store. I was back in the kitchen in less than twenty minutes. A perk of small-town living.

I cracked the bottle open and took a drink straight from

the bottle. It felt warm and tangy in my body, but the after-taste burned my throat. I pulled out the two-liter plastic bottle of Diet Coke and the bag of ice. I looked around, half-expecting to see Mother standing there shaking her head at me.

I blinked that image away. Brent had mentioned he had touched nothing inside the house yet, and he wasn't kidding. It was all there. Mother's knickknacks. Figurines. Glassware. The fridge was new. Probably another gift from the golden boy. The stove was the same since I lived there. This place was like a museum, frozen in time.

I noticed the calendar on the wall. One of those that you pull a sheet with every day. Didn't see those around much anymore thanks to the Internet and smartphones. It was one of those inspirational quotes calendars. Each day offered a cheesy inspiration. I couldn't help but shake my head at the irony that those quotes didn't inspire her to not take herself out of this world. The calendar page was three days old. The day she killed herself. It piqued my curiosity. What was the last quote Mother read before she took her life?

"Do what you can, with what you have, where you are." ——Theodore Roosevelt.

A chill went down my spine. Did that trigger Mother to do what she did? I chuckled at the notion that it was Teddy Roosevelt's fault.

I wanted nothing in this house. We would sell or junk all of its contents. And I really didn't need to read lame ass daily inspirational quotes. I took down the calendar and tossed it in the garbage bin. I opened the bag of ice, picked one of Mother's glasses from the cupboard, tossed a fistful of ice cubes into the glass, and made myself a stiff drink.

This ritual alone calmed my nerves. The sound of the ice cubes in the glass, the amber liquid of the whiskey. The fizz of the soda. I was actually licking my lips.

I downed the first drink fast as I put my stuff away in the bedroom. Heading back to the kitchen for drink number two. I drank it a little slower as I stared at the basement door. It took three drinks to muster up the courage to get closer to it. The hardwood floor leading to it creaked with every step I took. I placed the palm of my hand on the closed door as if I could feel it beating or something. My heart was about to explode from my chest. I finished the rest of my drink. Liquid courage, activate.

I stood there in front of it, staring at it like it was radioactive. I looked at the knob and thought about opening the door, looking down the long staircase leading down to the basement. Imagining it also frozen in time, like the rest of the house. But I chickened out. I made myself another drink, headed to the living room, and I plopped down in Mother's well-worn lounge chair with a sigh. The old chair had been a fixture in this living room for as long as I could remember, and it had certainly seen better days. The faded and frayed fabric and the shapeless cushions showed that. But damn, the chair was comfortable. Mother probably spent a lot of time in the chair, reading mystery books, knitting, watching TV, and taking naps. It had become a sort of sanctuary for her since I was a teenager, a place to relax and unwind after a long day.

I reached for the remote and clicked on the TV, flipping through the channels. She didn't have cable or Netflix, so I settled on the WCCO news channel. It had been a decade since I'd watched the local news anchors. One anchor was the same from when I was a teenager. Same golden pipes. He just got a little thicker and his hair was thinner.

There was a lot of weather talk. I forgot how weather obsessed Minnesotans are. The weather didn't change much in California and Nevada, so less to flip out over there about the weather daily, I supposed. Here you could freeze to death in mere minutes in the dead of winter or die from a heat stroke on the dog days of summer.

Back in the kitchen, I made myself another drink. I didn't think of picking up some food when I drove into town, so I looked for something to eat. I pulled out one of Mother's frozen dinners. Home-style meatloaf with mashed potatoes, gravy, and veggies, plus a brownie. Fancy, I said with a chuckle. I nuked it and headed back to the living room with my dinner and drink. The sportscaster was talking about the upcoming season of the Minnesota Twins. I scooped up some meatloaf and mashed potatoes. It wasn't as bad as I remembered. Besides, I needed to get food in my belly, even if it was this lab-made Franken-food.

As I finished my meal, something struck me as odd. Brent said Mother's Parkinson's had gotten so bad that it was probably the reason she took her own life. That he had to step up the care she needed. But I didn't see any signs of a sick woman's house. No pills except for the usual stuff: Tylenol, her blood pressure medicine, and a bottle of Xanax. I knew because I already riffled through her stuff and popped two of her Xanax pills to give me a pleasant buzz with the Jack and Coke. But I couldn't see any grab bars in the bathroom or in the shower. If she was having trouble getting around, as Brent claimed, it didn't seem that way. I expected to find a wheelchair or a walker, perhaps. But I didn't even see a cane.

Those thoughts floated away as the Xanax and Jack

kicked into high gear. I felt all chilled and fuzzy. The TV news anchor introduced a special report on the fifteenth anniversary of the mysterious disappearance of the young teen Mikey Dawson who vanished without a trace from Big Plaine. I cried seeing his picture on the television. I downed my entire glass of booze. I shouldn't have come back here.

TEN
BRENT

I CLEARED MY SCHEDULE FOR THE REST OF THE WEEK since I was going to be busy dealing with Mom's funeral, her estate, and with Cassie. No one complained, of course, since I was dealing with the loss of my mom. No one knew how she really died. I was evasive about it. "She's been struggling with Parkinson's and other health issues for years now. It's a blessing," I told them.

Most of the people I encountered in the Twin Cities were unfamiliar with my life before I went to college. Many wouldn't be able to find Big Plaine on a map, even though it was located an hour from the Cities.

None of my close friends or colleagues had ever met my mother. When they asked about her funeral, I told them that she had wanted it to be a modest affair—just a small gathering for family. This wasn't unusual in Minnesota, where the local ethos of being "Minnesota Nice" often meant people were reserved and preferred not to attract attention or cause a scene. It had been simple to shield them from the truth. Even if someone had happened to find the obituary, it was unlikely they would mention it.

I didn't want anyone from my upscale social circle or my patients to go to Big Plaine and see where I came from, and even more importantly, I didn't want them to know that my mother had hanged herself. It was embarrassing. Of course, Jillian knew—she was my wife. And Cassie knew too. I supposed the small-town rumor mill in Big Plaine would be abuzz about it soon enough. The first responder community there, small as it was, would probably spread the news about the former high school teacher and guidance counselor who had taken her own life in the basement. Gossipy nitwits.

I supposed there was a macabre irony that a guidance counselor killed herself? I didn't know. Frankly, I didn't care what they said in Big Plaine as long as it didn't make its way back to my community in the Twin Cities.

To anyone else, Jane Walsh was dead. People die every day. Cassie and I were the only family she had left. My dad died in a car crash when I was ten years old. Mom had an older brother, but I never met my uncle. He died in action during the Vietnam War when he was nineteen. I never met my grandfather either. He died of a heart attack while shoveling snow when Mom was a teenager. My grandmother died many years ago. That was it for my mom's immediate family. A small Irish-Catholic family in Big Plaine was a rarity, but that was us, so I wasn't expecting a huge turnout at the funeral.

I sent Cassie three texts. One before I went to bed, checking in to see how she was doing alone in that house. I did the same thing in the morning, after I finished working out at the gym. I sent a third text to let her know I should be there in about an hour. As usual, she didn't reply to any of them.

Maybe Jillian was right. Why did I even bother trying

so hard to connect with my sister? I think once we buried Mom and wrapped up the estate, Cassie could go back to Las Vegas with her inheritance and continue her pathetic nomadic drunken life, and I would wash my hands of her.

Mom's estate was also a sore subject with my wife. For years, I'd managed Mom's finances, so even though we wouldn't meet with the estate lawyer until after the funeral, I knew what her estate was worth. Between her checking, savings, a CD, and her pension, there was about $70,000 there. A few years ago, I paid off Mom's mortgage, so the house was clear. The estimated appraisal of it was $110,000. More than I expected. I figured we would list it for 90K for a quick sale as we didn't want to deal with an empty house longer than I had to, and Cassie sure as hell wouldn't deal with it, either. I didn't know about Mom's stuff. It wasn't like she had fine china or a Picasso on the wall. We might as well have given that all to Goodwill or tossed it in a dumpster that's arriving the next day. I thought about hiring one of those estate liquidators to handle selling it off. I doubted Mom's junk would bring in much cash, so that might not have been worth the hassle. Add it all up. After taxes, lawyer fees, and Realtor commissions, Mom's estate would probably net around $150,000. Mom had made it clear she wanted her estate split fifty-fifty between us. I told my wife I would like Cassie to get my half of the estate. That extra money could really help Cassie's life. For us, it wouldn't make much of a difference. My practice was doing well, and my investments had paid off, so I was in a good financial situation even though I was just in my thirties.

And my income would continue to go up. Cassie's income, not so much. But Jillian didn't think that was fair since Cassie had basically been MIA from my mom's and my life for years. And besides, she would probably piss it away on booze. Jillian wanted to accept whatever money was coming my way, and we could donate to a good charity vs squandering it on my ungrateful sister. She had a point. But still. She was my sister, and it was my mother's estate. And charity starts at home. I preferred my sister piss away the money than some stranger.

Cassie worried me. What she might do or say in her current state. So why not make her happy, if possible? What's stopping her from blathering away with someone in one of her drunken stupors about our family secrets? Sure, we'd all kept our mouths shut all this time, but obviously what happened was eating away at Cassie. I was ashamed to feel this way, but the way she lived her life with all that drinking, I didn't think Cassie was long for this world. If she left here with 150K, that might speed up the inevitable and I wouldn't have to worry about her telling tales out of school. And really, look at her life. It was a mess. And she seemed miserable living it. If she wound up drinking herself to death, she might just be better off, anyway. It would be like a slow-paced euthanasia.

I shook those dark thoughts from my head as I pulled up in front of Mom's house. It looked quiet. I didn't see Mom's car in the driveway, so either it was still in the garage or Cassie was out running errands. Who was I kidding? It was nine-thirty in the morning. Cassie wasn't out and about. I pulled into the driveway instead of parking on the street.

I suspected she'd had a long night with her best friend, Jack Daniels. Part of me wished my sister would choose a less brash way of drinking herself to death. I knew that was me being sexist, but my kid sister's go to booze was Jack Daniels Whiskey. So crass. Why not wine? Or vodka, like Mom. Anyway, I climbed out of my car. I looked around and luckily, none of the nosy neighbors were out and about. The last thing I wanted to do was have an innate conversation with them where they offered their stupid condolences. So sick of that already. I walked up to the front door with my copy of the house key in hand. But I stopped. Since Cassie was staying there, I should try to respect her privacy. So, I rang the doorbell. I waited a minute. Nothing. So, I rang it again. Nothing. I was going to send her another text letting her know I was outside, but screw that. This was my house now too. I used my key to let myself in.

ELEVEN
BRENT

I walked in slowly, calling out my sister's name, but I didn't get a response. I followed the sound of the television into the living room. The TV was on with one of the true-crime shows flickering on the screen. But the chair and couch in front of the television were empty. The TV tray was in front of the chair with a half-eaten dinner on it. At the end table were a bottle of Jack Daniels — half gone —, Diet Coke, a bucket of melted ice, and an empty glass.

I shook my head, then my attention went back to the bottle of booze. Did she start last night with a full bottle? I wanted to believe that couldn't be right. She must have brought an old bottle with her from home, or she found this somewhere around the house already opened.

But I knew that was my wishful thinking. I realized that Cassie's drinking problem was even worse than I imagined.

I called out her name again as I made my way to her bedroom. No answer. I saw her blue jeans and shirt strewn about the floor in the hallway.

As I got close to her door, I could hear snoring. The

door was ajar. I knocked on it, lightly. The smell of alcohol wafted over, making me flinch. Feeling angry, I knocked harder this time, which caused the door to open further, and I saw a body in the bed. I went inside and beelined up to her, calling out her name.

Cassie was laid out on the mattress, face down. An excellent position to pass out drunk, I suppose. It avoids choking on your own vomit like a rock star. She was lying on top of the sheets in her bra, underwear, and one sock. What happened to the other sock? I wondered. At least she wasn't naked. That would have been even more awkward.

"Cassie," I said louder. No movement. Good Lord, she would have a hard time waking up to a house fire or a break-in in that condition.

I called her name again. That time I was almost shouting. Finally, she stirred in bed, but that's it. I grabbed her by the shoulder, and I jostled her. "Cassie. Wake up. Come on, Cass, wake up." After about a minute of that, she finally came to life. She looked up at me with a bloodshot eye and a befuddled gaze. Her black mascara was smeared across her face, giving her raccoon eyes.

"Jesus, how much did you have to drink?"

She groaned and finally said: "Brent?"

She looked confused, and just awful, and the stench of morning breath and whiskey made me queasy. She was so out of it she must have forgotten where she was since she seemed genuinely surprised to see me. Cassie looked around the room, her eyes darting around, and I could tell her foggy brain was catching up. She sat up quickly. Must have been too quick since it made her groan even louder, no doubt regretting moving that fast. She looked down and noticed she was only wearing a bra and underwear. She pulled on the comforter and wrapped it around herself to cover up.

"We need to get moving, so go take a shower and get dressed. I'll make a pot of coffee." She just mumbled a bit. "Come on, Cass, get your shit together."

"Okay," she said, whining. Like my annoyance was unwarranted.

In the kitchen, I went to the cabinet and cringed. I forgot that Mom always bought the coffee that was the cheapest at the discount supermarket. Oh, well. I grabbed the container, filled up the teakettle with water, and I put it on the burner. I was left thinking about Cassie's messed-up life as I waited for the water to boil. I was about to go back and check on her to make sure she got out of bed, but I heard the shower going. Good. The kettle screamed. I poured some of the hot water into a cup, then I scooped some of the cheapest freeze-dried coffee money could buy into it and stirred. It smelled awful, but it had caffeine and that was what mattered. A jolt over taste.

The shower stopped, and I heard Cassie stumbling around in her bedroom. There was a loaf of bread in the pantry. I made sure it wasn't moldy. Looked good, so I grabbed two slices of bread and tossed them into the toaster. When it was toasted, I slathered peanut butter and straw-berry jelly on it. It wasn't for me. Jillian had made me a deli-cious and nutritious breakfast before heading down there, but Cassie needed some food in her stomach. And water. Lots of water.

I set the kitchen table for her: cup of coffee, plate of toast, and the largest glass I found in the cupboard filled with tap water.

I checked my emails on my phone while I waited for

her. Seemed like everything was under control at work. Ten minutes later, Cassie showed up in the kitchen, looking much better. Her hair was still wet from the shower. She had it pulled back into a ponytail. Even though she had been living a rough life the past few years, Cassie was still a beautiful green-eyed blonde, despite the years of alcohol abuse. She had been lucky so far. The hard-drinking, drugging party life ages you damn quick.

"Hey," she said in a raspy voice. She was wearing a white shirt tucked into faded blue jeans and black sneakers.

"How you feeling?" I asked her as I handed her a cup of coffee.

She thanked me for the coffee. Finally, I got a thank you from her. Not for paying for her airline ticket, picking her up at the airport, offering to pay for a hotel, but for handing her a cup of awful coffee. I smiled.

"Once you have some, you won't thank me. Mom only bought insta-crap, but it will do in a pinch," I said.

She tittered nervously as she took a sip, grimacing as the coffee touched her lips.

"You weren't kidding. This is awful," Cassie said. She took another sip.

"Well, there aren't any decent coffee shops in Big Plaine. Not even a Starbucks. So, think of that java as strictly for medicinal purposes."

She laughed softly. It was the first time I'd heard her laugh since I picked her up at the airport. Cassie took another drink and trembled.

I pushed the plate with the PBJ toast toward her.

She picked it up and took a bite. "Thanks."

I pointed at the glass of water. "Drink all of it. You need to hydrate."

There was no reason to talk about her drinking. Every time I tried, I just pissed her off. She knew it was killing her. I could see the shame in her eyes. There was no such thing as a proud alcoholic. I couldn't count how many times I'd offered to pay for rehab, but as usual, she wouldn't accept my help. Was I that awful of a brother that she wanted nothing to do with me? I helped that day when we were kids. Maybe I shouldn't have. I glanced at the closed door leading down to the basement. I doubted Cassie would have gone down there. Probably for the best. I wondered if we should talk about it now that Mom was dead? Well, not now in her current condition, I decided.

"We should get going to the funeral home," I said.

"I just need a minute." She took another bite of toast and drank some more terrible coffee and water, then she got up and went back into her bedroom.

She came back a minute later with her purse. "Ready."

We stepped outside. The air was crisp. It was a cool spring morning. Cassie was wearing white square Prada sunglasses. Not sure whether they were real or not. How could she afford them? Real or not, they didn't seem appropriate for visiting a funeral home. They screamed L.A., not Big Plaine. Neither did her white shirt and blue jeans, but I wouldn't say anything about her inappropriate attire. I just hoped she'd brought something decent for the funeral. If not, I'd buy her something. I didn't care if she got mad at me. I wouldn't let her bury our mom dressed like a beach bum.

As we walked into the driveway, I noticed a Chevrolet Malibu parked on the street. The driver's side door opened and a woman with black hair in a pixie cut climbed out. She was eyeballing us as she made her way from the street and up the driveway with a bold, edgy, and confident gait. She looked familiar, but I couldn't place her.

"Friend of yours?" Cassie asked.

"I was going to ask you the same thing."

"Good morning," the woman said as she joined us next to my car.

"What's this about? We're in a hurry," I said, appearing as dismissive and off-putting as possible, since that's the only way to address pushy salespeople. I already had real estate agents sniffing around Mom's house like an ambulance-chasing lawyer hanging out by the emergency room.

The woman smiled. "You don't remember me?"

I knew she looked familiar, but I still couldn't place her. I looked at Cassie, she just shrugged.

"It's me, Robin Moretti."

The name didn't mesh. Then I remembered Robin from high school. She had a different last name back then and long black hair. Pretty. A popular girl with the in-crowd. She had a rocket of an arm for the softball team. Good basketball player too. We ran in the same social circles in school, but she was three years older than me, so we had a different clique of friends within that social construct. Robin had lopped off her long curls, but still looked pretty good in that pixie cut. My stroll down memory lane came to an abrupt stop when I remembered about her brother, and what she did now for a living. She was a cop somewhere up in the Twin Cities. And she had been pestering Mom and had even emailed me a couple of times, which I ignored. Now here she was in the flesh.

"My maiden name was Dawson. Mikey's sister," she said after a few seconds of silence from Cassie and me.

Be cool, I said to myself, and I smiled wide and cheesy.

"I thought you looked familiar. Wow, Robin. I haven't

seen you in forever," I said, cool like Fonzi. I have nothing to be worried about, I told myself.

Cassie stayed quiet, so I glanced over at her and she wasn't playing it cool. The color she had regained since I woke her up hungover had drained from her body once again. I could see her trembling, and she looked like she was a perp that's about to take off running from the police.

TWELVE
CASSIE

My day started bad enough: being shaken awake in my bra and underwear from a drunken blackout by my brother. Humiliated, I dragged myself into the bathroom. The Karen Silkwood type shower helped. The crappy coffee and PBJ toast Brent made for me helped a little.

But I still felt sick and unsteady on my feet. The last thing I needed was to get ambushed in the driveway by Mikey's sister, Robin.

Seeing her standing in front of me was too much to bear. Suddenly, I remembered that the last thing I saw on television before passing out was a news report about the upcoming anniversary of the disappearance of Mikey Dawson.

That sent me over the edge of drinking until I forgot about him. And it worked. I had no memory of getting up from Mother's chair, making my way to the bedroom and doing a hallway striptease before I crashed into that tiny queen-size bed from my youth. That morning was all a blur. My head hurt, but I didn't remember the news report about Mikey Dawson, so he wasn't on my mind until his sister showed up in our driveway with a determined and confident look on her face.

Robin was five years older than me, but she was fit and toned, so she looked younger. I was envious of the confidence she radiated. I looked and acted the opposite of Robin. Sickly pale, with dark, puffy shadows under my eyes without an iota of confidence.

I wanted to crawl back inside to finish that bottle of whiskey. But I couldn't do that. Not yet. So, I set aside my fantasy to run away. I didn't say any of that. I just stood there, hoping she wouldn't notice that I was shaking like a leaf, unable to speak. It felt like I was having an out-of-body experience as I heard Brent talking to Robin after their awkward exchange of *long time no see* chitchat.

"You're a cop now, right?" Brent had asked Robin.

Robin nodded slowly. "Twelve years now with the St. Paul Police Department. Last six years, as a detective."

"Wow, congrats," Brent said.

"Listen, guys, I'm so sorry about your mom," Robin said.

"Thank you. We appreciate that," Brent said.

I tried to thank her as well, but I couldn't form coherent words, so I just stayed quiet as I slowly cowered behind Brent, trying to hide from her.

How did he do it? How could he be so nonchalant talking to her? A detective. Mikey Dawson's sister. I felt bile in my throat, and Brent was having a friendly conversation with her like it was no big deal. With her, of all people, without a care in the world. Old high school acquaintances reconnecting, that's all. But that wasn't what was going on and both of them knew it, despite the bullshit facade going on right there in my mother's driveway.

Robin cranked her neck to look at me standing behind Brent.

"Hey, Cassie. Haven't seen you here since you were a teenager," Robin said.

"I live in Las Vegas," I blurted out after a moment of awkward silence. I blathered on. "San Francisco before that." I didn't know why I said that. She didn't ask where I had lived.

"Awesome. Love both those cities. To visit," Robin said with a grin. "Say, I've been trying to get a hold of you for a couple months. You didn't get my text and voice messages?"

I tried to open my mouth to answer but my jaw clenched. It would take the jaws of life to open my mouth in order to speak.

Brent laughed out loud, breaking the awkward exchange between us.

"Good luck getting Cassie on the phone or to return a call or text," Brent said.

Robin laughed too. Her laugh was as fake as Brent's.

I didn't think I interacted much with Robin when we were kids. I was friends with her brother, not her. The five-year age gap between fifteen- and twenty-year-olds might as well have been fifty. But who was I kidding? I knew why she wanted to talk to me, and it wasn't to catch up or reminisce about our youth. Which was why I ghosted her when she reached out. It was much easier to ghost someone who's almost two thousand miles away. My precious buffer zone, gone.

Brent once again chimed in for me.

"Apologies, Robin, but we really must go. We were on our way to the funeral home to go over the final arrangements for Mom's service."

"I understand. Don't want to hold you up. But, please, Cassie, let's chat before you head back out west. Okay?" She handed me a business card.

"Okay," I said, looking at the card with the St. Paul Department logo with the state capital on it. I was lying to her. Meeting up with her was the last thing I wanted to do. I licked my lips, thinking about Jack.

Just as we were about to climb into Brent's SUV, Robin paused halfway down the driveway, turned around, and said, "By the way, I just wanted to say how much I appreciated your mom's help in trying to find Mikey. She was so helpful putting up flyers, baking brownies at the events we had to keep his case alive with the public. It meant a lot to me and my family."

"Thank you for sharing that. Mom always was eager to lend a helping hand in town," Brent said, as he got into the SUV. I was already inside with the door closed, wanting to burrow into that fine leather seat to hide from Robin.

Brent gave me a furtive glance as he fired up the engine. Unlike my old Corolla, which sputtered and shook when you turned the engine on, Brent's Mercedes Wagon purred to life. A sweet low hum. All outside noise filtered out like we were in a cone of silence from *Get Smart*. Very different from my car, which would rattle and vibrate loudly, every sound from the street bouncing around inside. But the feature I liked the most right then were the dark tinted windows. I could hide from Robin here.

Brent pulled out of the driveway. I looked back and saw Robin in her car, watching us.

"Do you think she knows something?" I asked Brent.

"About what?" Brent asked.

"Cut the shit, Brent." He smirked and looked in the rearview mirror.

"She's still parked on the street. We need to get going," Brent said, putting the car in reverse. He backed out of the driveway and turned toward town. He gave Robin's car a

friendly one horn salute as we drove past her car. I didn't
look out the window or anywhere in her direction. I was
staring down at the Mercedes logo etched into the floor mat,
counting its threads.

After about a minute, Brent spoke up.

"She's fishing, is all. Just keep ignoring her. You're good
at it," he said.

"But she's a cop."

"So?"

"A detective."

"So?"

"I don't know. It's not like dealing with a Barney Fife-
type cop in Big Plaine," I said.

"She's a detective in St. Paul. She didn't have jurisdiction here. So, whatever she's doing, she's doing it as a civilian, not as a cop," Brent said. He was still as cool as a
cucumber. It was like we were out for a Sunday drive. If
Robin had rattled him like she had me, he wasn't showing it.

"What the hell was Mother doing with her?" I
wondered.

"I told her to stay away from Robin and the Dawson
family. But she said it would look bad if she didn't help out.
She had a point."

"You knew?"

"Sure. Mikey's disappearance is a big deal around here.
Even statewide. Not as big as Jacob Wetterling, but big
enough. So, she helped the family out here and there.
Putting up flyers. Stuff like that. It's not a big deal."

"What was she thinking?"

Brent laughed. "What?"

"Are you serious?" I couldn't believe how cavalier he
was being about this whole thing.

"Don't worry about Robin. She emailed a while back

asking me some questions too. She's snooping, but she has nothing."

"What did she ask you?"

"Did I know Mikey said he was coming to our house the day he disappeared? Did I see him the day he went missing? Stuff like that," Brent said.

"Stop the car," I said.

"Why?"

"Pull over or I'm going to puke all over your fancy leather seat."

THIRTEEN
BRENT

It doesn't matter whether you're driving a $200,000 car, like I was, or a $1,000 beater. When your passenger shouts, "Pull over, I'm going to throw up," you pull over. Immediately!

As soon as I swerved onto the shoulder of the road, Cassie had the passenger side door open. The car was still rocking from being slammed into park, and she was outside, bent over. I could hear the retching sound, but she didn't vomit. She had dry heaves.

While Cassie was going through her ordeal, I thought about our encounter with Robin.

It was obvious she was just poking around. She had nothing solid. All we had to do wasn't let her rattle us, but Cassie looked ready to pass out when confronted by Robin, and it wasn't from the whiskey that she'd drunk the night before. Her entire body language and demeanor screamed, "I'm hiding something." If you were to do an image search for a guilty *person,* her face would have been the number one search result. I could see it on her face and her body demeanor, and I wasn't a skilled, trained police detective like Robin. So, I was certain Robin had picked up on that.

Although I hadn't seen Robin in person since high school, I knew she had been looking into her brother's disappearance more aggressively the past year. When she began to bug Mom in town and reached out to me, I hired a private investigator to check her out. She was a top-notch detective with one of the best case closure rates in the department. She worked on the missing and exploited children's squad, which was her area of expertise. There was even a nice write-up about her work with missing children in the *St. Paul Pioneer Press*.

It had a nice angle for a reporter, the sister of a missing child, now working to find other missing children as a detective while her own brother's whereabouts remained a mystery. That sold papers and got the clicks.

She wanted to know if I had seen her brother Mikey on the day he went missing. Mikey was Cassie's friend, not mine. They were both fifteen. I was seventeen. I downplayed how close Cassie and Mikey had become that summer. Back then, Robin was twenty and was an undergraduate at the university in Madison, Wisconsin, when Mikey disappeared. There was a lot of hoopla over Mikey's disappearance that first year, then it sort of died down after that. He would probably just be another of the many milk carton kids mostly forgotten, but his parents and sister were relentless in making sure the cops and the town didn't forget about Mikey's case. I got it. But what a pain in the ass that family had been. It'd been fifteen years. You would think they would move on by now. And now the sister was hot to trot on her brother's cold case. Just what Cassie and I needed, a trained police detective sniffing around.

Robin's investigation was on her own time. She was out

of her jurisdiction down there, and just a private citizen snooping around the notorious cold case.

Big Plaine's police department didn't have the resources for that type of investigation. The department had eight full-time officers and the police chief. They had one detective. And I doubted Mikey Dawson's disappearance was high on their to-do list unless an anniversary date rolled around and the media scrutiny increased. And that year marked the fifteenth anniversary of Mikey's disappearance, so it was a juicier one than normal, and that meant a lot of extra media attention. I was certain Robin knew that well, so she was trying to capitalize on it.

We just had to ride it out. Especially Cassie. She just needed to chill out for two more days. I was upset at myself for not thinking about Robin Moretti and how I gift-wrapped and delivered Cassie right to her. I should have just sent Cassie back to Las Vegas, but that would have looked terrible, and Robin would be all over it. No. The only thing we could do was press forward. Funeral. Estate business. Put Cassie on the airplane as planned in two days. Two days. It should work, I kept telling myself.

Cassie was a hot mess, but she had been like that since the day Mikey went missing. In a small town like Big Plaine, everyone knew each other's business. It was no secret that Cassie hated coming back to town. She had only visited a handful of times since she'd moved away. And that she had become estranged from Mom. I might live forty-five miles away, but I still had a few high school buddies that I kept in touch with — mostly over Facebook — who filled me in on the town's scuttlebutt about my family. How Mom and Cassie had some sort of falling out, which was why she hightailed it to the army at seventeen and then hardly went back for a visit. Cassie's teenage reputation wasn't a good one. She got into drugs. Cutting school. Cutting herself. A promiscuous teen. Arrested a few times. Nothing major: truancy, underage drinking, shoplifting, and mailbox smashing. Hanging out of the passenger window of a car with a bat to take out mailboxes was a rite of passage in small-town America. I did it. But Cassie always seemed to get caught. So, according to the rumor mill around town, Cassie's wild youth caused her and Mom to not get along and resulted in her being sent off to the army to get her life in order. Little did they know, it was Cassie who wanted to join the army to get away from Big Plaine and practically blackmailed Mom into signing the parental waiver needed for a minor to enlist.

After the army, word got back to town that Cassie was back to her party girl ways out west. Then came more legal entanglements. I told Cassie if she was going to engage in illegal activities, she needed to smarten up about it, because she didn't seem to be a very good criminal, always getting busted.

Did she want to get caught? If she had a prison wish, then that was up to her, but not for what happened here. Because that affected me. And I wasn't having my perfect life taken away from me because my sister was a screwup.

FOURTEEN
CASSIE

AFTER A COUPLE OF MINUTES OF DRY HEAVING BY THE side of the road, I climbed back into the car, still feeling woozy. Brent looked at me with worry—that was his usual expression these days. Initially, when I first arrived, his gaze held concern and pity. Now, it was filled with frustration and annoyance, even contempt towards me.

Although he tried to pretend he wasn't concerned about Robin, I could tell he was busy trying to figure out what was going on with her in his head, worried that I might mess things up badly.

"Ready?" he asked coldly.

I nodded, and he pulled back onto the road. On our way to the funeral home, he suddenly turned into the Hardee's parking lot.

"You need something more than PBJ toast in your stomach," he said. More of an order than a suggestion.

He pulled into the drive-thru. The teenager working there freaked out over the cool Mercedes Wagon. It seemed like not too many six-figure vehicles drove through his window in Big Plaine.

I didn't argue with Brent about eating. I ordered a bacon, egg, and cheese sandwich, and a coffee. Brent ordered the same, except he chose sausage and an order of Hash Rounds to share.

He pulled into an open spot in the parking lot, and we ate our food in silence. When I glanced at Brent, I quickly looked away; looking at him for too long brought back too many painful memories from the awful history we shared. It was a decades-long nightmare that he was meshed into with me. That's why I had tried to cut him and Mother out of my life. Whenever I saw them or even spoke to them on the phone, the worst day of my life replayed in my mind in high definition. Especially since he had managed to move forward and build a successful life for himself. I had thought Mother had put what happened behind her too, but maybe that's why she killed herself. She didn't leave a note, so we'd never know why she did it.

Ignoring what happened, not talking about it, had been our guiding principle for all these years. But that secret was killing me from the inside. I supposed if it hadn't affected me like it had, if instead I could bury it deep inside and move on with my life and achieve the success Brent had, I would. I just didn't seem to have that power in me.

When I first arrived at the airport, I could tell he was happy to see me. He had always tried to help me, seeking to reconnect with me. Now, I was seeing his gaze toward me turn colder by the minute. He was probably worried about what I might do. What I might say to Robin. I wanted to come clean so badly, because keeping the secret buried deep inside all these years had not worked well for me. But if I got everything off my chest, I would unleash havoc in Brent's life.

He was the one who helped me that day. I couldn't do

was dressed like he was one of the men in black. I wished he had that device that makes you forget things with the push of a button.

"Cassie," Lundegard said to me warmly as he shook my hand. "It's been so long. I'm sorry that it has to be under this solemn occasion, but it is nice to see you again."

I managed a weak smile. "Thank you, Mr. Lundegard." It was funny how even as an adult, I still felt compelled to address him formally. I supposed if I were to run into my English teacher, I would have addressed him as Mr. Goldfinch, not by his first name.

The next hour was surreal. Mr. Lundegard went through all the nuances of planning a funeral. At first, Brent tried to include me in the decision-making process. But I didn't care. Mother was dead. No matter what we did or how much money we spent, she wouldn't be impressed or disappointed by the service.

By we, I meant Brent. He was paying for it, after all. A little nugget I was sure was driving his wife nuts. But what the hell did Jillian want from me? If Mom's funeral and burial were up to my budget, I would have been forced to donate her body to the University of Minnesota's Medical School. Let their wide-eyed students have at her until they were done with the body, and they cremated what was left, for free.

Finally, we wrapped things up there. Brent had made Mr. Lundegard very happy with his expensive decisions on things like the casket and the other pricey accouterments of the funeral business. The average person from Big Plaine couldn't afford everything Brent ordered for Mother.

The wake would be the next morning. Followed by the funeral in the afternoon. In twenty minutes, we would meet with the estate lawyer to go over Mother's will. Everything

that to him. So, I bottled it up. I would not blow up hi
perfect Lake Minnetonka life. I needed to keep my mouth
shut like I had all this time. But we should clear the air, even
though we had made a pact to never speak about what
happened in the basement.

"I guess we should talk about the elephant in the
room?" I finally told him.

"With Robin sniffing around, it's probably a good idea,
despite the pact."

"We were teenagers. That pact ruined my life," I said.

"We did it to protect you," Brent said.

I didn't know what to say because he was right. It was
all my fault. And all Mother and Brent did was try to help
me walk away from my mess unscathed. But I regretted
going along with their plan, since I didn't walk away as
unscathed as they promised I would.

When you told such a big lie, you ended up telling more
and more lies to cover up one lie with another until it
became a hideous circle and you ended up having to drink
yourself into a stupor to forget, which was what I did every
day of my life. I wanted a drink then and it wasn't even ten-
thirty in the morning.

"Look, Cass. We're ten minutes late for our meeting
with the funeral director. Let's go bury Mom. Deal with the
estate. And figure out what to do next. We've lived with it
this long. What's another few hours?"

I rubbed my temples because they were throbbing. Not
sure if the pain was from the hangover, the need for a drink,
or the stress of being back in Big Plaine. In that house. Right
above the basement. But I was tired of having this over my
head. So, I agreed. We had a lot on our plate right now.

We arrived at the only funeral home in town. Norm
Lundegard, the funeral director, greeted us at the door. He

was wrapping up nicely and quickly. Brent was making sure of that. Seemingly, he had wrapped things up as quickly as possible. That worked for me. The sooner I was out of there, the better.

It was one o'clock. I'd been wanting a drink since the morning, but it was changing from, I wanted... to I needed a drink. I saw my hand trembling. It was subtle, but it was there. It made me self-conscious. Especially around Brent. Sure, he now spent his days lifting rich people's faces and giving women bigger boobs, but he was a doctor. A good one. He'd know why I was suddenly trembling indoors. Especially after he woke me up that morning.

———————

THE LAWYER'S office was just a mile away from the funeral home. In a small town, nothing was far from here to there. As we drove over, I looked out the window, and I saw Robin's Chevy Malibu pull out from a side street. I turned around and saw it fall in behind us.

"I think that's Robin behind us," I said.

Brent looked through the rearview mirror. "Same type of car. And yeah, a short-haired woman driving."

"Do you think she's following us?" I asked nervously, looking behind me.

"It's a small town, and she said she's in town for the weekend, so it's not too surprising we might cross paths on the road. I wouldn't worry about it," Brent said as he pulled into a parking spot on the street right in front of the lawyer's office.

We both looked as the Malibu drove on by slowly before it took the first right possible, disappearing from our sightline.

"See. She's gone. Just a coincidence. Nothing to worry about," Brent said.

I wished I shared Brent's lackadaisical take when it came to Robin snooping around town about her missing brother.

FIFTEEN
CASSIE

PATRICK RIORDAN HAD A CLUTTERED OFFICE. HE HAD been Mother's lawyer as long as I could remember. I was still reeling from seeing Robin drive by. Meeting with a lawyer didn't help with my nerves. I didn't like them. Last time I needed one, I ended up doing eighteen months in the Central California Women's Facility in Chowchilla. That lawyer kept reminding me that if it weren't for him, it could have been five years, as if I should drop to my knees in gratitude. I still got locked up. But on my budget, the public defender paid for by the taxpayers of the state of California was the best I could do.

Riordan had a massive desk which old-fashioned lawyers adored. The number of empty Styrofoam coffee cups on it would anger an environmentalist. A family sized bag of peanut M&Ms sat on top of a pile of red and blue folders. In the corner, there was an old Dell computer. I wondered if it was still using Windows 98.

He wasn't sitting at his desk, but I heard him mumbling and ruffling about under it.

"Sorry about that," Riordan said, popping his head out from

underneath. "I'm dealing with a rogue cable under there," he said with a smile. He didn't give a reason for the mess, like some odd phenomena occurred that unleashed a mini tornado only in his office. So, I assumed the mess was normal. He shook both our hands and directed us to a couple of chairs across from his beast of a desk. I sat down on a small wooden chair with a worn-out cushion. I was surprised Brent wasn't using one of his Twin Cities powerhouse lawyers, but I supposed Mother's estate would be pretty straightforward. And Mr. Riordan and Mother went way back. Nothing salacious, I didn't think. In Big Plaine, just about everyone went way back with everyone else.

As I sat down, I glanced up at the wall and saw his dusty degrees and licenses hanging crookedly on the wall behind his desk, the only sign of the profession practiced in this cramped space. A liberal arts degree from Mankato State and his law degree from Hamline. It was strange, it seemed to me, that the law profession was one of the only fields where its practitioners felt compelled to display their degrees on the wall.

The room was stuffy and warm, and I could hear the faint hum of the furnace struggling to keep up.

"Sorry for your loss. Your mother was a wonderful woman," he said.

I tried not to roll my eyes. But what was he going to say? Your mother was an insufferable shrew?

Riordan was in his sixties. He was bald but still had that crown of hair on the sides that he kept way too long and messy, giving him a mad scientist look.

"How are things looking?" Brent asked.

"Pretty straightforward stuff," Riordan replied. He plucked a folder from the pile and opened it as he got down to brass tacks and explained what was going on.

that to him. So, I bottled it up. I would not blow up his perfect Lake Minnetonka life. I needed to keep my mouth shut like I had all this time. But we should clear the air, even though we had made a pact to never speak about what happened in the basement.

"I guess we should talk about the elephant in the room?" I finally told him.

"With Robin sniffing around, it's probably a good idea, despite the pact."

"We were teenagers. That pact ruined my life," I said.

"We did it to protect you," Brent said.

I didn't know what to say because he was right. It was all my fault. And all Mother and Brent did was try to help me walk away from my mess unscathed. But I regretted going along with their plan, since I didn't walk away as unscathed as they promised I would.

When you told such a big lie, you ended up telling more and more lies to cover up one lie with another until it became a hideous circle and you ended up having to drink yourself into a stupor to forget, which was what I did every day of my life. I wanted a drink then and it wasn't even ten-thirty in the morning.

"Look, Cass. We're ten minutes late for our meeting with the funeral director. Let's go bury Mom. Deal with the estate. And figure out what to do next. We've lived with it this long. What's another few hours?"

I rubbed my temples because they were throbbing. Not sure if the pain was from the hangover, the need for a drink, or the stress of being back in Big Plaine. In that house. Right above the basement. But I was tired of having this over my head. So, I agreed. We had a lot on our plate right now.

We arrived at the only funeral home in town. Norm Lundegard, the funeral director, greeted us at the door. He was dressed like he was one of the men in black. I wished he had that device that makes you forget things with the push of a button.

"Cassie," Lundegard said to me warmly as he shook my hand. "It's been so long. I'm sorry that it has to be under this solemn occasion, but it is nice to see you again."

I managed a weak smile. "Thank you, Mr. Lundegard." It was funny how even as an adult, I still felt compelled to address him formally. I supposed if I were to run into my English teacher, I would have addressed him as Mr. Goldfinch, not by his first name.

The next hour was surreal. Mr. Lundegard went through all the nuances of planning a funeral. At first, Brent tried to include me in the decision-making process. But I didn't care. Mother was dead. No matter what we did or how much money we spent, she wouldn't be impressed or disappointed by the service.

By we, I meant Brent. He was paying for it, after all. A little nugget I was sure was driving his wife nuts. But what the hell did Jillian want from me? If Mom's funeral and burial were up to my budget, I would have been forced to donate her body to the University of Minnesota's Medical School. Let their wide-eyed students have at her until they were done with the body, and they cremated what was left, for free.

Finally, we wrapped things up there. Brent had made Mr. Lundegard very happy with his expensive decisions on things like the casket and the other pricey accouterments of the funeral business. The average person from Big Plaine couldn't afford everything Brent ordered for Mother.

The wake would be the next morning. Followed by the funeral in the afternoon. In twenty minutes, we would meet with the estate lawyer to go over Mother's will. Everything was wrapping up nicely and quickly. Brent was making sure of that. Seemingly, he had wrapped things up as quickly as possible. That worked for me. The sooner I was out of there, the better.

It was one o'clock. I'd been wanting a drink since the morning, but it was changing from, I wanted... to I needed a drink. I saw my hand trembling. It was subtle, but it was there. It made me self-conscious. Especially around Brent. Sure, he now spent his days lifting rich people's faces and giving women bigger boobs, but he was a doctor. A good one. He'd know why I was suddenly trembling indoors. Especially after he woke me up that morning.

THE LAWYER'S office was just a mile away from the funeral home. In a small town, nothing was far from here to there. As we drove over, I looked out the window, and I saw Robin's Chevy Malibu pull out from a side street. I turned around and saw it fall in behind us.

"I think that's Robin behind us," I said.

Brent looked through the rearview mirror. "Same type of car. And yeah, a short-haired woman driving."

"Do you think she's following us?" I asked nervously, looking behind me.

"It's a small town, and she said she's in town for the weekend, so it's not too surprising we might cross paths on the road. I wouldn't worry about it," Brent said as he pulled into a parking spot on the street right in front of the lawyer's office.

We both looked as the Malibu drove on by slowly before it took the first right possible, disappearing from our sightline.

"See. She's gone. Just a coincidence. Nothing to worry about," Brent said.

I wished I shared Brent's lackadaisical take when it came to Robin snooping around town about her missing brother.

FIFTEEN
CASSIE

PATRICK RIORDAN HAD A CLUTTERED OFFICE. HE HAD been Mother's lawyer as long as I could remember. I was still reeling from seeing Robin drive by. Meeting with a lawyer didn't help with my nerves. I didn't like them. Last time I needed one, I ended up doing eighteen months in the Central California Women's Facility in Chowchilla. That lawyer kept reminding me that if it weren't for him, it could have been five years, as if I should drop to my knees in gratitude. I still got locked up. But on my budget, the public defender paid for by the taxpayers of the state of California was the best I could do.

Riordan had a massive desk which old-fashioned lawyers adored. The number of empty Styrofoam coffee cups on it would anger an environmentalist. A family sized bag of peanut M&Ms sat on top of a pile of red and blue folders. In the corner, there was an old Dell computer. I wondered if it was still using Windows 98.

He wasn't sitting at his desk, but I heard him mumbling and ruffling about under it.

"Sorry about that," Riordan said, popping his head out from

underneath. "I'm dealing with a rogue cable under there," he said with a smile. He didn't give a reason for the mess, like some odd phenomena occurred that unleashed a mini tornado only in his office. So, I assumed the mess was normal. He shook both our hands and directed us to a couple of chairs across from his beast of a desk. I sat down on a small wooden chair with a worn-out cushion. I was surprised Brent wasn't using one of his Twin Cities powerhouse lawyers, but I supposed Mother's estate would be pretty straightforward. And Mr. Riordan and Mother went way back. Nothing salacious, I didn't think. In Big Plaine, just about everyone went way back with everyone else.

As I sat down, I glanced up at the wall and saw his dusty degrees and licenses hanging crookedly on the wall behind his desk, the only sign of the profession practiced in this cramped space. A liberal arts degree from Mankato State and his law degree from Hamline. It was strange, it seemed to me, that the law profession was one of the only fields where its practitioners felt compelled to display their degrees on the wall.

The room was stuffy and warm, and I could hear the faint hum of the furnace struggling to keep up.

"Sorry for your loss. Your mother was a wonderful woman," he said.

I tried not to roll my eyes. But what was he going to say? Your mother was an insufferable shrew?

Riordan was in his sixties. He was bald but still had that crown of hair on the sides that he kept way too long and messy, giving him a mad scientist look.

"How are things looking?" Brent asked.

"Pretty straightforward stuff," Riordan replied. He plucked a folder from the pile and opened it as he got down to brass tacks and explained what was going on.

Mother appointed Brent as the Executor. No surprise there. I expected Riordan to remove Mother's will from a leather briefcase, put on some reading glasses, clear his throat, and begin to read her "Last Will and Testament" out loud. But I guess that's what they do in the movies, not in real life. Because he just handed us our own copies and told us to read it at our leisure and to let him know if we had questions. So why was I there? He could have just emailed this shit to me. I looked at the ancient computer back there but figured he must use email. Probably an AOL email account, but still.

He must have seen the annoyance on my face.

"Like I said, pretty straightforward stuff," he said, clearing his throat, then he gave me the CliffsNotes.

"Your mother had a checking and savings account with Wells Fargo with a combined balance of $43,254.19. She had a ten-thousand-dollar CD, also with Wells Fargo. In her pension account, there is $21,576. Those are liquid assets. There is a $15,000 life insurance payable for both of you. Brent, as the Executor, needs to file that claim with the insurance company. However, since suicide is listed as the cause of death," Riordan cleared his throat, "the insurance company probably won't pay it out."

He quickly moved on to the house. "Your mother's house has an estimated value of $110,000. You might get a bit more or less if you decide to sell. So, the entire estate's value is about $185,000."

I felt a little excited. My half came to around 92K, maybe a little less after the lawyer's fees, taxes, and stuff. Brent could buy another watch. For me, that was a windfall, especially if I played it smart.

"Thank you for the recap, Mr. Riordan," I said with a

smile. My mood vastly improved. Riordan offered me a thin smile.

"There is one more item left to discuss," Riordan announced, pushing his chair back from his desk. The sound of plastic wheels rolling on the plastic carpet protector filled the room as he slid back to a filing cabinet. He opened one drawer and fished out an envelope. He rolled his chair back to his desk, and he handed Brent the envelope, doing all this without getting out of his chair.

"Your Mother instructed me that after her passing, I was to hand deliver this sealed envelope to both of you in person. This is why I made this appointment with you kids."

I hadn't been called a kid in a long time, but I was intrigued by this mysterious envelope that Riordan handed over to Brent. I looked over at Brent and I could tell from his expression that he had no clue what this was about, either.

"You're both to read it in private, together. At her home. That was her wish, at least," Riordan said, knowing he couldn't enforce that.

"What's in it?" I asked Riordan.

"I don't know. It was sealed by your mother with strict instructions that it not be opened by anyone but her children after her death and no one else is to read it, myself included," he explained.

With that, the lawyer got up from his creaky chair, shook our hands, and told us he'd see us at the funeral.

BACK IN BRENT'S SUV, we looked at the envelope like it was toxic.

"Open it," I said.

"Mom wanted us to open it at her house."

Seriously?

"Mother is dead. She won't know the difference," I snapped.

"It's a five-minute drive," Brent said, firing up his car. "Let's honor her wishes."

Everything in Big Plaine was five minutes away. I supposed he was right, so I didn't feel the need to get into it with him right there, right then. He backed out of the parking spot and headed toward Mother's house. I was looking at the envelope, wondering what Mommy Dearest was up to from the grave.

SIXTEEN
CASSIE

WE SAID LITTLE DURING THE DRIVE BACK TO THE house. Brent pulled into the driveway, and we made our way inside.

We took a seat across from each other at the kitchen table. Brent removed the envelope from his laptop bag and placed it on the table.

I hadn't had a drink since the previous night, and I needed one badly. I looked at my hand. It wasn't trembling, at least. The drink would have to wait. I wasn't going to drink in front of Brent.

I shifted my gaze between my brother and the envelope. I told him to open it.

Brent reached for it and, using his index finger, he tore it open.

"Be careful," I cautioned him, worried that he might rip the contents. He gave me a "no shit" look before returning to the task at hand. He carefully pulled out a folded piece of paper. It looked like Mother had left us a letter. I imagined its contents: "Dear Kids, sorry I beat you and locked you up in the cellar, but you know the saying, 'spare the rod, spoil the child.'" That one seemed to be her favorite Bible verse, since it excused the abuse at her hands.

Brent looked inside the torn envelope to make sure he hadn't missed anything else in there. It was empty. He unfolded the paper. It was a single sheet.

"It's a letter," he said, confirming my thoughts. I was disappointed. I wasn't sure what I had been expecting. Maybe a map showing the location of gold coins buried in the backyard.

"It's dated nine months ago," he added.

I could see it was handwritten and recognized it as Mother's. She had always been so proud of her penmanship. She called it a lost art form in the age of computers.

"Read it," I said, feeling anxious.

Brent did that.

Dear Brent and Cassandra,

Brent stopped and looked at me as if to apologize. He knew how much I hated my full name. And no one called me Cassandra but Mother. *It's the name I gave you*, she would tell me. And now even in death, she used the name I loathed.

He continued reading the letter.

I apologize for burdening you two with this. If you're reading my letter, that means I'm gone, and I failed to take care of something I should have, many years ago. I don't know why I didn't get rid of this albatross from our lives. It's a moot point now.

Please understand that I did what I did as a temporary solution while I figured out a permanent solution. But then a day became two, then a week, a month, a year, ten years. Until now.

I suppose I lost my nerve to do what needed to be done and now, I'm sorry, but you need to act to ensure our secret remains just that.

I don't want to get into details in this letter. But you must know what I mean.

The one secret I made you both swear we would never discuss ever again. I told you I had taken care of it, and it would no longer be a problem, but I lied.

My failure to act means I have to break our pact now that I'm dead. You children need to go down to the basement. In my freezer, you'll find it. Do what I failed to do and get it out of there and finally get rid of it, forever. Then burn this letter.

You need to do this quickly, because Robin Dawson has been relentless, and she won't stop.

Regards,
Your Mother.

I felt my heart pounding in my chest and my blood pressure dropping. I looked at Brent and, for the first time in a long time, he appeared frazzled. His face was ashen. He put the letter down. And he looked at me.

"What do you think is in there?" I asked, not wanting to contemplate what was going through my head.

Brent shrugged. He took a deep breath, then, "Only one way to find out." He tapped on the table with his knuckles, and he got up from the chair, turning towards the basement door.

"You don't think..." I couldn't say what I was thinking out loud.

"We need to check it out right now," Brent said.

"I can't," I said, feeling sick.

"We have to, Cass. Come on. We can do this together."

"Don't make me go back down there," I begged.

"Cassie, whatever Mom left in that freezer might come back and bite us in the ass. We have no choice. Come on. I'll be there with you."

I felt wobbly, but I got up from the chair. Brent took the few steps to the basement door. I followed him. My legs felt like lead. I looked down, thinking my feet had been encased in buckets of cement.

But they weren't.

He opened the door, and of course, it had to creak like we were in a horror movie.

I stood behind him and peered down the long steps that led down to the basement. It was pitch dark down there, and I could feel a dank coldness wafting up from below. Even though I had spent time at Mother's house over the years, I hadn't gone down into the basement in fifteen years.

After what happened, Mother tried to force me down

there, telling me I needed to face my fears, but I refused. It was the first time I stood up to her. She beat me with that leather strap she always used to discipline us with, but I wouldn't budge. When I was sixteen, I told her she would have to beat me to death and drag my dead body down there if she wanted me down in that basement. After that, she stopped. She never beat me again. Not that I gave her much of a choice, since seven months later, right after graduating from high school, I was gone.

I knew I shouldn't have gone back here. Nothing but bad memories for me in Big Plaine and now this. I supposed Mother was finally getting her way. She finally was getting me down in that damned basement from the beyond. Maybe that's what this was all about. Mother always had to have her way. She just wanted to scare me. To face my fear and get me down in that basement. That's what this was all about. Another one of her life lessons she loved doling out.

Brent flicked the light switch on, and the steps leading down to the basement became awash with fluorescent light. He made his way down the steps, normally. It was obvious he didn't let the memories of the awful thing that had happened down there affect him. But for me, taking those steps down to the basement felt like I was jumping into a pool full of sharks with chum hanging around my neck.

The basement was unfinished. A cold concrete floor and even colder cinder blocked wall ominously welcomed me back. There were a couple dozen boxes, half of them cardboard, the other half plastic, stacked against the walls. A lifetime of stuff crammed inside of each one. A Polaris workout machine from the 90s gathered dust in one corner.

The only natural light came from the half window up on the wall. Its light came in like a spotlight, with dust bunnies dancing in the light.

I felt my anxiety surging and my body begging for booze. I couldn't believe I was back down there and I was feeling angry and resentful toward my dead mother.

There were two sections in the basement. On the right was a door that led to the utility room and a root cellar. It was where you would find the furnace and water heater. It was also where Mother had put her washing machine and dryer. There was a laundry sink and a cabinet. And the door to a root cellar where Mother stored vegetables, fruits, and other perishable items. And where she would mete out her punishment for our more serious infractions by locking us in that cold, dank room to reflect on what we did wrong. I shivered, thinking back to it.

All the boxes and junk were stored in the other half of the basement, which accounted for most of the space. Back when we were kids, Brent had set up his bedroom in the corner right by the window.

It wasn't up to code, so it wasn't a legal bedroom, but this had been his fiefdom. His bed and posters were long gone. But I remembered his setup.

Mother didn't have the money to convert it into a legal bedroom. Brent didn't care. He wasn't about to share a room with his little sister.

He had put up two large privacy screens made of bamboo that divided his corner of the basement into his de facto bedroom. The room divider was completely opaque, providing complete privacy. Although they weren't anchored in or anything and were actually quite flimsy, it felt like I was looking at the Great Wall from Game of Thrones. And I wasn't supposed to enter his space without permission. Behind the great wall of bamboo, Brent had his bed — a full size mattress — a study desk, bookshelf, stereo with speakers, and a workout bench with a rack of weights and dumbbells. It was his kingdom.

It was vivid in my memory even though it was all long gone and I was looking at open space. A stack of boxes in the corner that was once his bedroom. My knees buckled as I stared at the corner where it all happened.

"You okay?" Brent asked.

"Terrible memories," I said.

"That was a long time ago, Cass. Come on, let's go into the utility room to see what's up with that freezer."

"Fine. Let's get this over with," I said.

We both headed to the utility room where Mother kept that big chest freezer. It was dark. Brent reached for the cord dangling above without even have to look for it, and pulled on it, turning on the bare lightbulb and only source of light back there. That part of the basement was more utilitarian where the furnace and water heater were located. It had a brick wall and uneven slabs of concrete for flooring. The washing machine and dryer were in there, too, right next to a laundry sink. Across from the sink was the half door into the root cellar.

I shivered, looking at it, remembering how cold it was in there and the memories of Mother locking me inside when I needed to be punished.

Next to the dryer was the chest freezer, pushed up against the brick wall. Mother always had this freezer down there. It was white with dents incurred over the years.

As a kid, before I stopped coming down to the basement, that freezer was a source of joy. A treasure trove filled with all kinds of frozen goodies, like hot pockets and ice cream.

I could hear it humming. Brent opened the lid. Fog seeped out, and I felt the chill of the freezer. I peered in, crossing my arms around my chest for warmth. I shivered, not just because of the cold air emanating from the freezer, but because of the memories and the fear of whatever Mother wanted us to find in there.

I stood behind Brent, and I looked closely inside the freezer as a sense of dread came over me.

SEVENTEEN
CASSIE

My knees were shaking as I looked inside the freezer, and I was staring at... Mother's groceries. Her go-to foods had always been pizza, Chicken Kiev, meatballs, frozen TV dinners, veggies, vanilla ice cream, and ice cream sandwiches. Her eating habits seemed unchanged since I was a kid. I felt a sense of relief. I had been expecting to see a body in there.

It was surreal to see her food there, frozen in time — literally and figuratively. Waiting for her, but she was never coming back for it. For someone who had killed herself, she must not have planned it out in advance since there was enough food in there to last her through the summer. Strange.

"There's nothing there," I said to Brent.

He looked inside. I was ready to run back upstairs, but he leaned inside the freezer and started moving items around. For a few minutes, he shuffled the contents around, but there was only food inside, nothing sinister.

I didn't know what Mother was trying to do. I supposed

I was right, and this was just her way of tricking me back down to the basement. She always had to have the last word; even in death.

I was done with these stupid head games from someone who was dead and whom we were dumping into the ground tomorrow.

"Another of her mind fucks. I'm outta here," I said to Brent.

I was halfway out the door, heading for the stairs.

"Hold on," Brent said.

I stopped, turned around, and gave him an impatient shoulder and hand shrug. A silent what do you want gesture.

"The tone of Mom's letter was serious. Real. She's not messing with us, Cass. She hid something in here and we need to find it before it bites us in the ass," he said.

I begrudgingly walked back to the freezer, looked inside, and pulled out a bag of frozen peas. I showed it to him. "What do you want to do? Go through every item, see if she hid something for us inside?" I tore open the bag and spilled the frozen peas on the floor. It was dramatic, but I had had it. "Wow, peas. The horror," I said, laying down the snark thick.

Brent rolled his eyes. "Don't waste food," he told me like he was talking to his nine-year-old son. I figured that making a mess on the floor triggered his OCD for cleanliness.

"Help me get everything out of the freezer so I can inspect inside," he continued, as he removed the frozen food items from the freezer and laid them out on the floor neatly.

I scoffed. But I helped him.

It took a few minutes, but now we were both standing over and looking into an empty freezer.

"Nothing. See. Mind fuck," I said as I crossed my arms over my chest.

Brent bent down into the now empty freezer. His chest touched the lip of the top of the freezer as he reached down and put his hand on the bottom panel. As he did that, it teetered loosely. He looked over his shoulder up at me. I was still standing there with my arms crossed.

"It's loose," he said.

Brent ran his fingers through the edges until he found a gap in the corner, which he lifted.

"The bottom comes up," he said.

Now, I was once again wondering what Mother was up to. "A false bottom?" I asked as I felt my heart beating a mile a minute once again.

"Looks so," Brent replied from inside.

He was on the tips of his toes as he continued lifting the plastic panel until he could get a decent grip on it, then it easily came up. He gently put the plastic panel on the floor and then we both peered down inside once again.

This time, we were looking down at the real bottom of the freezer and there was something in there, wrapped up tight. It was about four feet long. I remembered before Dad died, that he liked to buy a side of beef from the local butcher. It was more tasty and less expensive that way, he would say. And he would store it in the freezer. Was that what this was? I closed my eyes, hoping that's what it was, some forgotten side of beef, but knowing that was just dreaming.

Brent looked at me, then said, "We need to get that out of there and see what the hell is going on."

I felt like crying and running back up the stairs and not stopping until I was back in Las Vegas. Instead, I helped my brother remove that wrapped-up package. Doing it was difficult since it was frozen solid at the bottom of the freezer for who knew how many years. I felt duct tape and brittle frozen fabric. We took a few minutes, but we were able to pry it loose. We stepped back, short of breath. After a brief rest, Brent reached back inside and lifted the package and put it down on the cement floor.

It was bigger than I thought at first, looked around five feet long. And now I could tell what it was wrapped up in. Bed linens and towels held together with silvery gray duct tape.

I took several steps back. Brent hunched down, bent at the knees, and peered down at the thing on the floor.

"What is it?" I asked. My eyes were closed. I could feel a tear trickling down, warming my cheek from the chill of the basement and the freezer.

Brent said nothing as he began to pull and yank at the frozen materials wrapped around whatever was in there.

"It's frozen good. Give me a hand," he said.

I shook my head, just standing there looking away. I didn't have the mental energy to help him. Brent must have been okay with my unhelpful inaction because he didn't ask me again as he pulled at the frozen fabric and chunks began to crack and break off.

"It's breaking up like peanut butter brittle," Brent said, as he continued tearing at the frozen fabric.

I looked down at it, and I recognized the fabric's pattern. Mother's old linen, bed sheets, and those pink hard towels we used when growing up. Remembering how it felt like I was drying off with a Brillo pad as a kid.

I recoiled until my back hit the door. Brent stopped for a moment. He said nothing, but I knew he, too, recognized the fabric. He went back to the task at hand and continued for a few more minutes. Suddenly, he jumped up.

He turned and looked at me.

"What is it?" I asked. The tears were now free flowing.

"Go back upstairs, Cassie. You don't need to see this," Brent said, his voice soft.

"Is it him?" I asked.

"Go now!" he said.

EIGHTEEN
CASSIE

Fifteen Years Ago

I wasn't supposed to be down here, unless I was doing chores, like helping Mother with the wash or if I was in the root cellar, either fetching something for Mother or being locked inside it for misbehaving.

And I sure as heck shouldn't be in Brent's bedroom, if you could even call it that. There were no walls or doors, just an eight-panel folding partition screen made of cheesy-looking bamboo separating it from the rest of the basement area. But to Brent, that flimsy partition might as well be Fort Knox, making his bedroom impenetrable to anyone without his explicit authorization. I certainly didn't have Brent's security clearance to enter, which made being down here even more exciting.

The partition screen was tall, about six feet, and about sixteen inches wide, with solid slats providing complete privacy to anyone looking at it from the other side of the bamboo wall.

Behind it was his room. He had a sweet set-up with a full-size mattress, which seemed enormous compared to the little single bed I slept on upstairs in my bedroom. He also had his own TV with a DVD player and a mini dorm refrigerator. On the wall underneath the half window, he had three posters: two were from his favorite movies: *Darkman* and *Gladiator*. The third one was of Torii Hunter hitting a home run for the Twins.

Against the other wall was a desk, lamp, and a monitor with a docking station for his laptop, where Brent, an excellent student, did his schoolwork. Next to the bed was a flat weight bench and a storage rack for his dumbbells. As always, his living space was impeccably clean. Brent would be angry to find me not just in his bedroom, but on his bed in his soft, lavender-smelling comforter. Even more dangerous than trespassing into Brent's space was that I wasn't alone. I had snuck down a boy.

Brent would have a meltdown over trespassing into his room. Mother over having a boy over at the house, alone.

She would probably whip out her leather strap and beat me and the boy to death if she caught us down here messing around.

Despite feeling nervous about breaking so many rules by being down in the basement in Brent's room with a boy, I found the excitement of it all to be thrilling. Made me wonder if there was something wrong with me.

I reminded myself that I was not a sadist wanting to get caught. There were practical reasons for bringing him down to the basement instead of my bedroom. My tiny bed could barely fit just me, let alone the two of us. The other reason was that the basement was the best place for a quick escape if needed. In my room, I wouldn't have been able to tell if Mother or Brent were back home until I heard the garage door open, and it would have been too late - we would have been caught like a deer in headlights. Down here, although you couldn't see much out of that half-window, what you could see was worth the risk. If Mother or Brent's car turned into the driveway, I'd hear the familiar rumble of the engine and see the flash of headlights sweeping across the glass and tires of the car. We'd have plenty of time to run upstairs, and for the boy to sprint out the front door and for me to race up to my bedroom before Mother or Brent came in through the side entrance off the garage, none the wiser.

I wasn't worried about Mother coming home soon. She was at work. And Brent was at the track, so I had the entire house and this boy to myself.

He was cute and we'd been flirting a lot lately, but he wasn't really my boyfriend since Mother said I was too young to go steady. We were sitting on Brent's bed. My heart was beating fast, and my hands were sweaty, which made me self-conscious. We were making out. And gross, was he a sloppy kisser; I thought he learned how to kiss from watching porn videos online, whereas I wanted to kiss like they did in the Romcom movies I liked. But I went along with it his way, a lot of tongue flicking, felt kind of intense. But after a while, I felt his braces nicking my mouth, making me wince. The sexiness of it was fading fast. We finally pulled apart, both of us flushed and breathless. I giggled, and he leaned in for another kiss. Okay, one more round, I said to myself as we kissed deeply. I ran my hands through his hair as he wrapped his arms around my waist. His hands were moving up towards my chest and then down into my crotch. I yelped. He'd gone too far. Fun's over. So, I broke away from him and told him to stop. But he wasn't listening, so I told him to stop again, this time more forcible, but he ignored me. I pushed him away with my hands.

"You have to leave. My mom will be here any minute." But he knew I was lying, because I told him we had the whole house to ourselves for hours. He leaned in again. But I was done with this entire experience, so I leaned back and folded my arms across my chest so as to make it clear. The party was over.

"I want you to leave, now," I said to him. That made him snap. He transformed into something else that I'd never seen before.

He called me names. That I was a cock tease. This ugly side of him made me angry, but it also scared me. I was down here all alone with someone who was bigger and stronger than I was. I needed to end this, so I got off the bed to leave, but he lunged at me. His weight brought me crashing back down into Brent's bed. His hands running wild on my body, making my skin crawl. I tried to shove him off me, but he was stronger than me. It was so confusing. I'd known him since grade school. He was so sweet and cute up to a few minutes ago, and now had his hands all over me and wouldn't leave me alone and he wouldn't stop even though I'd asked him many times.

My initial anger was now a panic. How far was he willing to take this? I knew about date rape. Was that what was going to happen to me? Then what? I couldn't tell Mother and Brent. And he'd tell everyone that I wanted to do it.

I reached my arm to the side of the bed, trying to pull myself up, but I couldn't. My hand brushed up against something cold and hard on the floor. I glanced down and it was one of Brent's dumbbells. I wrapped my hand around it, and I picked it up, swinging it to the back of the boy's head. He let out a groan and his body tumbled off to the side. At first, I was relieved. He was off me, and he'd stopped assaulting me. But then, fear. He was not moving.

I called out his name, but he didn't answer. I shook his

body, but he was still. Tears were now streaming down my cheeks. I couldn't have hit him that hard. I was scared that I'd hurt him really badly and that I was going to be in so much trouble with Mother, Brent, the boy's parents, school, the police.

I was sobbing and in a mad panic as I ran up the basement stairs so fast that I tripped, skinning my knee on a step. But I picked myself up and I made it to the kitchen. I had to call the police. But I didn't reach for the landline phone in the kitchen, instead I ran for the front door. Perhaps a neighbor could help me without getting the police involved. I was about to reach the door when it opened and in walked Brent. I crashed into him, causing him to jump back.

"Watch it," he said, annoyed with me. Then he saw me with my long, disheveled hair, and I was sobbing.

"Whoa, what happened to you?" Brent asked.

I tried to tell him what had happened, but I was so hysterical that it took me a moment to calm down enough to tell Brent that a boy was trying to rape me, so I hit him with one of his dumbbells and he wasn't moving down in the basement.

"Wait here," he said as he headed downstairs.

"No, don't go down there," I begged him between sobs. Pleading that we get an adult to help us, but he waved me off and told me to wait while he checked on the boy.

"I'll go check on him," he said before he ran down the steps and slammed the door shut. I heard his footsteps quickly stomping down the creaky wooden steps down to the basement.

I didn't remember how long I waited, but it felt like a long time. What if the boy woke up and he hurt Brent?

I slowly opened the door to the basement, but I couldn't go back down there.

"Brent?" I whispered from the top of the stairs. I heard noises, but he didn't reply. So, I called out his name again, this time louder.

"Don't come down here, Cassie," Brent said. I was relieved to hear his voice.

"What's going on? Do you need my help?"

"No! Just hold on. I'm coming right up."

"Is Mikey okay?"

Brent didn't answer me, but a moment later, I heard shuffling toward the steps, then the sound of feet clomping up the stairs. I heard the familiar creak of the top step and Brent was there in the kitchen. He looked somber as he closed the door.

"Is he okay?"

He shook his head slowly.

"Come on, he's okay, right?"

"No, Cass. He's not okay. You killed Mikey."

NINETEEN
CASSIE

I PUSHED THAT TERRIBLE MEMORY AWAY AS I'D DONE for years, but it was different now that I was standing in this cursed basement almost fifteen years to the day that I killed Mikey Dawson.

Brent was with me, just like he was all those years ago, when we were teenagers. He was on his knees, frantically scraping the frozen fabric away like an archeologist who had just discovered an ancient mummy. But he wasn't being careful as they were since this wasn't a discovery bound for a museum. It was evidence that could land both of us in legal trouble.

Brent frantically pulled and tore at pieces of frozen fabric when he suddenly stopped. He balanced his weight on the balls of his feet, his toes pressing into the ground to support him as he looked down at what Mother had hidden in that freezer. I had been standing behind him, too afraid to look, but I had to, so I slowly got closer until I could look over his shoulder to see what he was seeing.

At first glance, it looked like a forgotten side of beef covered in freezer burn, but I could see its chest and part of its arm, mummified. There was no question what I was looking at and it wasn't meat from a cow or hog. It was a human body. I felt my body jerk away and a scream escaped from deep inside me; it must have come from the same place where I'd tried to bury these awful memories that were now coming out of me like a volcano erupting lava after years of being dormant. I didn't realize how loud I screamed, until Brent flinched, before he quickly covered the body up with the still-frozen fabric he had pried loose as he told me to leave.

But I couldn't. I just stood there, crying.

"Go back upstairs, Cassie. You don't want to see this," he told me again.

"Is it him?" I asked.

It was a stupid question. How many dead bodies would Mother store in her chest freezer? Brent went through its pocket and pried something out of the front jean pocket.

I was still standing there looking down at the body. All I could see was part of the torso and arm. I couldn't see the body's face since it was still covered by frozen fabric. But I recognized the T-shirt on the body. An AC/DC shirt, just like the one Mikey had worn when he came over that day. The body didn't look like I would imagine a fifteen-year-old cadaver would look like. It wasn't skeletal. It looked leathery, covered in freezer burn, although it had glistened from the melting ice. I saw what Brent had in his hand, what he pulled loose from the body's jean pocket, a blue velcro wallet emblazoned with the logo of the heavy metal band, The Scorpions. Mikey's favorite band. I started to sob. "Mikey's wallet!" I shrieked.

Brent grabbed me by the arm, gently but firmly, as he pulled me away toward the door that led away from the utility room and out to the main part of the basement.

"Let's go upstairs. We both could use some fresh air," he said. We made our way up the stairs and went to the kitchen. Brent took two glasses from the cabinet and filled them with tap water. He handed me one as I eyed the bottle of Jack Daniels on the counter. It was less than half full. I could drink it all right now. I licked my lips. Brent must have wondered what I was staring at because he glanced back in the direction I was looking and saw the bottle. He turned back to me with disdain. "Drink the water."

I felt ashamed. Ashamed for what I did to Mikey Dawson. I thought of his sister, Robin. Ashamed for being part of covering it up, so that his family continued searching for him to this day, holding hope he might still be alive. And that whole time he'd been in Mother's freezer less than three miles from the Dawson home. His parents still lived there. They'd refused to move. They'd kept the same land-line phone number. Just in case their missing child would call. And I was ashamed for wanting a drink so badly. Then I thought about Robin. Now a hotshot detective from St. Paul was sniffing around Brent and me. What did she know? I drank the water. As did Brent.

We sat at the kitchen table in silence for a moment. My hands trembled. And I didn't think it was the shakes, it was from the freezer discovery.

"Why would she just leave him there?" I asked after a moment of silence.

Brent shrugged. "I don't know. She told me she got rid of the body that night. I didn't realize she just wrapped it up in linens and dumped it into the chest freezer," Brent said, shaking his head.

"All this time," I said in disbelief.

"All those frozen pizzas, Hot Pockets, peas, carrots, the Thanksgiving turkeys we've eaten since then, all stored in that freezer with that thing underneath," Brent said. He couldn't stop shaking his head in shock.

Thinking about all those meals I ate pulled from the same freezer that served as Mikey Dawson's frozen grave made me want to throw up. It wasn't like my childhood was full of happiness and joy before that day. My dad was taken away from me in a car crash. Mother becoming a widow with two young children on a measly public high school teacher salary put enormous stress on her, which she seemed to take out on me. Was it because I was Daddy's Girl, as he would tell me all the time? The apple of his eye was another thing my dad would say to me. Is that why Mother turned so cold and nasty toward me? She had spanked us before my dad died, but it wasn't until after his death that her punishment became disturbing. Locking me in the fruit cellar for a couple of hours. Using that leather strap to whup me in the back of the legs.

Perfect Brent didn't incur her wrath like I did.

I remembered that day the fear I felt of what Mother would do to me after what happened to Mikey. I had begged Brent not to call Mother. I was ready to take my chances with the police. But Brent disagreed. "Mom will know what to do," he had told me back then.

So, he called Mother at the school asking her to come home right away. "It's an emergency," he told her.

She arrived fifteen minutes later. She went down to the basement and saw what I had done. I would never forget that look of horror on her face. The disbelief that a child she had given birth could do that to another human being.

I wanted to tell her that it was an accident, that I just wanted Mikey to leave me alone, but I couldn't speak. I sat at the kitchen table in a daze.

I waited for her to call 911, but she didn't. She said

since I had gotten Brent involved, he was now culpable for not calling the police right away. At seventeen, he was already considering the many college scholarships that were coming his way. Mother would not let my actions ruin Brent's future. And what about her future? she demanded.

She had finally gotten out of the classroom and started working as a guidance counselor a year ago. "How would it look?" she kept asking me.

Her own daughter killing a boy. In her house. She could all but hear the snickering around the town of the guidance counselor with the killer daughter in prison. They would probably fire her. No. She would not let what I had done ruin their lives. So, she told Brent and me to leave.

"Get in the car and don't come back until I text you that it's okay to return. It will be a few hours," she had told Brent. We did as Mother told us.

A few hours later we received the text that we could go home. Mother told us not to ask what she did with the body and that we would never discuss this again. Ever.

After what happened with Mikey Dawson, Mother turned even more cold and distant toward me. She stopped the whupping and locking me in the cellar. It was as if she had given up on me, or perhaps I scared her as she saw what I was capable of. My estrangement with my family began on that day. For two years, I lived in that house, and I never again set foot in the basement until today. Mother tried to get me down there to help with the laundry or get stuff from the root cellar, but I refused. Brent would play mediator, going down there in my stead. He also continued using the basement as his bedroom. I never understood how he could sleep down there. But we didn't discuss it, because Mother told us never to talk about what happened down there ever again, which was what we did until now.

"We need to get rid of it. For good this time," Brent said.

"You must be kidding," I said.

"I wish I were, but I'm serious, sis. And we have little time. The funeral is tomorrow. And then I have that junk hauling and cleaning crew coming to the house the following morning and that Realtor is also stopping by. That can't be here," Brent said, pointing down toward the basement. "And we have Robin out there sniffing around. We need to do this tonight."

"We? I can't—"

Brent stopped me. "I'll take care of it. You just hang tight up here."

I was used to him being cool and collected. He was always the confident one. In control. But this wasn't some normal shit life throws at you. We weren't saying it out loud, but we were talking about getting rid of a body. How could he be so nonchalant about it? So, I asked him.

"I dissected plenty of cadavers in medical school. I cut up bodies for a living. It's not a big deal for me. And I know how to make sure it's gone forever. I just need to get some supplies. And I can get to work later tonight."

I couldn't believe we were having this discussion. But it was my fault we were having it. I put us in this predicament. And even though I was the killer, Brent helped cover it up for all these years.

It was an enormous risk. His life as he knew it would be over. His pretty little socialite wife would probably divorce him. All because of what I did to Mikey Dawson. I couldn't do that to Brent, even though the guilt and keeping it all inside for all these years was slowly killing me. That guilt must have also been rotting away at Mother until she couldn't take it. Maybe that's why she killed herself. Oh, God, I started bawling again.

"Cassie. You need to keep it together."

I nodded slowly, unable to meet Brent's gaze. "Okay," I said, not really believing it.

As I felt Brent's eyes on me, I looked up at him. I was so scared.

"Don't worry, Cassie. I'll take care of everything. It soon won't be a problem, trust me."

Brent avoided using terms like "body" or "Mikey" and instead referred to him as "it," "the thing," or "the problem." I suspected this was his way of trying to distance himself emotionally from what he was planning to do. All of this was because of what I did all those years ago. And Mother leaving that body in the freezer all these years. What was she thinking?

TWENTY

BRENT

PLANNING A FUNERAL, A WAKE, EXECUTING MOM'S estate, dealing with my alcoholic sister, and putting the house up for sale had already been running me ragged between the Twin Cities and Big Plaine. Now I had to add getting rid of a body to the list. I took deep breaths and centered myself. I could handle this as long as I remained calm and focused. Just another thing I needed to add to my to-do list, so I could then cross it out.

Cassie was the wild factor. She was a mess. Having never dealt with what happened, burying it deep inside her only for it all to come back up in this way was going to send her on a downward spiral. How far was she going to go? And was she going to take me down with her?

The body of that little shit went on the top of my to-do list. So, I needed to make some changes to my plans. What I had planned to do was head home to the family, then go down to Big Plaine in the morning with the family for the funeral. But now I had to get rid of that body tonight. And it was going to take time, and I would need some tools which I didn't have with me. Why would I? I wasn't going to drive to the Walmart that's ten miles away to buy tools with Robin in town investigating. She was my chief concern. Robin had already been following us around, wanting to question us. For all I knew, she was watching me now. I looked around, feeling paranoid.

I needed to get home, get my tools, and get Jillian down there tonight instead of in the morning. I left Cassie at the house with strict instructions to not let anyone inside the house.

I DROVE onto highway 169 and I called Jillian to let her know of the new plans.

She wasn't happy about the last-minute changes. I blamed it all on Cassie — which wasn't technically a lie. I told Jillian she was having a breakdown, and the drinking had gotten worse. Also, not lies. So, I was heading home, and she needed to get herself and the kids ready and packed for an overnight stay in Big Plaine with a change of clothes for the funeral in the morning. I let Jillian vent for a while, then she agreed to be ready by the time I got home in about an hour.

I WAS home for less than fifteen minutes. Got my toolbox, then packed up my things and the family in Jillian's Porsche Cayenne. I told Jillian it was best if we drove separately since I would need a car for the couple of busy days I had in front of me. Didn't tell her about the late evening plans I had for that night, of course. Turned around and headed back down Big Plaine.

. . .

I PUT Jillian and the kids at the Festival Inn Xpress in Big Plaine. They wrinkled their noses at the subpar accommodations, but it was the only choice in town. I'd spoiled my family with our usual hotel choices being more like The Ritz Carlton and the Four Seasons. But this was as good as it got in Big Plaine, so they needed to make the best of it. It was just for one night, I reminded them.

I drove over to the house. This whole fiasco was playing in my head, but I did my best to remain calm. Once I got rid of the body tonight, then we could move on with the funeral and the estate business. As soon as Mom was in the ground, I was sending Jillian and the kids back home to Minnetonka. She wouldn't argue, eager to head back to the Twin Cities.

I would stay behind with Cassie to wrap things up and deal with the estate. I had already been planning to do that anyway, so Jillian wasn't suspicious that something nefarious was going on. Like me having to get rid of that frozen human popsicle Mom left for us in the basement.

What was she thinking? Obviously, she wasn't. I was amazed Mom had gotten away with it for fifteen years. It was that sturdy old American-made freezer that kept going like a tank. Today's freezers would have long ago stopped working. The motor petering out, melting and thawing out Mom's secret. We were lucky that the freezer never broke down. It just went on ticking for all those years.

I just needed it to work for a few more hours. Once I took care of its contents, the freezer, along with all of Mom's other stuff in the house, would end up in the junk hauler's truck after the funeral. Once all the household goods were out of the house, I had a high-tech cleaning crew coming in to scour the place. This company specialized in deep cleans. Cleaning up a crime scene was their specialty. Of course, they wouldn't know there had been a body in the freezer for over a decade and that they were cleaning up a crime scene.

I needed that basement scrubbed clean before I handed the keys over to the real estate agent.

It was going to be a busy couple of days down there while I took care of our problem for good and dealt with Mom's estate.

I headed over to the house in the Mercedes Wagon. In the back was my portable Craftsman toolbox containing the tools I needed to take care of the Mikey Dawson problem.

What had me more worried than the dead body in the freezer was Cassie. She was a complete wreck emotionally, and that had me on edge. The fear of her spilling our family's darkest secret consumed me.

Concealing a murder was bad enough, but if the media ever discovered the truth—that Mikey Dawson, the town's long-lost missing child, lay entombed in my mother's chest freezer for fifteen years beneath a mound of frozen food— my high-society life would shatter. And that was merely the beginning. The revelation would undoubtedly trigger a relentless police investigation, leaving no stone unturned. I could play dumb, hey, that's Mom's freezer and her secret. But even if I evaded law enforcement punishment, my reputation and practice would still be ruined.

I was wobbling on the high wire as I shouldered the responsibility of permanently disposing of the body, but I also had to navigate Cassie's deteriorating mental state, ensuring she remained tight-lipped. All the while, I had to orchestrate my mother's wake and funeral and prepare the house for sale.

. . .

THE BURDEN of all I had to do was heavy on me as I walked into the house. The first thing that hit me, yet again, was the smell of alcohol. It was strong and pungent.

I followed the smell down the hallway and into the living room, where I found my sister sprawled out on the couch in front of the television. She had passed out with an empty bottle of whiskey on the TV tray and an empty glass in her hand. I took the glass and laid it on the table.

I tried to wake her, but she was out cold. I thought this was for the best. I could go downstairs and take care of our problem without dealing with Cassie's frail state of mind. I grabbed my toolbox and went to the kitchen.

I stopped cold. The door to the basement was open. I was certain I had closed it before I left. I looked back toward the living room. Did Cassie open it? She wouldn't go down there by herself. Until today, when I practically had to drag her down to the basement, Cassie had refused to go back down there after what happened with Mikey.

I considered going back to Cassie to ask her, but she was dead to the world, so what was the point? With so much on my mind, I supposed, I could have left the door open. I headed downstairs to do what Mom refused to do and take care of our Mikey problem for good.

TWENTY-ONE
BRENT

I set my toolbox down next to the freezer, knowing I needed to work quickly. I opened the freezer door and peered inside. I felt a chill down my spine, and it wasn't from the sub-freezing temperature from inside.

Mikey's sunken face was looking back at me. I had covered the body back up with the fabric I removed. I didn't see the point of putting it back into the hidden compartment, but I covered it up with the food packages I had removed. Now, someone had been moving them around inside the freezer and also took off the fabric that had covered his face.

This confirmed it - Cassie had been down there. Who else could it be? It sure as hell wasn't Robin, because there would be a cadre of law enforcement there. I never would have thought Cassie would have had the wherewithal to go down to the basement, alone. She had avoided it like the plague since that day.

But it was clear that Cassie had been down there while I was gone, and she removed the fabric from its head. Why did she do that? Morbid curiosity? Did she know?

I wanted to run back upstairs and throw her into a cold bath to wake her up and demand that she told me why she went down here and messed with the body.

But I couldn't do that right now. Getting rid of this damn body once and for all was the most important thing to do and I needed to do it quickly before Cassie woke up and started getting in my way. I could deal with Cassie later.

I put on a hairnet and changed into blue scrubs and surgical gloves. I removed the electric autopsy bone saw and the 40-volt DC power supply source, which I plugged into the wall. Once it was plugged in, I hit the button to test the saw. This was a top-of-the-line model; it purred almost silently. Next up, I removed a manual bone saw, a large finely sharpened butcher's knife, and a dust vacuum. I took the extra-large blue plastic tarp from the toolbox. I unfolded it and laid it on the floor next to the floor drain in case there was fluid seepage.

I reached inside the freezer and lifted the body from it, laying it out on the tarp. Mikey Dawson was fifteen when he died. And he had been frozen in that freezer for fifteen years, so the body wasn't as large as I expected. That was a plus. It would be easier to work with than if it was a six-foot, two-hundred-pound man. Since my goal there was to make the body vanish, I didn't have to let it thaw as a medical examiner would do before cutting into it for an autopsy.

A body frozen for that long would take a few days to thaw out. But for my purposes, it was easier this way.

I put on a face shield visor and just got to work.

I worked fast, now and then stopping to listen if I heard Cassie stumbling around. Then I went back to the task at hand. When I was done, I had quartered the body and removed the head and hands.

I placed each section on thick brown paper along with a

twenty-pound weight and wrapped it up, like a butcher does. I then secured the bundle with duct tape so it wouldn't come loose.

I put that in a black heavy-duty contractor trash bag. I drew the flap tie tight to close it and then went around it a few times with duct tape until it was tightly wrapped.

I repeated this four times. Until I had five bags ready to go.

I checked the time. It had taken me two hours. I was sweating and my arms, hands, and back were sore. But there was no time to rest. I had to get rid of these bags.

I wished Mom had one of those big old-time furnaces, but she didn't, which meant I had to drive into the country to get rid of them.

There was still no sign of Cassie. My electric saw was quiet, but she would have heard it upstairs, so she must really have been out of it. Same when I had to use the manual saw and the knife. She would have heard all that. It didn't matter that I was experienced and I worked fast, chopping up a body makes noise. But apparently not enough to rouse her from a Jack Daniels-induced coma.

It was dark out, but the night sky would soon begin to lighten with the approaching dawn, so I got going.

I peeked out the front door. It was the dead of night. No one was around. I loaded the bags into the back of my truck and drove onto the empty highway.

The first stop was a small bridge over the Minnesota River, a few miles outside of Big Plaine. With a quick glance around to ensure that I was alone, I heaved the bag over the side of the bridge and into the dark waters below.

Continuing on my journey, I took the Minnesota River Valley Scenic Byway toward Highway 25, stopping halfway to dispose of a second bag. From there, I turned toward the many large lakes that dotted the landscape within a forty-mile radius of Big Plaine. I found a secluded spot to rid myself of the third and fourth bag.

With a sense of finality, I tossed the last bag with the head and hands, into Silver Lake. I drove back to Big Plaine, the weight on my shoulders much lighter.

As I pulled into the driveway of the house, the digital clock on the dashboard read 3:30 a.m. I was exhausted. The house was dark, just as I had left it. I called out for Cassie as I made my way inside, but there was no response.

I went to the living room where I left her, but she wasn't there. I called her name. No answer. I checked her bedroom. She wasn't there. Where the hell was she?

I checked the garage, and Mom's car was gone. "Dammit, Cassie."

I called her phone, but it went straight to voicemail.

Where could she be? Money was tight for her until we settled the estate, so she couldn't really go anywhere else, like up to the Twin Cities. The two bars in town had closed hours ago, and Cassie's suitcase and belongings were still in the bedroom, so I didn't think she took the car and drove back to Las Vegas. I felt exhausted and hungry. I went to the kitchen and made myself a sandwich, hoping that Cassie would show up.

I thought of the places Cassie could have gone to while I ate a PB&J sandwich and drank milk at the kitchen table. I knew that Mom and I weren't the only connections to Big Plaine that Cassie had all but severed. She hadn't kept in touch with any of her high school or town friends, so it was unlikely that she would stay at any of their homes. I chewed my sandwich thoughtfully, trying to think of anyone else who might know her whereabouts. I supposed she could have left town and gone up to the Twin Cities. Plenty of places to stay up there. She must have a credit card she could use even if she couldn't afford a hotel up there. Maybe she just needed to clear her head and stay away while I took care of our basement problem. She was likely still wasted. The last thing I needed was for her to get pulled over by the police driving in her condition.

It was now three-forty in the morning. I needed to sleep. It had been a long and hectic day. Although worried about where Cassie was and what she was up to, the primary source of my worries that night was at the bottom of five different bodies of water. A perk of living in the Land of Ten Thousand Lakes. Even if Cassie were to speak to someone about what had happened, there was nothing left in the house to implicate me anymore.

In just a matter of hours, the cleaning and junk-hauling crew would arrive, and I intended to have them start in the basement by getting rid of that damned freezer that had caused me so much trouble and scrubbing the basement and root cellar top to bottom. The crew would arrive, and I intended to have them meticulously scour every surface, every nook and cranny, as if trying to erase the sins of the past.

But right now, I needed to sleep. I had been on edge for so long, and sleep was much needed. I told Jillian I was spending the night there with Cassie. So, I collapsed onto the couch. I was worried about Cassie, but I must have been more tired than worried, because right away, I was out.

TWENTY-TWO

CASSIE

THE HUMAN MIND IS AN INCREDIBLE AND COMPLEX machine, capable of twisting and burying unpleasant memories in order to protect us from the pain of the past. I had been doing this for so long that I hadn't even realized it. But now, being back in Big Plaine and facing the memories of what had happened to Mikey Dawson all those years ago, I found myself overwhelmed by a flood of long-forgotten memories.

It was as if I was watching a home video of myself from fifteen years ago.

Then

I was fifteen years old, and I was so scared over what I had done to Mikey. Brent had been down in the basement with Mikey for what felt like an eternity. Suddenly, I thought I heard Mikey's voice, and my heart leapt with hope. He was alive.

I walked over to the closed basement door and pressed my ear against it, trying to make out what was being said. I could hear muffled voices on the other side, two of them, and although my heart was pounding and my knees felt weak, I slowly opened the door.

I heard a thudding sound. And a groan. From there, it became fuzzy again. I remember calling out for Brent.

"Don't come down here, Cassie," he shouted from the basement.

I stepped back until my back hit the wall of the kitchen across from the basement door, and I slowly slid down to sit on the floor with my knees to my chest.

A few minutes later, Brent reappeared in the kitchen. He was looking down at me with curiosity. "Are you okay?" he asked.

"Is Mikey okay?"

Brent slowly shook his head. "No, sorry, Cass. He's dead. You killed him."

I sobbed. "Are you sure?"

Brent squatted down so we were face to face. He was disheveled, which was a rarity for him to have a single hair out of place. He looked at me for a moment then said, "Yes, I'm sure. I tried to save him. I did CPR, but it was too late. He's gone."

"We need to call 911," I said to Brent.

"They'll lock you up, Cassie. Maybe even Mom since as the adult, you're her responsibility. She'll lose her job. The town will hate us, and this will ruin my college chances if it's in the news that my sister is a killer. No, this has to be our secret," Brent said.

I was hysterical. "No, Brent, we have to call 911."

Brent left and came back with a couple of pills and a glass of water. "Take this. It will help calm your nerves," he told me.

I hesitated. "Come on, Cassie, do it now." I took the

pills and drank the water. It didn't take long for me to start feeling woozy. "What was that you gave me?" I asked, feeling fuzzy.

"Just some of Mom's happy pills. Don't worry, you'll be fine. It will help you chill out while I figure out what to do."

"Call 911," I said, hearing myself slurring.

I remember feeling like a zombie when Mother came home. Brent and her talking in hushed tones, looking at me with concern and disgust before I looked away in tears then faded off.

———

I WOKE up in the passenger seat of Brent's car. I turned my head, and he was sitting behind the wheel eating a burrito.

"Hey, welcome back," he told me with a smile. His face was back to what I was used to. The dead eyes and darkness with which he looked at me back in the kitchen had dissipated.

"I feel funny."

"Yeah, sorry, I shouldn't have given you Mom's pills. A bit too much firepower at your height and weight. But you needed to calm down."

After a moment, he handed me a bag from the backseat. "I got your favorite from Taco Bell."

I hoped it was all just a terrible dream. I looked out the window but didn't recognize where we were, so I asked Brent.

"Red Wing. Eat your tacos."

Red Wing was more than an hour from Big Plaine. We have no connection to this town. "What are we doing in Red Wing?"

"Eating tacos," he said with a smile, without a care in the world.

I looked at the food and felt like vomiting again. "I don't understand what's happening."

"We're just killing time," he gave a devilish grin. "Oops, sorry, poor choice of words."

I started to tear up, and Brent rolled his eyes at me.

"Enough with the waterworks, Cassie. It's getting annoying. Mom and I, we've been taking care of your mess. Show some appreciation."

"I wanted to call for help."

"If you called the police, you wouldn't be far from here then, you know that, right?" Brent laughed.

I didn't know what he was talking about. "What do you mean?"

Brent smiled widely. "The state juvenile correctional facility is in Red Wing. It's around here somewhere, close. Had we called 911, it's probably where you would be right now. Not here with me eating tacos. Your ass would be in jail for who knows how long. Until you're eighteen, I suppose then they would send you to adult slammer in Stillwater."

"But... it was an accident. He tried to rape me."

"I suppose that might work. If everything aligned perfectly for you, the right lawyer, judge, and jury. Maybe. But if one of those cogs misfire, then you're fucked, and your ass goes to prison. And your future is over at fifteen. So be smart about this, Cassie. Mom and I are helping you stay out of jail."

"I didn't ask for you and Mother to do that," I said.

"Don't be an ungrateful shit," Brent hissed. The face of my brother once again was gone, replaced by someone I did not know. I looked at him, feeling terrified. His hard glare softened. His whole body loosened, it was like he could transform back and forth into two different people.

"I'm sorry, Cassie. I didn't mean..." he sighs loudly. "Look, I'm trying to be calm about all this, but I'm also scared. For what might happen to you. And, I won't lie, what might happen to me. I'll be able to pick which Ivy League college I want to go to in the fall. Now that I've helped cover up a murder and clean up a crime scene, destroying evidence, they'll lock me up. And I'm eighteen. I won't end up here in Red Wing in juvie hall. They'll lock me up in Stillwater. And Mom, too. After the legal system is done with us, all our lives would be destroyed. I won't be able to go to medical school. Mom won't be able to get another job in the school system. She'll lose her house. She'll lose everything. All because of what you did. And sure, I believe you, it was in self-defense. But now we've gone too far. If you go to the police, you're taking Mom and me down with you. So please, I beg you. Don't say anything to anyone about what happened tonight.

"Don't ruin all our lives over someone who tried to rape you, for Christ's sake. Soon we'll go back home and talk to Mom and figure things out. But for now, let's just chill out, okay?"

I slowly nodded and agreed to go along with what they wanted me to do.

Now

THOSE MEMORIES KEPT FLICKERING in my head. I blinked hard, and I looked around, trying to get my bearings. Where was I? I wasn't fifteen-year-old me in Red

Wing anymore. I sat up, and my head was spinning. One thing was for sure, I wasn't at the house either. It hurt my head, but I looked around at the empty walls and the thick door in front of me and noticed I had been lying in an uncomfortable metal cot attached to a cement wall. I got up, slowly, looking around — I was in a tiny room. There was a metal door with a little square window. I ran to it, but there was no handle. I pushed at it, but it was locked. I screamed.

TWENTY-THREE
CASSIE

I FLUNG MYSELF AGAINST THE THICK DOOR. "WHAT AN idiot," I said to myself as I felt shooting pain in my shoulder. I looked out the small window. It was as thick as the door. As my head cleared, I knew where I was. I had been in a room like this before. I pounded on the door with my fists. After what felt like an eternity, I saw a man's face appear at the window, looking at me. I screamed at him to let me out. Suddenly, the door unlocked and slid open violently. The man, a police officer in uniform, stood in front of me, holding his hands up.

"Take it easy, Cassie," the officer said sternly, but there was kindness in his tone and body language. Another cop, a woman, stood behind him, eyeing me with a look of pure loathing and disgust. Her hand rested on a can of OC spray attached to her utility belt.

"Where am I?" I asked, feeling groggy and sick. I was pretty sure I knew the answer, but still... Big Plaine? Minneapolis? Somewhere else? I couldn't remember last night. Another blackout.

"What a freaking space cadet," the female officer scoffed.

"You're in the city jail, Cassie," the male officer said. The sternness in his voice eased some.

"Am I in Big Plaine?"

The female officer guffawed at my question, but the male officer seemed kinder. There was concern on his face, not contempt like the other officer.

"Yes, Cassie, you're in a holding cell in Big Plaine," he said.

He used my name like he knew me. I looked at him. He was all grown up, but I recognized his face, especially his brown eyes.

"Charlie?" I asked. The officer smiled.

"Long time no see, Cassie. Sorry it had to be like this," Charlie said.

Charlie Bell and I had been friends in school. He was Mikey Dawson's best friend, and I remembered reading an article on one of the anniversary dates of Mikey's disappearance where Charlie said that, like Mikey's sister, Robin, he had become a police officer, partly because of what happened to Mikey. Now there he was, a cop, not knowing that he was looking at the person who had killed his best friend. Maybe deep down, he knew.

At first, I felt reassured, a friendly face, unlike the other cop, but then I noticed it in his eyes, and the way he was looking at me. There were no mirrors there, but I must have looked like death warmed over as I usually did coming out of a blackout. What Charlie was doing was pitying me. I got that a lot in my pathetic life, and I couldn't stand being pitied. My relief at seeing Charlie soured. I felt embarrassment and anger.

"Why the hell am I in jail? I didn't do anything," I

snapped. I felt dumb as soon as I said it. It was what cops hear all day long when they're arresting someone: I did nothing wrong. Why are you arresting me?

I had no recollection of last night. For all I knew, I ran over someone or killed someone in a car crash. Oh, God. I panicked. Did I kill another person?

The other cop laughed out loud. "That's a good one. She didn't do anything. Cut her loose, Charlie."

Charlie turned back to face the other officer with an annoyed look. "It's okay, Crystal, I've got this." The female cop shrugged. "Alright, Sarge, she's all yours." Her contempt toward me was thick as mud as she turned and walked away from my cell.

Charlie turned his attention back to me. He still had thick black hair, although in school it was a Billy Ray Cyrus mullet that hung down past his shoulder blades. Now it was short and neat. A cop haircut. He was sporting a well-groomed beard, and I noticed he was wearing a gold wedding band on his finger. I assumed, like most of my classmates, he had gotten married, had kids, and was living a decent life, which was more than I could say for myself.

Charlie said, "They arrested you last night for DWI, Cassie."

"What?" I was so confused. Freaking blackouts. But I got these flashbacks. I heard the sound of a buzz-saw coming from the basement. Faint at first, then louder. It woke me up from my stupor. I slowly got up from the couch and wobbled over to the window and saw Brent's SUV parked there. He was back, and from the sound of that motor whirring, I knew what he was doing down there. I almost threw up right there in the living room.

I ran back to the couch and buried myself under a blanket. I didn't want to think about what Brent was doing in the basement.

Then it was just a series of flashbacks. Moments of lucidity in my blackout. Brent looked at me. He left. I stumbled off the couch. I was out of my booze, so I took the fifth of vodka Mother had in the icebox and her car keys.

I was already way too drunk to drive, but that didn't stop me. I had to get away. I downed the vodka in a few swigs. The car fishtailed when I took a curb too fast. A few cars blew their horns at me, and I recalled wanting to sleep. The memories of being a teenager in Red Wing and then waking up in jail.

"You were in bad shape, Cassie. We got two 911 calls about you driving erratically. Crystal found your car on the side of the road. It was running. Lights on. And you were passed out behind the wheel. Luckily, you could put it in park before you passed out. But the car was running with the doors locked. Crystal and another officer tried to get you to open the door, but you were out of it for a while. Finally, they were able to rouse you, but you tried to drive off. You hit the accelerator, but the car was in park, so you were spinning wheels. That's when they broke the window and pulled you out. You resisted a bit once on the ground until you passed out again."

I cried, not remembering any of that. I had been drinking and I was sure I was over the limit and like an idiot, then I got in Mother's car and drove. But I was an old pro drunk. I couldn't be that smashed. There wasn't enough booze left in that bottle to get into the blackout zone.

I felt so ashamed. "Charlie, I know I shouldn't have..." He put his hand up interrupting me in mid-sentence.

He looked around, making sure no one else was nearby. "Don't say anything, Cassie. You have the right to remain silent. I suggest you exercise that right because anything you tell me right now, I have to report."

Charlie was trying to help me. Even though I was out drinking and driving. Resisting. A piece of shit who knew where his best friend was right now.

I nodded and sank back down onto the uncomfortable cement bench.

A moment later, I heard a voice I recognized coming from behind Charlie. "Good morning, Cassie." I looked up and saw Robin standing next to Charlie. This was the last school reunion I would have wanted to be a part of, but I had no choice, since I was in jail.

Charlie closed the door to my cell, and I could see him and Robin talking through the windowpane, but I couldn't hear them because the cell was soundproof. After a moment, I saw Charlie turn his head and look through the glass pane at me. His expression showed that he was conflicted, but he nodded his head. Robin gently patted him on the back, as if thanking him.

The door opened and Charlie stepped inside. "Robin wants to talk to you," he said. Then he leaned in close and spoke in a low voice. "Remember what I told you." I looked at him, and I could see a warning in his eyes, and I remembered his words: "You have the right to remain silent. I suggest you exercise that right." He exited the cell as Robin entered.

Charlie closed the door. Robin leaned against the wall. She was dressed in blue jeans, a black shirt tucked in, and a black Patagonia jacket. She was beautiful.

"How are you feeling?"

"Like shit."

"Not too surprising. I watched the cop's body camera footage of your arrest. You were out of it."

Great, that will probably end up on YouTube someday.

"I checked your record. Not your first DWI."

I didn't like the feeling of being so exposed. An open book. But they call it a public record for a reason. And as a cop, it was easy for her to dig up all the legal dirt in my life.

"Only one other time. A long time ago," I said, sounding way more defensive than I intended.

"Four years ago," Robin corrected me.

"Okay, whatever," I said. "I have the right to remain silent," I blurted out.

She laughed. "You sure do. Besides, I'm not a member of the Big Plaine police department. I'm not here as a cop."

"So, what are you doing here?" I asked her.

"You know."

I looked away. I knew. "How did you find me here, anyway?"

"Charlie knew I was in town, looking into Mikey's case on my time. I told him I've been trying to talk to you, but you refused to meet with me. So, when they brought you in here under arrest, he called me," Robin said.

I felt angry. That must be some kind of privacy violation. Robin must have sensed what I was thinking, because she added, "Let's not get Charlie in trouble with his police chief. Like me, he just wants to know what happened to Mikey. He didn't call me cop to cop, on official business. He called the sister of his missing best friend. That's it."

I looked at her but said nothing. She had a very easygoing, calming presence in the way she spoke and looked at me. I had to remind myself that it was part of her act. It was how she became a detective in St. Paul in her early thirties. She was a talented investigator who could bring me and Brent down, and that's what this was about. Official or not, she was investigating a missing child's case, her own brother, and she didn't care about my well-being. She was fishing, just like Brent kept telling me. I wasn't taking the bait.

After a moment of silence, Robin asked me, "Don't you?"

I looked at her, confused. "Don't I what?"

"Don't you want to know what happened to Mikey? You were close. I know he liked you. A lot."

"I don't know what you expect from me. I don't know anything," I lied.

She sat on the concrete bench next to me. "I think you know more than you're telling me. More than you've told anyone about what happened to Mikey."

I told myself to stay silent like Charlie and Brent had advised me.

Robin continued. "I know Mikey was going to your place. He told Charlie he was going to hook up with you because you had the house to yourself. So, Mikey goes to your house. It's just you and him. And no one's seen him alive since."

I swallowed hard, unable to even look at her. I started to tremble.

"Cassie, I've looked at your record and files. You've lived two lives. You were an A-student. Great at soccer. A popular girl in school. Funny. Spunky. A bright future ahead of you. Then a drastic change. You become a D student. Withdrawn. Your appearance changes. You cover up your body with bulky dark clothing. Hanging out with the potheads and the juvie hall crowd. You drink. A lot. And I can track the change clear as day. It's like flicking a switch. The day Mikey vanished, so did the old Cassie."

TWENTY-FOUR
BRENT

I ONLY SLEPT A FEW HOURS, BUT I FELT REFRESHED. The burden that was in the freezer was now at the bottom of five lakes. Then I remembered Cassie. I got up and ran over to her bedroom. She still wasn't there. The bed was a mess, but that was typical for Cassie; she probably hadn't made her bed since she was in the army. But it was the same messy bed as last night. She hadn't slept there.

I walked to the door leading to the attached garage; I opened it and looked inside. The car wasn't there. So, I thought she might have driven back to Las Vegas, or maybe she had crashed somewhere and was dead or in the hospital. I checked my phone. She hadn't called, but there was a text from a number I didn't recognize, with a 952 area code, so it was local.

The text read:

> This is Charlie with Belle Plaine PD. Just wanted to let you know Cassie is here in jail. DWI arrest. She's not hurt. No accident, but she's in pretty bad shape. Passed out cold. We will keep her in custody for a while. Not official notice. Just an FYI.

Okay, well, that solved the mystery of Cassie's disappearance. I had to get her out of there as soon as possible before they got to talk about our family secrets.

I texted Charlie back.

> Thank you for letting me know. I was worried sick, wondering where she was. When can she get out?

He texted back right away:

> She's doing better now. Should be okay to bail her out soon. She's talking with Robin now.

My blood ran cold. I almost dropped the phone. But I managed to text back:

> On my way

Since I had slept in the same clothes I wore yesterday, I was out the door within seconds of sending that text. I jumped into the Mercedes Wagon, backing out of the driveway quickly and peeling off toward the police department. I parked in front of the police station a few minutes later; thankful that in tiny Big Plaine, nothing was too far away.

I ran inside. Less than ten minutes after I read that first

text from Charlie, I was talking to the desk officer. Since Big Plaine was so small, I knew or recognized most people, but I didn't know him. I told him who I was and that I was there to bail out my sister.

The officer reported that they had arrested Cassie for DWI and resisting arrest. *Dammit, Cassie.*

"I'm here to bail her out," I repeated to the officer.

"Well, that's fine, but we're not at that part just yet," he replied dismissively.

"Can I see her?" I asked.

"Take a seat," the officer said as he stepped out into the staff only area.

As I waited, Charlie popped out from the back and greeted me. We shook hands.

"Thanks for letting me know she's here," I told him. "I'm afraid Cassie's fallen on hard times with her drinking. I'm trying to get her into rehab."

He nodded solemnly. "That's good to hear," Charlie said.

"Is she still with Robin?"

Charlie nodded.

"Why? She's St. Paul PD, not Big Plaine."

Charlie looked worried. "Well, um. You know she's trying to find out what happened to Mikey. And I am too, so she said Cassie might know something that can help figure out what happened to him. So, I called her to let her know Cassie was here."

"I understand where she's coming from, being Mikey's sister and all, but she's been hounding my family a lot. First Mom, now Cassie. I didn't know what she thinks Cassie knows about Mikey, but I'm getting sick and tired of Robin harassing my family."

Charlie's brows rose. He looked nervous as he hemmed and hawed for a moment.

"Um... well, I didn't know... it's just that Cassie and Mikey were close, though. And well, he told me he was going to see Cassie when he disappeared," Charlie said, stammering.

"You were close to Mikey. The way I remember it, he was supposed to see you that day, not Cassie. Is Robin hounding you non-stop?"

My comment took Charlie aback. Good. See how he likes it.

"I've had enough. It feels like Cassie's rights are being trampled on. Is Neil here?" I asked, referring to Neil Hansen, the chief of police whom I knew well.

I was a big financial contributor to the Big Plaine police department and union, so I had some sway, which I was prepared to use.

"No, he's not in yet," Charlie said, clearly worried about his job.

"I want to see Cassie right now, Charlie. Mom's wake is in a few hours. I want her out of here."

I saw Charlie fidget, but he relented. "Sure, follow me."

I followed him to the back of the station. It was a small department, with only a few officers and admin staff. It didn't take long to get to the jail section. These were only holding cells used for temporary detention. They called them sober tanks since they were often used to hold drunks overnight before releasing them.

There were only four cells. The station had been remodeled six years before, and I had contributed signifi-cantly to that project. Charlie led me back to the cell where they were holding Cassie. Through the windowpane, I could see Robin and Cassie sitting side-by-side on a metal bench. Charlie opened the door, and both Robin and Cassie flinched and turned to look at me.

"You don't have the right to talk to my sister, Detective," I said curtly to Robin.

"She's not a minor," Robin retorted with a snort.

"Cassie, you don't talk to cops who have arrested you, ever. They are here to collect evidence against you, that's it. I don't care how far back we go with Charlie and Robin. They're not your friends. You know the drill. Don't talk to the police without a lawyer," I said, my anger towards the police and Cassie bubbling up. She should have known better than to speak without a lawyer present.

Cassie looked away from me, and I wondered what she had already told Robin.

"This isn't St. Paul, Detective. What are you even doing here talking to my sister, anyway?" I demanded.

"I'm here as a private citizen, that's all," Robin replied.

"Oh, really? So, any private citizen can just come into my sister's cell for a friendly chat?" I raised my voice, causing other cops nearby to turn their attention to us. I glared at Charlie.

Robin stood up from the bench. "I didn't mean to upset you guys," she said as she made her way out of the cell.

"It's all you've been doing, Detective. Bugging my mom. Now my sick sister in jail. And Mom's wake is in a few hours. I'm taking her home."

Robin raised her hands in a gesture of surrender. "My apologies, Brent, I didn't mean to upset you."

"It's Doctor Walsh, Detective," I barked at her, fed up with her intrusion into our lives. I wasn't above playing the rich, entitled asshole doctor card when necessary, and what was happening there was certainly necessary.

"My apologies, Doctor Walsh. Ms. Walsh," Robin said

as she walked away. I glared at Cassie. "I'm going to bail you out of here right away. Just hang tight and don't talk to anyone else. Clear?"

She nodded but said nothing. So, I leaned in close and said more forcefully, "Clear?"

"Yes, clear," she finally whispered.

TWENTY-FIVE
BRENT

IT DIDN'T TAKE LONG TO BAIL CASSIE OUT OF JAIL. They set the bail at ten thousand dollars. Higher than I expected, but considering Cassie's criminal history, it wasn't too shocking, I suppose. It was unconditional bail, which was a relief since that meant Cassie didn't need to follow any special rules before her court date. Meaning she could carry on as usual once I got her out of jail. I paid the bondsman in cash, and they released Cassie.

I waited for her in the lobby. She walked out with Charlie. Even though I had been tough on him as well, I thanked him for texting me she was there, though he seemed upset at the fuss I had made. But hey, I did what I had to do to get Robin to leave Cassie alone so I could bail her out and get as far away from there as possible before she could sink us both.

We sat in the car for a moment. She stared out the window, hunched her shoulders, and squinted at the morning sun, looking forlorn and lost, as if the weight of the world was pressing down on her. A single tear rolled down her cheek. The sadness emanating from her was palpable, filling the car with a sense of despair. I started the car's engine and pulled out from the street parking spot in front of the police station, headed back to Mom's house.

"I know this is tough, Cassie," I said, trying to keep the frustration out of my voice. "But did you say anything to Robin that could come back to haunt us?"

"No," she replied, shaking her head.

"How long did she have you cornered in that cell?" I asked, trying to get a sense of what had happened.

"It wasn't like that," Cassie protested.

I couldn't help but let a sarcastic laugh escape my lips. "Right, just two old friends catching up. She knew she had you trapped and pounced. Come on, Cassie, you need to smarten up."

She said nothing.

"How long did you and Robin talk for?"

"They locked me up for hours, but Robin was only in there with me about fifteen minutes before you showed up."

Okay, some good news for a change.

I pulled into the driveway.

"What about Mother's car?" Cassie asked.

"It's impounded. The driver's side window was busted out by the cops so they could drag you out and arrest you."

"I'm sorry that I've made things even worse."

"You're not making things any easier, that's for sure."

She started crying again.

"Don't worry about the car. Once the police release it, I'll go pick it up," I reassured her, though my mind raced about having to deal with the impending repairs to the car and the trouble of dealing with the police.

Back inside, we made our way to the kitchen. Cassie looked at the closed basement door.

"What did you do with him?" she asked me.

"I got rid of it. That's all you need to know."

"I heard like an electric saw last night," she said.

"You want the play-by-play, Cass?"

She looked down at her feet.

"Didn't think so. All you need to worry about is keeping it together for a couple more days. You can then head back to Vegas with your inheritance and then never come back here."

She looked at me like what I said was hurtful.

"What? It's what you've always wanted, anyway. You get your wish. Once you're gone, stay gone. I won't bother you again trying to maintain our tenuous sibling connection. After this shit show, it's severed for good."

Before she could say anything, the doorbell rang, which made her yelp. I glanced at my watch.

"Relax. It's the crew I hired to get this place ready for sale." And to wash away any possible DNA evidence lingering in the basement. But I didn't tell Cassie.

"I'll have them start in the basement. You need to wash the stink of booze and jail from your body and get ready for the funeral in two hours."

Cassie nodded and headed to the bedroom.

I welcomed the crew inside. I had used them before for the rental properties I owned. Hugh Stacy was the owner—a big burly man with an unruly ZZ-Top beard. He had brought four scrawny Latino men with him, no doubt day laborers that Hugh had hired from the Home Depot parking lot in the Twin Cities before heading down there. Then there was the three-person cleaning crew, a man and two women.

I led them all to the kitchen. "I want you to start in the

basement," I said, opening the door and turning on the light. We all went down the stairs. Everyone looked around.

"I want all this stuff cleared out," I instructed, waving my arms around the basement.

It used to be a sweet pad for me. I had my privacy down here. All the accouterments that had made my corner of the basement into a comfy bedroom were long gone. I couldn't recall what Mom did with my bed and partition wall. I had sold my gym equipment on Craigslist during my senior year in college. Now the basement truly resembled a space where cobwebs hung in the corners, and the sound of dripping water echoed through the dank and musty atmosphere filled with the smell of mildew and old, forgotten things stuffed in aging cardboard boxes with frayed and fraying edges and battered and bent corners.

I could see that the bottom of most of the boxes was sagging, as if the weight of its contents was too much for it to bear. The boxes had been through a lot, and they were on the verge of collapsing in on themselves. I had already looked inside of them soon after Mom died and discovered that they were filled with junk that she should have gotten rid of a long time ago. Like that body in the freezer.

"You want to get rid of everything?" Hugh asked, surveying the task at hand as he stood in the laundry room's doorway, one foot in the main basement area, the other foot in the laundry room section where just a few hours ago I had cut up Mikey's mummified frozen body.

"All of it," I replied firmly.

"Even the appliances?" Hugh asked, looking at the freezer. I could hear its motor humming.

"All of it," I repeated. "Start with this freezer. Toss whatever is inside and then junk it. I want this basement cleared one hundred percent. I don't want to see a single cobweb. Then I want it cleaned and disinfected with bleach."

Hugh nodded. "Got it, boss. No problem."

"I'm going to be upstairs," I said. "Holler if you have questions."

As I made my way up the steps, I could hear Hugh giving instructions to his crew in broken Spanish.

I SAT at the kitchen table, sipping on a glass of water. The sound of Cassie's shower running in the background was soothing. Everything was falling into place perfectly. Robin could snoop around as much as she wanted, but she wouldn't find anything there anymore. However, Cassie was still a source of worry for me. I meant it when I told her that after this was all over, we were done.

I didn't care if she stayed out West and drank away her inheritance, but I wondered if that was the best course of action. After all, you didn't give a loaded gun to an unstable person and let them go on their way. And the information Cassie had about what happened there was like a loaded gun that might harm me. I would not let that happen. She could ruin her own life, but she wasn't dragging me down with her. I had told her that many times. She refused to listen. It might not be wise to just let her leave. And now, with this DWI case hanging over us, we were even more intertwined.

A sigh escaped from my lips. Time to untwine us for good. And maybe it was for the best.

TWENTY-SIX
CASSIE

I stepped into the shower and let the hot water cascade down my body. It felt like a calming balm to my frazzled nerves. I closed my eyes, letting out a sigh of relief as the tension of the last couple of days washed away down the drain.

The hot water pulsed against my skin. I couldn't shake the feeling that I was being torn in two. On one side, there was the guilt about what had happened in the basement; that really hadn't worked well for me. On the other side, I just wanted the truth out there, to see what would happen.

But my decision wouldn't just affect me. If it were only about me, I might have unloaded my guilt on Robin while in jail.

Suddenly, there was another burst of light that made my knees wobble. A memory from last night's blackout came back to me like an electro-shock bolt.

I remembered going down to the basement last night before Brent returned. I was already three sheets to the wind. It was the only reason I mustered the liquid courage to go down there. I walked to the freezer and opened it.

Looked inside. Brent had placed the body back and covered it up with food packages we had removed.

I didn't know why or where I got the strength to do this. I felt a powerful pull that told me: look at what you did to Mikey. So, I did. I removed the stuff from the upper half of the body. Brent had covered up his face again. I removed the fabric from the face and what I saw horrified me.

As the warm water of the shower cascaded over me, I hyperventilated, thinking about what I saw in that freezer. Mikey's head had been bashed in. And even though I was looking at a fifteen-year-old frozen mummy, I could tell as clear as day that he had been violently and horrifically attacked. I knew that I hadn't done that. I hit him one time on the back of the head with the dumbbell. And even though I didn't think I hit him hard enough to kill him, I had hit him with enough force to knock him out.

I knew the head was a finicky thing. I'd read about folks getting shot in the head and surviving. And then someone gets punched once in a drunken bar fight, falls back, hits their head on hard concrete in just the right spot, and dies.

So certainly, my single blow could have hit the right spot to kill Mikey. I was certain of that much, and it was why I believed Brent when he told me that I had killed Mikey. But the damage I saw to Mikey's frozen, mummified face, I was certain I hadn't done that. I didn't know much about forensic stuff, but I highly doubted a skull could cave inward like that because of decomposition. It looked exactly as you would expect to see something that had been bashed by a rock or some other blunt object.

But the body had been frozen for so long. What did I know? I wasn't a doctor like Brent. Maybe he could explain it to me. Did that damage occur over the years, or did someone inflict it?

I closed my eyes, letting the water soothe me once again. All these memories from fifteen years ago kept flooding back to me in little flashes. I felt one coming as I placed both my hands on the shower wall, hung my head low, with eyes wide shut, going back fifteen years to that day.

Then

I was on Brent's bed with Mikey. We were fooling around. I opened my eyes and looked up at the window and saw Charlie, scrunched down, looking in on us.

He seemed startled when we made eye contact. I was startled too, but I didn't stop kissing Mikey. I didn't tell him that Charlie had been peeping on us. I just looked up at him and he seemed despondent. I felt bad for him; I knew he had a crush on me.

Mikey broke away, perhaps sensing I was distracted. I looked at him and then back up at the window, but Charlie was gone. I didn't tell Mikey about it. Maybe if I had, he would have been angry and creeped out about Charlie, and he might have left and would still be alive. But I didn't. We carried on kissing and within minutes of seeing Charlie in that window, I asked Mikey to stop, but he wouldn't until I reached for that dumbbell.

Now

I opened my eyes, and I wasn't a fifteen-year-old girl in the basement anymore. I shut off the shower and got out. As I toweled off, I thought about the guilt of that day that had been eating me up inside for all those years.

But what would have happened if I hadn't fought back against Mikey's unwanted advances?

I would have become another of the many girls who become victims of date rape.

I would have probably never told anyone, like most victims do, and lived with that horrible memory.

It seemed I was doomed to be messed up mentally that day regardless of what I did.

I got dressed in the steamed-up small bathroom. I kept hearing weird noises that sounded like feet shuffling and the walls pulsating. Then came the sensation that I was being watched. My body trembled. I felt someone coming up behind me.

I spun around, my heart racing, and I saw Mikey standing there. But he didn't look like he did when he was fifteen, how he looked when I thought about him, forever stuck like how he looked on that fateful day. This time, he looked like he had crawled out of the freezer. His skin was leathery and wet. I felt the cold from the freezer wafting toward me, and his sunken face stared back at me.

I screamed and closed my eyes for a moment. When I opened them and looked again, there was nothing there. Just me. Alone. Was I going crazy?

I ran to the safety of my bedroom, fumbling with the doorknob before finally locking it behind me. I leaned back against the door, trying to catch my breath and calm my racing heart.

But just as I felt safe, I heard a knock on the door that made me shriek out loud. "Cassie, are you okay?" came the voice from the other side of the door. It was Brent.

I hesitated for a moment, my mind racing. I took a deep breath and opened the door a crack. Brent stood there with a concerned look on his face.

"Are you okay?" he asked again, his voice laced with

worry. "I heard you scream, and I just wanted to make sure everything was alright."

"I'm fine," I said, forcing a smile. "Just a little jumpy, that's all."

Brent nodded, his face relaxing. "Well, the crew is downstairs clearing and cleaning up the basement. In a couple of hours, they'll tackle the upstairs. A couple more days, and we could put this all behind us." He looked at me with concern.

"Are you sure you're okay?" Brent asked.

"Yeah, I'm fine. Just need to finish getting ready," I replied, trying to reassure him and perhaps myself as well.

"We need to talk, privately," Brent said, looking over his shoulder. I could hear the crew working downstairs; perhaps that was the noise I had heard in the bathroom. My mind was twisting things. Just like I was doing to Brent, when all he'd ever tried to do all my life was help me from myself. He always tried to be a good brother, and I pushed him away.

Even now, he had just paid to bail me out of jail without hesitation or making me feel guilty about it.

"I know. I'll be out in a few minutes," I said, closing the door.

I sat on the bed. What I had seen was just my mind trying to absolve me from what I did to Mikey and put the blame on Brent.

As I walked into the kitchen, I saw Brent sitting at the table, a mug of coffee in front of him. He looked up at me and smiled. "Do you want some of Mom's shitty coffee?" he asked.

Despite the pounding in my head and the desperate need for caffeine, I couldn't help but smile at the joke. "Sure," I said, grateful for the offer. Brent got up and grabbed another mug, pouring me a cup of the freeze-dried abomination.

I took a tentative sip, my face contorting at the bitter taste.

We sat down at the kitchen table, the same one that had been there for as long as I could remember. I took another sip of coffee, trying to push down the headache that was threatening to take over.

As we sat in silence, I couldn't help but feel grateful for Brent's presence. He may have been joking about the coffee, but he was always there for me when I needed him, even if it was just to sit and drink terrible coffee together.

I heard the crew down there working in the basement, making my skin crawl.

"Let's go for a walk so we can talk," Brent whispered.

TWENTY-SEVEN
BRENT

We walked from Mom's house down to the Big Prairie city park. Despite having "Big" in its name, it was a small patch of land that was the pride of our tiny town. I had hated growing up there in small-town America, but now that I lived in the big city, like I always wanted, I found something comforting about being in a place where everything was small and manageable.

My life in the Twin Cities was so hectic, big, and loud, that it was nice to slip into third gear.

We sat on a bench, the late morning air still crisp and wet with the springtime dampness. It felt good, pure in a way that only small towns could provide. But as much as I loved the peacefulness down there, I was grateful to have escaped its suffocating limitations.

"So, what happened last night, sis?" I asked, trying to catch my sister's eye. She looked down at the ground, avoiding my gaze. I wasn't sure if it was shame from her DWI arrest or something else.

"I don't remember much. I drank... a lot," she finally said, her voice heavy with guilt. "I must have fallen asleep."

She said she fell asleep. What she did was pass out from drinking too much. But I wasn't going to get into those nuances with her.

"I woke up to a buzzing sound. It took me a bit to get my bearings, but I figured out you were back down in the basement with..." she stopped herself for a moment then took a deep breath. "I freaked out and ran off. The next thing I know, I woke up in jail."

"Charlie said they found you on the road passed out with the car running. When they woke you up, you tried to flee," I said.

"I don't remember any of that. All I remember is leaving the house, then blackness, then jail."

I stared directly into her eyes. I knew it bothered her. My ability to make direct eye contact with people freaked out many of them. But I didn't care. I needed to figure out what Cassie said to Robin and Charlie.

"Now that you have a chance to clear your head. Did you say anything to Charlie or Robin about Mikey that I need to worry about?"

"No, I swear," she said. I believed her. She hadn't told them anything today. But what about tomorrow, the day after, next week, three years from now? That worried me.

"I'll get you an excellent lawyer from the Twin Cities on these charges," I said, trying to sound reassuring. "Are you still on probation from out West?"

Tears welled up in her eyes as she nodded. "They're going to send me back to prison," she said, her voice shaking with fear.

"Not necessarily," I told her, even though I knew that she had screwed up badly. They could enforce stricter restrictions or return her to prison.

"I don't see how I can avoid that."

"Not with the pit bull of a lawyer I'll get for you. The type of lawyer that gets off O.J. Simpson, Bill Cosby, and Robert Blake, but you have to keep your mouth shut about everything. What happened fifteen years ago and what happened last night. Do you understand?"

She nodded. I think I was finally getting through to her.

"What exactly did Robin say to you?" I pressed.

"She's fishing like you said. She knows from talking to Charlie and others that we had been hooking up for a couple of months, and that he was coming to the house when you and Mother weren't there. And that's the last they know as to his whereabouts. I told her it was true about Mikey and me messing around before, but not on that day. I told her he was supposed to come over, but he stood me up."

"Excellent. That's good. What else did she ask you?"

"She wanted to know why I stayed quiet all these years about Mikey and I and how he was coming over on the day he disappeared. But before I could say anything, you showed up. So that was it, I swear."

I felt relieved that I got there in the nick of time to put an end to Robin's sneaky interrogation of Cassie. But now I needed to make sure we locked the hatch tight to prevent this leaking boat from sinking.

"Okay, good. But from now on, you don't speak to her or anyone else but me about any of this. Is that clear?"

"Won't I look guilty for refusing to talk to the police?"

"It doesn't matter. Never talk to the police without first consulting an attorney, period. Police officers like Robin were trained to get confessions, admissions, and inconsistencies. The more you talk to her, the more you're putting both of our well-being at risk. I'll get you an attorney right away. If Robin or Charlie or anyone from law enforcement wants to talk to you, all you have to say is that you would like to invoke your right to remain silent and talk to your attorney. I'm serious about this, Cassie. We need to get smart about this, okay?"

She looked at me, then back to the ground.

"Okay?" I repeated more firmly.

"Yes. Okay," she finally said, tears streaming down her cheeks.

I looked around the park, half expecting to see Robin hiding behind a tree, but there was no one around. One thing was for sure, Cassie would not spend another minute in that house. It would break her. I was done trying to accommodate her. It was too risky for me to continue doing that anymore. Now, it was my way, all the way.

"We'll go back to the house and pack your bag. I'm getting you a room next to mine at the hotel. That way, you're not in the way as they clear up the place."

She gave me that mule-headed look. I shot it down instantly.

"It's not up for debate, Cassie. Let's go get your stuff. We're burying Mom today."

TWENTY-EIGHT
BRENT

WHILE CASSIE PACKED, I CALLED JILLIAN AND TOLD her about Cassie's night in jail.

"On the eve of her mother's own funeral. She has no bottom left to sink to," Jillian remarked.

I let Jillian know that I had come to the realization that Cassie wasn't good for me. When this was all over, I was cutting my sister out of my life. She sounded relieved. "I know this is hard for you, sweetheart, but you're making the right choice."

We got into the car and headed to the funeral home for the wake.

Cassie cleaned up nicely, but she was still unsteady on her feet and her eyes were glassy and red. I wasn't sure if that was still from the booze from last night or all the crying she had been doing the last two days. It was beyond me how weak she had become.

I figured Cassie's reddened eyes would be fine for the wake. People would assume she was grieving for her dead mother, not knowing that was the last thing that had turned her into this blithering thing she had become.

As we drove to the wake, I reminded Cassie that we could see the finish line. Two more days and she would be back in Las Vegas with money from the estate so she could move forward and not think about Mikey or Big Plaine ever again.

She looked at me askew. "I've tried to forget for fifteen years. And look at the mess I've made of my life."

I said nothing because it was a valid point.

"How do you do it?" she asked me. I glanced over at her. She was looking at me childlike. So sad.

"How do I do what?"

"Carry on with your life like nothing happened with Mikey."

The question took me aback. Our long-held pact to never talk about what happened was now broken.

"You suck it up and you put it away and you carry on. What other choice do you have? Confess? Go to prison?"

She said nothing as she turned away and looked out the window.

"You killed that boy, Cassie. Everyone in town has been looking for him for years. Including his sister, a police detective. You want to come clean? You think they're going to let you off the hook because you were a teenager? And you didn't mean it? He felt you up, and you didn't want him to, so you killed him? It will not fly after lying about it for fifteen years. Just keep your mouth shut for two more days. Because you coming clean will blow up my life. So yeah, suck it up. It's not all about you."

She stayed quiet. I knew that was harsh, but I needed to reach her. She had to understand that there was no coming clean and finding absolution without affecting my life. And I wouldn't have it. Everything I'd done for her. All that I'd accomplished. It wouldn't turn to shit. I wouldn't allow it. No matter what I had to do.

When we arrived at the wake, Cassie was still a little unsteady on her feet, but she managed to compose herself and could even make small talk with the visitors. There was an awkward and tense reunion between Cassie and Jillian, and my two children, who barely knew their aunt.

It was a small gathering. I found myself hoping more people would attend my wake. The service was short and intimate, with a few prayers and a few words from the pastor. I said a few words about how Mom had raised us as a single mother after Dad died and about the thousands of kids she had helped educate and later find their purpose as a guidance counselor. Cassie didn't speak, which was probably for the best in her delicate state of mind.

We made the rounds. I stayed by her side the entire time, making sure she had everything she needed and helping her through the more difficult moments until one visitor split us up.

Mrs. Helmer, one of my mother's colleagues from the school and my former social studies teacher, cornered me and talked nonstop about my mother and how proud she was of my accomplishments as an adult, just as Cassie walked away toward the exit. Mrs. Helmer had a mixture of pity and annoyance in her voice as she asked about Cassie and her perceived waste of a life. "Such a shame. She was so smart," Mrs. Helmer said to me, as if Cassie were the one lying in that coffin.

I forced a smile and nodded, but my attention was caught by Robin entering the funeral parlor. Damn, the last thing I needed. I was actually surprised, after our tense conversation in the jail that morning, that she had the nerve to show up at Mom's wake.

Mrs. Helmer was still blathering on as I watched Robin heading towards Cassie like a lion ready to pounce on the weak zebra that had been separated from the pack.

In Cassie's state, I knew Robin would crack her open like a walnut, and I couldn't let that happen. So, I gave Mrs. Helmer my thousand-watt smile and patted her liver-spotted, wrinkly hand gently, like a politician. What I was actually doing was prying her fingers from my arm. Success. I was able to break free from her grip as I clasped both my hands over hers. "Thank you for coming, Mrs. Helmer. I'd better check on Cassie," I told her, finally freeing myself from her grip.

"Of course," she said as I headed straight toward Cassie and Robin.

Robin was already speaking with Cassie, her intense gaze fixed on her face as she seemed to probe deeply into her thoughts. I knew exactly what she was doing—she wasn't offering her condolences or checking on Cassie's well-being. She was digging, just like a detective did.

As I approached them, the sound of Robin's voice reached my ears. "You know you can trust me, right?" That bitch. She was attempting to deceive my emotionally vulnerable and hungover sister at our mother's wake. Oh, how I wished I could unleash my high-priced lawyer from the Twin Cities on her, to teach her a lesson for messing with my family. But going after the sister of a missing child, especially one I had just chopped up and dumped in lakes, wouldn't exactly bode well for my public image. No, I needed to protect Cassie from her. So, I mustered a smile, baring my pearly whites, as I positioned myself none too subtly between them. At this delicate juncture, I couldn't care about subtlety.

"Robin, I'm surprised to see you here after this morning, but thank you for coming. It means a lot to Cassie and me that you came to pay your respects to our mother," I said, stealing a glance over my shoulder at the sight of our embalmed mother, dressed in her Sunday best, resting in the open casket.

"Of course. You're welcome," Robin replied. "I still want to catch up with you, Cassie. How about coffee tomorrow?"

"Robin, please. Cassie is going through an incredibly difficult time. You know the circumstances of our mother's passing," I interjected, fully aware that Robin had dug deep into the Big Plaine police department's records and was privy to the details.

Annoyance flashed across Robin's face, but she knew better than to cause a scene at a funeral. Reluctantly, she backed off. Seizing the moment, I swiftly wrapped my arm around Cassie. "Excuse us," I said to Robin dismissively as I guided Cassie away from her reach.

I was determined to keep Cassie as far away from Robin as possible. After the funeral, I planned to sic the lawyers on her, ending this silly charade of fake politeness between us.

TWENTY-NINE
BRENT

THE FUNERAL WAS SCHEDULED AN HOUR AFTER THE wake. It was a private event, for family only, so at least we didn't have to worry about Robin showing up.

It would be a somber drive from the funeral home to the cemetery. The hearse carrying Mom's coffin led the way. Jillian and the kids were in Jillian's Porsche, while Cassie and I were in the Wagon.

I could feel some of the weight of the past thirty hours ease up. The wake was over. Soon Mom would be in the ground. The body from the freezer was in five different lakes. And the cleaning and hauling crews had been working in the house all day. Soon all this would be behind me.

But now it was time to say our last goodbyes and lay her to rest so we would finally get all this behind us.

I told Jillian to take the Wagon. I would drive alone with Cassie in Mom's car and meet her and the kids at the cemetery. Jillian protested, but I explained about Cassie's fragile state. That didn't exactly elicit much sympathy from Jillian, but she agreed to my request.

I climbed into the driver's seat and buckled my seatbelt. "How are you holding up, Cass?" I asked her as she climbed into the passenger seat.

"I'm fine," she said, her voice weak and sad. "Don't worry, I won't ruin your life." It was a relief to hear her say that, even though she sounded broken, so I wasn't sure I could count on that just yet.

"We're almost done with all of this, Cassie. I promise." She didn't respond to that.

It was dusk when we arrived at the cemetery. A few chairs were set out in front of the open grave, with faux bright green grass draped over the edges. The metal lowering device was already set, waiting for the casket.

It took a few minutes to transfer the casket from the hearse onto the lowering device above the grave. We gathered in front of the casket where the pastor stood facing us. The graveside service lasted about twenty minutes. We watched as the casket was lowered into the ground and that was it. Cassie remained aloof throughout the ceremony.

After the funeral, Cassie and I walked back to the car in silence. Jillian had taken the kids and headed back up to the Twin Cities. Cassie and I drove back to the house in silence.

I couldn't help but smile when I saw Hugh's hauling truck filled to the top, pleased at how quickly they had worked. My smile faded, however, when I spotted Robin's Chevy Malibu parked across the street.

"Jesus," I muttered under my breath.

"She won't quit," Cassie observed.

"Well, it's getting ridiculous the way she is hounding us. On the day we buried Mom," I said, my annoyance growing. I pulled up into the driveway and got out of the car, shooting Robin a hard glare. She had pushed my patience to the limit.

Robin got out of her car and slowly made her way up the driveway as we exited ours. "I know I'm being a pest, but we need to talk."

"No, we don't, Robin. Come on, our mother hasn't been buried for an hour," I snapped.

"I'm sorry. I'm just trying to bring closure for my family. So we too can have Mikey buried and resting in peace with a gravesite for us to visit," she said.

"Not sure why you think we can help with that. We don't know what happened to Mikey," I retorted. I was so upset with her relentless intrusion that part of me wanted to blurt out that I had chopped up her stupid brother last night. But of course, I kept that to myself.

"I wouldn't be bothering you if it wasn't important. Mikey told my mom that he was going to ride his bike with his buddy, Charlie, who had told the police for years that Mikey never showed up as planned and did not know what happened to him. Charlie finally told me the truth. It turns out that he lied to avoid getting Mikey in trouble. But when Mikey went missing, and it was a serious situation, he became afraid of being punished for lying to the police and to our parents. He's now finally willing to tell the truth. He and Mikey went to visit your mom's house," Robin said, turning her attention toward Cassie. "Isn't that right, Cassie?"

Cassie opened her mouth, so I quickly stepped between her and Robin.

"Get inside the house, Cassie," I said, almost pushing her through the front door. I turned back to face Robin. "Not possible," I said. "First, Mom would never allow Cassie to hang out with a boy in the house. Second, I was here on that day. I was down in my room doing homework.

Cassie was upstairs in her room. Neither Mikey nor Charlie was here."

"You seem so certain about what happened fifteen years ago," Robin said.

"Everyone in Big Plaine knows the day of Mikey's disappearance. And I'm telling you, I was here with Cassie all afternoon. Then Mom was here after work. Mikey never showed up here. And if he had, I wouldn't have let him inside because Mom wouldn't have allowed it. And there was no way he could have sneaked inside. The house isn't that big," I said, gesturing towards the house with my thumb. I turned to go back inside when Robin then said, "I know about the flyer your mom had put out when she died. Why did she do that?"

I turned to Robin and glared at her. "I'm trying to be respectful of your loss, Robin, but now you've gone too far. You don't work for the Big Plaine PD. So, the only way you know about that is because someone in the Big Plaine PD is talking to you about my mom's death, violating my family's privacy. So, we're done here. I'm calling my lawyer. If you or anyone from law enforcement has more questions, call my fucking lawyer." I tossed my attorney's business card at her. "Now kindly fuck off and get off my property." I turned and went inside.

"Everything okay, boss?" Hugh asked. He had obviously overheard my terse exchange with Robin.

Luckily, Hugh wasn't from town, and although I was sure he was familiar with Mikey Dawson's disappearance like most people in Minnesota, he did not know that we were intertwined in that mess.

"Nothing. Small town stuff," I said to him with a smirk, eager to change the subject. "You've done a phenomenal job here," I added quickly.

Hugh smiled proudly. "Yeah, not too shabby. Picked up a good crew this morning. It's hit and miss these days," he said.

"What's left to do?" I asked, looking around the place. It seemed to me the job was done. I glanced over at Cassie, who stood by the window looking out at the driveway.

"We're all done. We'll be out of your hair in ten minutes," Hugh replied.

That was music to my ears.

THIRTY
CASSIE

Brent practically pushed me into the house. I closed the front door behind me. Hugh Stacey stood there looking confused.

"Brent will be with you shortly," I said, turning away from him. I knew I was being rude, but I didn't have the energy to talk. Besides, I wanted to see what was going on between Brent and Robin, right outside the door.

My anxiety was rising. She knew about Mikey and Charlie. I couldn't believe Charlie was talking to her.

Whenever I saw Robin, the image of her brother Mikey came to mind. They even looked similar in the eyes and mouth. Looking at Robin was like seeing what Mikey might have looked like had he made it out of the basement alive.

What did Robin have that was making her so aggressively question me and Brent?

I stood behind the ajar front door and pressed my ear against the open space, trying to listen in on their conversation.

I could hear Robin speaking in a firm and more direct tone, asking Brent about a flyer that Mother had put out before her death. I couldn't see Brent's face, but I could hear the anger in his voice as he lawyered up, and then told her to fuck off.

As Brent came inside, I stepped back to let him in. His face was flushed, as it always was when he got angry. When things in Brent's life tilted out of his control, he became flustered, not used to being anything but in charge.

Then I heard Hugh asking him if everything was okay. I wanted to ask Brent what the hell was going on with Robin, but I couldn't with Hugh and his crew still milling around.

I was looking at my empty bedroom when I heard Hugh and the crew finally leaving. I was startled when one worker, who had walked up behind me, spoke.

"Excuse me, miss," he said in broken English. Having taken Spanish in high school and improved it living in Nevada and California all these years, I responded to him in Spanish, asking where he was from. His face lit up with a wide smile.

My Spanish wasn't flawless, but it was better than his English. He introduced himself as Ángel and said he was from Oaxaca, Mexico. We chatted for a minute, mostly about the horrors of his first Minnesota winter, before he handed me a leather document pouch.

I took it and looked at it as he explained in Spanish: "This was in your mother's bedroom, under the mattress. There are some papers in there. I wasn't sure if they're important, so I thought you would want to go through them since the boss wanted me to toss it in the garbage pile with everything else."

I thanked Ángel as I slid the pouch into my backpack, not wanting to let on that my plan was to toss it in the garbage as well. But I would wait until he wasn't around. There was no need for him to know that my relationship with my mother wasn't a good one. That Brent and I were getting rid of just about everything inside the house probably clued him in, though. I often envied those who had strong, loving relationships with their parents. Even when they complained about their mothers and fathers, it was clear they cared deeply for them.

My father passed away when I was a young child, so I have few memories of him. It took me a long time to come to terms with the fact that I didn't feel the same love for my mother that I had for my father. I supposed that's why it was easier for me to become estranged. Aren't children supposed to love their parents? Is that a hard and fast rule?

My mother was cold and indifferent towards me my entire childhood. She beat me and locked me up in a root cellar. I didn't think I blindly owed her love just for giving birth to me. I didn't ask to be born. And it takes a hell of a lot more than giving birth to be a good mother.

I never shared this with anyone. I was adept at keeping the true feelings I had for my mother bottled up, just as she had taught me. People were understanding about certain things; they could accept my faults, of which I had many, but most would deem my lack of love for my mother as unforgivable. What kind of sick person didn't love their mother? Those who would judge me didn't have a mother that beat them with a leather strap, locked them in a cold root cellar, or hid a dead body in a freezer.

Brent and I stood by the front bay window as Hugh and his crew drove away, leaving us finally alone to talk.

I asked Brent what he had discussed with Robin, but he ignored me and walked towards the living room.

"Talk to me, Brent."

He looked annoyed. "What a pain in the ass, that one," he muttered almost to himself, his voice echoing off the walls in the now empty house. I noticed the drastic change in our surroundings too, but that wasn't what was on my mind.

"What did she mean about the flyer Mother put out?" I pressed, trying to understand the strange conversation I had overheard.

Brent's head snapped towards me, and he brushed off my question. "It's nothing. She's just trying to play mind games," he dismissed.

I didn't believe him. "It didn't sound like anything to me. Come on, Brent. Tell me what's going on."

Brent walked to the kitchen and poured himself a glass of water, drinking it in silence. I followed him, pressing for an answer.

"Brent, what about the flyer?" I asked again, my frustration growing.

He stood with his back to me, leaning against the kitchen sink. After a deep sigh, he finally turned to face me.

"I was just trying to protect you," he said softly.

I snapped back at him. "I don't need you to protect me. Just tell me the truth."

Brent raised an eyebrow, his face showing incredulity. "Oh, really?" he retorted sarcastically.

"Just tell me what Robin meant about the flyer Mother had put out. What did it say?" I demanded.

Brent turned away from me, putting the empty glass in the kitchen sink. He stood there hunched over the sink for a moment. Finally, he turned around and looked at me directly.

"The police found one of those missing children flyers of Mikey on the floor near where she killed herself which raised some questions."

"She felt guilty for what I did to Mikey," I said. "She

couldn't handle the guilt of what I had done and her role in covering it up."

"You don't know that, Cassie. None of us know why she did it. And mom didn't put it out like Robin claims. It had partially slid under the washing machine. You heard how much she helped put up those flyers all over town, so one of them must have slipped under there and she never noticed."

"You said it was Parkinson's that drove her to it. I suppose that was bullshit. You were trying to protect me."

He nodded his head slowly.

"Did she even have Parkinson's?"

"She did, but her symptoms were still mild," he admitted.

"So, I drove her to kill herself for what I did to Mikey."

"Hey, look at me," Brent said sternly. "That piece of shit tried to rape you. You reacted in self-defense, and it was an accident. That's it."

"Why didn't you and Mother let me call the police like I begged?" I asked, the weight of guilt and secrecy crushing down on me. "They wouldn't have locked me up and thrown away the key. Maybe I wouldn't have self-destructed under the weight of this guilt if I could have talked about it. Gotten help to deal with what happened. Instead of being forced to keep it all inside."

Brent shrugged. "Maybe you're right. We all screwed up that day. But we couldn't change what happened. Mom is gone. So, it's just you and me now. We just need to keep this between us."

I looked at Brent. His eyes were boring into mine. It was the only time he had admitted that we did this all wrong fifteen years ago.

Brent left me standing in the empty kitchen as he went down to the basement. He returned after a couple of minutes, his demeanor noticeably changed. He was smiling, his confidence seemingly restored.

"They did a good job down there. You can eat off the floor, it's so clean. And that damn freezer is gone. We're in the clear, Cass," Brent said with a grin.

I didn't share his optimistic outlook.

We left the empty house for what felt like the last time in our lives. Brent dropped me off at the hotel, and I headed to my room alone. He reminded me that we were meeting with the lawyers and a broker in the morning to wrap up Mother's estate and figure out the DWI hanging over my head. He also told me for the millionth time to keep it together and lay off the booze.

As if that was easy for me. But I told myself I needed to keep my drinking in check. I needed to keep my head clear. Memories fluttered in my brain, blurring the line between reality and the tricks my mind played on me. The image of the sunken skull I saw in the freezer haunted me.

One thought kept bouncing around in my head, refusing to be silenced. What really happened to Mikey that day?

THIRTY-ONE

CASSIE

I SAT ON THE BED IN THE HOTEL ROOM, ALONE. ON THE television, Steve Harvey was yammering about a survey on Family Feud, but I wasn't really paying attention. I just needed the TV on for background noise. Fragments from the last two days circulated through my head like an out-of-range radio station.

Mother's note. Finding the body in the chest freezer. Brent peeling away the frozen linens, revealing a body preserved as well as those Incan child mummies I'd seen on National Geographic.

The Incan child mummies found at the summit of a volcano on the Argentina-Chile border were one of the most significant and haunting discoveries related to the Inca civilization.

The preservation of those mummies was exceptional because of the cold temperatures and dry conditions at such high altitudes. This had allowed researchers to study the clothes, hair, and even the contents of the stomachs of these children, providing invaluable insights into the Inca's diet, health, and practices.

Mikey Dawson, like those mummies, had preserved himself for fifteen years in Mother's freezer, until we found him.

Unlike the Incas, who were carefully preserved to be studied, Brent had mutilated Mikey's corpse and dumped it into the lake like trash. It seemed like further punishment towards Mikey.

Brent had mentioned that Mikey was still wearing the same clothing from fifteen years ago, and he could still see the dried blood encased all over the front of Mikey's Rush T-shirt.

I searched for a mini bar, but this hotel didn't have one. Resigned, I took three Advil, hoping to temper the headache that was growing in intensity.

I sank into the bed, the fabric cold against my skin, and my eyelids fell heavily. Even though the television was on, the silence felt deafening, punctuated only by the erratic drumming of my heart and the throbbing in my head.

I thought back to that day. In the chaos of the moment, with adrenaline clouding my senses, I had noticed no blood. Certainly not the torrent that Brent described, a vivid crimson soaking the front of Mikey's shirt. The dumbbell had connected with the back of his skull, not the front. It made little sense.

The image of Mikey's face in that freezer jolted through my body. It was as if someone had bashed his head in an orgy of violence. Far more brutal than the single knock I had inflicted on him.

It was evident now, after seeing the condition of the face with my own eyes and learning about the bloody T-shirt, I was starting to wonder. Did I really kill Mikey? For years, I'd clung to a sliver of doubt, a desperate hope that the blow hadn't been fatal. A desperate hope I had kept to myself since until yesterday. I hadn't discussed this with anyone.

If it wasn't me that killed Mikey, that meant it had to be... Brent? No, that couldn't be. I saw Charlie peeping through the window. He had lied about that day until recently, as he confided in Robin. What did she know about what happened?

I drifted away, my eyes heavy with fatigue. In front of me appeared Mikey Dawson, not as the frozen mummy but as he was back when we were kids. That day he came over wearing his white Rush T-shirt, blue jeans, and black Van sneakers. He looked at me and didn't seem angry that I had killed him.

"You know the truth. Don't you?" Mikey asked.

"What truth?" I responded, confused.

He repeated, "You know the truth. Don't you?"

I shook my head in denial.

"Yes, you do. You know the truth," he insisted.

I shook my head again, unwilling to accept.

"Deep down, you know. It's why you looked in the freezer," Mikey continued.

"Looked?"

"You came down to the basement and looked at my dead body. Because you know the truth. Don't you?"

"I'm scared," I admitted, tears welling up in my eyes.

"You need to stop being scared. Be strong, like you used to be. The truth can't hurt you. The lies have been killing you since the day I died," he urged.

I sprang up from the bed, my brow sweaty. I had fallen asleep. The dream was so vivid that until I woke up, I could have sworn I was having a conversation with Mikey. I pondered over it. Although I knew it was just a dream, Mikey's words resonated with me. I couldn't carry on like this. I needed to know the truth about what happened. And if I was the one who killed Mikey, then I could live with that truth being out there. Not like this, shrouded in lies.

It was a fifteen-minute walk from the hotel to Mother's house. The streets were empty, and the lights were off in most of the houses late at night.

Once off Main Street, the lack of streetlights made the darkness startling. I had forgotten how dark it got there without the incessant glow of big city lights and the neon madness that was the Las Vegas Strip.

Walking when you have no other options was strange. Mother's car was still in the city impound lot, and public transportation there was practically nonexistent. I hadn't even checked the ride-share apps; I doubted they had drivers in Big Plaine, and I couldn't really afford it anyway. So, I walked. The DWI hanging over my head scared me—I couldn't be without a car in Las Vegas. For now, I still had my driving privileges, at least temporarily.

In Minnesota, if you're arrested for DWI, the police take away your license on the spot. They had given me a temporary paper license to drive while I sorted things out legally, but I could lose my license permanently. That thought terrified me. My studio apartment was seven miles from the Strip. How would I get to work without a car?

Brent had promised to help me find an attorney and figure out my options, and I was determined to do everything in my power to get my Nevada driver's license back.

I turned into Mother's street. I didn't know why I felt this compulsion to leave the hotel and return to that house. It was like a bird flying south—it just did it.

I let myself in. Standing in the empty house, a wave of

sadness washed over me. Despite the tumultuous childhood I had endured there, this was still the home of my youth, and a part of me felt attached to it. Or maybe it was just Stockholm Syndrome.

I hadn't been there but a few minutes when a knock at the front door made me jump in surprise. A visitor was the last thing I expected. Could it be Brent checking on me? No, he would have just walked in. Peering out the now curtain-less window, I saw Charlie Bell waving at me with a sympathetic smile.

THIRTY-TWO
CASSIE

I hesitated before opening the door. Brent's warnings to not trust Charlie or Robin echoed in my mind—because they were cops, he said, and I should remain silent. After a moment of internal debate, I unlatched the door.

The last time I had seen Charlie was at the police station; he was in uniform, and I was under arrest.

Now, he stood before me in civilian clothes: a long-sleeve black Under Armour shirt, blue jeans, and a well-worn Minnesota Twins baseball cap.

As I looked at him, a surge of embarrassment over my drunken arrest bubbled up inside me, but I masked it with a façade of confidence.

"Charlie," I said, my voice steadier than I felt, "what are you doing here?"

He shrugged, biting the inside of his right cheek—an old habit of his when he was nervous. "I was driving home and saw you turning down your street alone, late at night. Thought I'd make sure you're okay."

I managed a smile, though I felt foolish. Walking alone at night, going into an empty house—it was reckless.

"It's stupid. I shouldn't have come here," I muttered, more to myself than to him.

Despite the awkwardness of our last encounter where he had seen me at one of my lowest points, I couldn't help but feel a slight relief at his presence. Instead of judging, he had checked on me to ensure I was okay.

"Hey, you've had a rough few days, Cassie. Don't be so hard on yourself," he said gently, his tone soothing.

Charlie had always been the good guy, even when we were kids. His kindness at the jail, when he'd been more humane than the other officer and even contacted Brent to let him know I was arrested, hadn't gone unnoticed.

"Thanks, Charlie. I'm okay," I managed a smile as he peered curiously inside the house. "Wow, it's all empty," he remarked.

I knew I should tell him not to worry about me and close the door. But deep down, I needed to know what happened that day, and Charlie was there. Against what Brent would want, I invited him inside. I was tired of the lies, tired of not knowing. I needed the truth.

Charlie walked in and looked around, noting the bareness of the now empty house.

"All your mom's stuff is gone. You guys work fast."

"Neither Brent nor I cling to things because they have sentimental value," I explained casually.

"You're putting it up for sale?" he asked.

I nodded. "We're meeting with a real estate agent tomorrow. I hate to sound crass, but I need the money fast."

"People are always looking for affordable starter homes like this one. I don't think you'll have problems selling it," Charlie reassured me.

I remembered Charlie's gentle demeanor from our childhood days, how he and Mikey were always together.

Suddenly, two images flashed through my mind—the sight of Mikey's mummified body in the freezer, his skull horribly caved in, and a younger Charlie peering through the window as Mikey and I fooled around.

Feeling dizzy with the rush of memories, my knees buckled.

"Are you okay, Cassie?" Charlie's voice was filled with concern as he reached out to steady me.

"I'm fine," I lied, brushing off his help. "Just dealing with a lot of memories."

Looking up at Charlie, I noticed how much he had changed into a handsome man—tall and lean, with a neatly trimmed beard and full lips. For a fleeting moment, an urge swept over me to kiss him, to escape my dark thoughts and feel something good, even if just for a little while. But then my eyes caught the glint of the wedding band on his finger.

That small, shiny reminder snapped me back to reality. I pushed the reckless thought away as quickly as it had come. I couldn't afford to make things more complicated than they already were, not with everything else crumbling around me.

"Charlie," I started, my voice steadier than I felt, trying to steer away from my sudden impulse. "It's nice to see that life has treated you well," I added, forcing a smile, trying to mask the turmoil inside me.

He smiled back, seemingly unaware of the brief, tumultuous moment that had just passed through my mind. "Thanks, Cassie. Life's been pretty good," he replied warmly.

We continued talking, and I listened as he shared stories about his family and life in Big Plaine since I had left.

It was soothing to hear about normal, happy lives—it was a sharp contrast to the chaos of my own. As he spoke, I found myself momentarily distracted from the bleak thoughts that had been plaguing me.

But no matter how much we chatted, the reality of my situation lingered in the back of my mind, unyielding and oppressive. The conversation was a brief respite, but it was just that—temporary. And soon, I would have to face all the dark corners of my life again.

"How long have you been married?" I asked, trying to distract myself from the turmoil swirling inside me.

Charlie smiled, his eyes briefly touching the wedding band on his finger. "Four years," he answered.

"Did you marry someone from around here that I know?" I continued, clutching at strands of normal conversation.

He laughed, a sound that seemed so out of place in this house.

"No, I met my wife at St. Cloud State. We were college sweethearts."

"That's great," I said, feeling a twinge of something like envy.

"She's a nurse at a hospital in Chaska."

"That's a haul," I said.

"It's a bit of a commute, but not too bad—sixteen miles. There aren't any hospitals closer." His voice was casual, just two old childhood friends catching up.

"Any kids?" I asked, my curiosity piqued despite myself.

His face lit up. He pulled out his phone and showed me the screensaver—a picture of a beautiful child. "Yeah, a two-year-old girl," he beamed. "Her name is Chelsea."

Seeing the joy in his eyes, I felt a pang of jealousy for the stable life Charlie had managed to build. "She's beautiful," I managed to say, my voice tingling with a mix of admiration and underlying sorrow.

The image of his daughter and the evident happiness in his life made me reflect momentarily on the paths not taken, on the life I might have led if circumstances had been different. It was a fleeting thought, quickly suppressed as the reality of my current situation pressed in on me again.

"Look, Cassie, I just felt bad that I reached out to Brent and Robin without asking you first if you were okay with that," Charlie admitted, his tone earnest. "It's just... you were so out of it at the station. I was worried about you. Seeing you brought in like that—it was shocking. I never thought I'd see you back here, especially not like this... not after your mom passed."

I could feel the weight of his words, the concern in his voice, and it made the room feel even more hollow. "I've made a mess of my life, Charlie. I'm surprised you even recognized me, looking like shit."

Charlie smiled gently, and it was the kind of smile that seemed to push some of the shadows in the room away. "I recognized you right away. And despite the situation, I was happy to see you again," he said. His voice carried a hint of wistfulness that filled the space between us.

There was an awkward silence then, made all the more palpable by the bareness of the house—no furniture to sit on, nothing to offer him to drink, nothing to do but stand there and face each other.

I felt a wave of shame surge through me, shame about him seeing me in that condition. It was too much, and I couldn't bring myself to meet his eyes. I turned slightly away, staring at where a picture used to hang on the wall, trying to hide the flush of embarrassment that I knew was creeping up my neck.

"I know I need to get my drinking under control," I confessed, my voice heavy with the mix of guilt and a newfound self-awareness. "Coming back here... it stirred up a lot of raw emotions, and I've been drinking too much, trying to handle them."

"I understand that," Charlie replied. "But mixing alcohol with opiates—that was really dangerous, Cassie. We're grappling with an opiate problem here in Big Plaine, like so many other places. I just want to make sure you're not in over your head. You could have overdosed that night."

I furrowed my eyebrows, confused. "Opiates? I didn't take any pills. Just booze."

"They drew your blood at the station, Cassie. The results came back—you had both alcohol and fentanyl in your system," he explained, his concern evident in his tone.

"I didn't take any fentanyl. I don't even know where to get that, especially not here in Big Plaine," I countered, feeling a chill crawl up my spine.

Charlie sighed, the look on his face showing he might not believe me. "I know it's none of my business—we haven't seen each other since high school. But I've seen too many people go down that path," he said, his voice filled with genuine worry.

"I admit I was drinking, but I didn't take any fentanyl," I insisted.

He just looked at me, skeptical—the same look I'd gotten from friends when I said I didn't have a drinking problem.

"It must have been a mistake at the lab," I suggested, though a part of me wondered if that could really explain it.

"Cassie," he started, in that tone that meant he wasn't convinced.

"I swear, Charlie."

He paused, then seemed to make a decision. "Alright," he said finally. His voice was kind but still held a hint of doubt. "Just take this, though. For safety." He handed me a small box.

"What's this?" I asked, taking the box but feeling a knot form in my stomach.

"Narcan," he said. "It could save your life if there's a next time."

I took the box without further protest, knowing arguing would get me nowhere.

I wanted to ask him about the day he and Mikey came over, about him peeking through the window, but the conversation had already turned too awkward, and he mentioned he needed to get home after his shift.

"I'll give you a ride back to the hotel," he offered.

I turned him down. It was a nice night out, and I could use the fresh air.

He handed me his business card with his cell number scribbled on the back. "If you need to talk, or need help, call me anytime."

Charlie left then, and I was alone with my thoughts, more confused than ever. I didn't remember taking fentanyl, but that might explain why I blacked out that night. I usually could handle much more alcohol than I had drunk but mixing it with fentanyl could knock anyone out. How did it get into my system, and why?

THIRTY-THREE

CASSIE

AFTER CHARLIE LEFT THE HOUSE, I WALKED BACK TO the hotel. A sense of relief washed over me when I was safely in my room. Here, in this anonymous room, I was free from the stranglehold of the past that still gripped me tightly, even though the house was empty and void of anything from my past. But it wasn't the stuff inside that held on to your psyche, it was the house itself. As if it was its own entity. I laughed at myself. *I've watched too many scary movies.*

I turned on the television for white noise and took a shower. I sat in bed, wanting a drink. But for the first time in a long time, I was determined to not have one. It had been hours since I'd had a drink. I couldn't even remember the last time I had gone that long without it. But I needed to be clear headed, even though I felt my body going through the early stages of withdrawal.

I wondered if Brent had slipped me the fentanyl. But why would he do that? Maybe he thought it would be best to have me knocked out while he did what he had planned to get rid of Mikey's body in the freezer. It wasn't a stretch to think that Brent could get the stuff since I knew he could prescribe medications, so getting a hold of fentanyl shouldn't be too difficult for him. I didn't know what to think. I had to stop thinking the worst of my brother who had tried to help me my whole life.

I reached for my backpack to get my laptop when I saw the leather document pouch Ángel had given me earlier today. I'd forgotten it was there, so I hadn't come around to tossing it into the dumpster on the curb of the house as I had planned.

Curious, I opened it and took out the documents inside. They didn't look important, just loose pieces of papers that were printouts of news articles from the last couple years. I thumbed through the stack — twelve in total. The articles discussed multiple murders in the state and suggested a connection to the same killer.

I wasn't sure why Mother was interested in these stories. Had she become a true crime junkie like everyone else in this topsy-turvy world?

What was she up to? Planning a podcast? I laughed at the thought. Maybe she knew one of the victims? I read the first article. By the time I finished reading them all, I was still at a loss why these articles had piqued Mother's interest enough to save them like this. Since I didn't recognize the names of the victims, I didn't think they had a personal connection to Mother.

Although the bodies were found not too far from Big Plaine, none of them were actually discovered within the town limits or had any connections to the town.

I went to Google and began searching for more information. The police believed one person was responsible for all the murders. Because the bodies were found in different counties, the Minnesota Bureau of Criminal Apprehension, which was a statewide criminal investigative bureau under the Minnesota Department of Public Safety Police, had joined the investigation.

The victims' bodies had been discovered in southwestern Minnesota. All had been strangled and bludgeoned. *How awful,* I thought.

I leaned back in the bed with the laptop balanced across my knees as I began going down the infinite rabbit hole that could be the internet. I came across some interesting stories about the cases, mostly from local news outlets. There was a TV news segment about the killing on KSTP. I clicked on the link and watched the news report on YouTube. The reporter was turning up the drama, warning viewers of an active serial killer on the loose in rural Minnesota. The way the victims died was horrific. The reporter going over the dastardly deeds in a slow, rhythmic cadence. A slight Southern drawl to his accent. This guy wasn't from Minnesota, I thought as I watched him lay out how the victims died.

The victims were beaten and strangled. Their faces bashed into oblivion by the brutal killer, thus the crass nickname the media had given the killer: The Basher.

That was it for me. I closed my laptop. I lay in bed trying to fall asleep, but those articles and that reporter's voice were on an auto-play loop in my mind. It was stupid to read about all that carnage before going to bed.

Then I thought about the past and the memories I had been trying to forget but that came back.

Mikey's body in that freezer. I should have never gone down into the basement and looked inside that damn thing.

How I removed the linens from his face. Why did I do that? That caved-in face looked back at me.

Then suddenly, I felt a jolt of awareness coming over

me. My heart beat fast as I sat up in bed. I got out of bed and began looking through Mother's clippings on those murders.

The reporter's vivid description of what those victims endured before death played in my head like a movie.

I felt my blood run cold. I looked around the room which had begun to spin.

I saw something sticking out of my bag on the floor. I bent down for it. And I looked at it. It was Charlie Bell's business card.

"I HOPE I didn't get you in trouble with your wife," I said to Charlie, who came over right away after I called him. He sat on the edge of the bed. I was in the chair, across from him.

I figured telling his wife that he was meeting an old high school female friend at her hotel room at ten o'clock at night might not have gone over well with her.

Charlie smiled. "Sara understands. She has a lot of experience with cops. Her father was the chief of police in Inver Grove Heights. Her grandfather was a cop in Minneapolis and her brother is on the job in Minneapolis. So, she understands and trusts me."

"That's wonderful, Charlie. Looks like you found your-self a great gal there," I said.

"So, what's up?" he asked, looking around the hotel room at the articles strewn about.

"Have you heard about this serial killer they call The Basher?" Charlie nodded his head slowly, looking at me in confusion. "They briefed us about it since the bodies turned up in the woods close to here. Why are you asking about this?"

I heard Brent's voice: Charlie isn't your friend. Don't talk to the police. Ever.

I wanted a drink so badly. How could I tell Charlie about any of this without blowing mine and Brent's life up?

My hands were shaking. I wasn't sure if it was the stress of everything I was going through or whether it was the tremors, a common sign of alcohol withdrawal.

"Jesus, Cassie, you're shaking. What is it? You can tell me anything. You can trust me."

"I'm a horrible person," I blurted out, crying.

"Hey now, you are not a bad person," Charlie said.

"I know what happened to Mikey." There I said it. The first time in fifteen years that I'd talked about this with anyone outside of the family.

Charlie looked at me with surprise.

"I'm finally ready to tell the truth about everything that happened and about The Basher case too."

I thought saying those words to Charlie would make me crumble into tears, but I felt relieved. An odd sense of calm overcame me.

Charlie looked at me with surprise as he got up from the bed. He looked at the articles on The Basher strewn on the bed, and then he turned his attention back to me.

"That's going to be a problem, then."

THIRTY-FOUR
ROBIN

I was at work when I received a cryptic text from Charlie: "You need to get down here. It's about Mikey." I was about to knock on a suspect's door in the North End of St. Paul, so I could only glance at the message and feel my heart start to race. I couldn't respond right away.

An hour later, I finished up with the witness and tried to call Charlie back, but my call went straight to voicemail. I left him a message explaining I still had two hours left on my shift and it would take me another hour to drive to Big Plaine, so it would be nearly four hours before I could get there. I urged him to call or text me back with any updates.

The rest of my shift dragged on painfully slowly. I didn't hear from Charlie again. As soon as I was off, I got into my car and drove straight from St. Paul to Big Plaine.

I tried calling Charlie several more times and texted him, but frustratingly, he didn't respond. Driving down Highway 169 as the sun set, turning the sky orange above the farms and small towns, I felt a mix of impatience and worry. It was unlike Charlie to ignore my calls; he'd always been reliable, especially when it involved something as serious as this.

With each unanswered call, my anxiety grew. Something wasn't right. I pushed my Malibu faster along the highway, the fields and houses blurring past as my mind raced with possibilities.

What if something had happened to Charlie? Or worse, what if he had found out something about Mikey that put him in danger? My thoughts were grim, but I couldn't help but fear the worst. Deep down, I had always suspected that Brent and Cassie knew more about Mikey's disappearance than they let on. But suspicions alone weren't enough; I needed proof, and I needed to know what Charlie had discovered.

I drove faster, the urgency gnawing at me. I needed to find out what was going on, not just for my peace of mind but for my brother. I needed answers so that maybe, just maybe, my parents could finally have the chance to bury their son.

For six months, I had been relentlessly pressing for information from everyone connected to Mikey—Charlie, Cassie, Brent, even their mother, Jane, before she tragically took her own life. I sometimes wondered, guiltily, if my persistent questioning had pushed her over the edge.

For fifteen long years, my family had been trapped in a torturous state of not knowing. My parents clung to the slim hope that Mikey might one day return, but deep down, I knew he was gone from the day he disappeared. My years in law enforcement had taught me the harsh reality of these cases. The perpetual uncertainty was a constant agony, an open wound that refused to heal.

I devoted my spare time to the investigation, driven by a desperate need for justice for Mikey and some peace for my aging parents. They continued to distribute missing person flyers around town, unable to move forward with their lives, holding on to the hope that Mikey might find his way back to them.

The day I received the call about Mikey's disappearance, I was a student at the University of Wisconsin-River Falls. It was a call that shattered the innocence of our small-town life, much like the Jacob Wetterling case had done for the entire state of Minnesota years earlier.

Jacob Wetterling was an eleven-year-old boy from St. Joseph, Minnesota, who was abducted at gunpoint and remained missing for nearly twenty-seven years before his remains were finally found and his killer brought to justice. His story inspired me to never give up on finding Mikey, holding on to the hope that we might also find closure.

Initially, I suspected a stranger abduction. But that didn't make sense. Mikey was only fifteen, but he was strong, and in good shape from his wrestling and football training—a seemingly unlikely target for a random stranger kidnapping.

As the years passed and after going through the lives of every pervert sex offender with a penchant for young boys within a 100-mile radius of Big Plaine, I started to get a clearer picture that the stranger angle didn't hold water.

It seemed increasingly likely that whatever happened to Mikey happened at the hands of people he knew. That he hung out with and trusted. People with whom he would be comfortable to let his guard down. Like his friends Cassie and Charlie.

So, I began with Charlie, his closest friend, and worked my way out, scrutinizing everyone in their circle.

I always ended up back at one place: the Walsh home.

Two MONTHS before Jane Walsh died, I met up with Charlie at the Starbucks in Chaska. He didn't want to meet in town, so he picked a place near the hospital where his wife worked.

I didn't blame him for being discreet. He didn't want to meet me in Big Plaine, since in about eight seconds after being spotted together, the whole town would be abuzz with gossip that Mikey's big sister was seen in deep conversation with his best friend.

Charlie had faced repeated questioning about Mikey over the past fifteen years. And the town's rumor mill had him somehow involved. That all went away, and now he was a respected police officer in town. Meeting with me was like opening up old wounds that had never healed, they just scarred over with time.

Despite coming to town often to visit my parents, I hadn't seen Charlie in years.

I could never imagine doing police work in a small town like Charlie, especially where I grew up. I had longed for something bigger and better. So, I joined the St. Paul Police Department. As the anniversaries of Mikey's disappearance piled up and the case became as cold as a Minnesota January, I obsessed about my brother's case.

I spoke with all the law enforcement agencies that had touched Mikey's case files over the years: the FBI, the Minnesota Bureau of Criminal Apprehension, the County Sheriff, and the Big Plaine Police Department had all investigated at one time or another.

Officially, it was Big Plaine PD's case. The entire police department comprised fifteen police officers and only one dedicated detective. They assured me the case was an active one, but come on, I was no fool. Even if they wanted, they just didn't have the resources to spend time working on Mikey's cold case.

So, I got more aggressive with my private investigation. I knew that upset the police chief. I could see how it annoyed him that he had to tread lightly around me since I was the sister of a missing child and a fellow police officer, but Chief Strand didn't want me, a family member, and detective for a big-city police department butting into his fiefdom. Not that I blamed him. I would have felt the same way if our roles were reversed.

Strand was a good cop. He did twenty years with the Milwaukee Police Department before retiring and taking the job of small-town police chief, so he was no hick from out of the sticks.

I imagined it was a nice change of pace for him to go from the rough and tumble mean streets of Milwaukee to sleepy Big Plaine.

But Strand was an outsider and my brother's cold case meant nothing to him. So, I had to be his advocate. I had to push. And that's why I reached out to Charlie, Jane, Brent, and Cassie after all these years.

Charlie was the only one who had agreed to meet up with me in person to discuss the case.

Charlie was already sitting at a table by the window when I arrived at the Starbucks. He wore a red and green flannel shirt and blue jeans. He looked up at me as I approached the table.

"Hey, Robin. Nice to see you," he said, probably lying.

"Likewise," I said. I excused myself, went up to the counter, and ordered a black coffee. I joined him back at the table. He was sucking on the straw of what looked like a huge milkshake.

"What the hell is that?" I asked him, pointing at the drink.

He blushed and smiled. "It's an Iced Caramel Macchiato. Three pumps. Wanna try it?" he said, pushing the drink toward me.

He might as well be speaking to me in a foreign language. I just drank black coffee. Hot. Iced coffee was an abomination to me.

"No, thanks."

"Your loss. It's delicious."

I smiled.

We chatted for about ten minutes about our lives and how we both ended up in law enforcement.

"How do you like working for the hometown PD?" I asked, genuinely curious.

He shrugged. "I know every nook and cranny within our jurisdiction, which is nice. And I know most folks in town. But that can also be awkward. Pulling over an old buddy whom you used to underage drink with for DWI is bizarre."

I laughed. "Any arrests from anyone that would shock me?" I asked. Charlie looked around to make sure there wasn't anyone he knew.

"We're in Chaska. No one from Big Plaine is here. You can gossip freely," I said, grinning, as I tried to reassure him we could talk freely here.

"Last year, I arrested Mr. Stockton for peering into a young woman's window."

"Mr. Stockton is a Peeping Tom?" I said, laughing.

Charlie nodded his head. "Later on during the investigation, they found a bunch of way out there porn on his computer. Real pervert, that one," he said.

Mr. Stockton was our music teacher. A real blowhard,

stick up his ass type who was a stickler for rules and for handing out detentions. He loved to tell everyone how much he loved God, his wife, and his six kids, in that order. So, it didn't surprise me he was a pervert. A lot of the time, those were the type of people that were that way since they're trying to hide who they really are.

I segued into the reason for our meet up and asked him about Mikey.

"I'm ashamed," Charlie said.

"You were fifteen," I said, trying to reassure him and to get him to open up about what happened the day Mikey disappeared.

"Mikey was going to Cassie Walsh's house, like I told the police back then. But..." He looked away from me in shame.

"I'm not going to judge you, Charlie," I said after he stayed quiet for a while.

"Like you know, the official story I told the police was that we were supposed to hang out that day, but he ditched me. But that wasn't true."

"Yeah, he went over to Cassie's house," I said, already knowing about that.

Charlie fidgeted with his cup. "I went with him to Cassie's house."

I almost fell off my chair, but I had to stay calm and keep still. It was like feeding a hummingbird by hand. You couldn't make sudden movement or you'd scare it away.

"You actually went inside? You saw Cassie on that day with Mikey?"

Charlie nodded. *Holy shit. Keep it together, Robin.* That was huge. In her official statement, which I know from memory, Cassie told the police that Mikey never showed up at her house on that day. And Brent vouched for her. Why would they lie about that? As a kid, I supposed she didn't want to get in trouble for having a boy over at her house. Most parents would frown about their teenage kids hanging out alone without adult supervision at home, especially from the opposite sex and everyone in town knew that Cassie's mom was a bit of a looney tunes about her kids being prim and proper — whatever that meant. Maybe that's why Cassie lied. And Brent was trying to protect his sister? But from what? Whatever the reason, I knew one thing for damned sure. I needed to talk to Cassie Walsh as soon as possible.

"So, what happened?"

"We drank a beer I stole from my dad's fridge. Shared a joint. We were watching Beavis and Butthead on TV. After a while, I noticed that Cassie and Mikey were getting frisky. I felt like a third wheel. The two of them went down to the basement to mess around. I felt stupid waiting in the living room by myself while they were down there screwing around. So, I left. I never saw Mikey again."

THIRTY-FIVE
CASSIE

I woke up feeling the familiar grogginess usually followed by a night of heavy drinking, but I hadn't touched a drop in over twenty-four hours. Confusion clouded my mind as I tried to figure out where I was; this wasn't my hotel room. Everything around me was blurry at first, and my thoughts felt slippery and elusive. My head throbbed.

The surface under me was hard and bitterly cold, chilling me right through the thin layer of my clothes. As the mental fog slowly began to lift, the harsh, clinical light above me stung my eyes, forcing me to squint and try to piece together my surroundings.

A shiver ran through me—not just from the cold but also from the sudden, sickening realization of where I might be. My head throbbed with a dull, relentless pain that fogged my ability to think clearly. I attempted to sit up, but dizziness overwhelmed me, sending me sprawling back onto the cold metal. I felt like a tiny pin stuck on a magnet.

With a deep breath, I mustered the strength to sit up

again, despite my trembling arms and pounding head. As my vision finally started to clear, I was able to get a good look at where I was, and the grim reality hit me—I was inside a steel shipping container. The walls were stark, bare metal, streaked with rust and the drip of condensation. The air was stale and heavy, laced with the tang of iron and a faint, unsettling undercurrent of fear or maybe despair coming from me.

In the corner lay a bucket and two water bottles, which only added to the bleakness of the setting.

Panic started to take hold, and I had to remind myself to breathe—slow, deep breaths to calm the storm of fear rising inside me. I was trapped in this cold, impersonal metal prison, and I had no memory of how I ended up here.

My recall was fragmented, slipping through my mind like water through fingers. But I started to slowly remember. I asked Charlie to come over. I told him about what had happened – the truth – and he seemed concerned. Then... nothing. Where the hell was I and where was Charlie? Did he put me in this fucking metal coffin?

I got up, but I heard a clunking sound of metal against metal, and I felt something heavy around my ankle. I looked down and that's when I saw the heavy chain. A leather restraint bound my ankle with the chain firmly attached.

I stooped and reached for the ankle restraint with both hands to remove it, but it wouldn't budge. I picked up the chain, pulled it, and saw that it was attached to a metal loop bracket mounted on the floor. The chain and bracket were heavy duty, stainless steel. I felt the tears down my face as I realized what had happened to me. I was chained to the floor inside this shipping container. There were no windows, so I did not know where it was located or if it was day or night. I wasn't even sure how long I'd been there. I yanked at the chain and the bracket, but it would not budge.

I tried for the door but there wasn't enough give from the chain. I stretched my arms for it, but my fingers brushed against the doors. I screamed out of fear and frustration.

Even if the door was wide open, I wouldn't be going anywhere with that damn chain tying me down like a junk-yard dog.

I yelled at the top of my lungs: "Help! Get me out of here," as I flashed back to the times that Mother would lock me up in the root cellar in the basement.

Time outs. That's what she used to call the cellar punishments. She had read in a magazine how putting misbehaving kids in time outs was a suitable form of punish-ment. Make them sit in a corner. Or have them go to their room for ten minutes. I doubted those articles in the self-help for parents' magazines intended a time out to be locked in a cold root cellar for a day. But Mother never used restraints and chains like this, she didn't have to. Fear kept my childhood self there until she allowed me to leave the cellar.

I examined the metal bracket bored into the steel floor. It was scratched and kinked from the chain rubbing up against it. No doubt a sign of its heavy use. I also noticed scratch marks on the floor from dragging the chain across it. My God, how many others like me had been chained up like this in here? I screamed again. But no one came.

The only other thing in there besides me and that chain was the large plastic bucket and the two water bottles. How long was I going to be kept locked up in there? I wasn't going to the bathroom in a bucket.

After screaming and trying to yank the chain from the

brackets for thirty minutes straight, I felt dejected and exhausted as I sat down on the floor, breathless. I was trying to be strong, but all I felt was despair and fear.

I had no clue how long I'd been locked in there. And I had no one to come look for me, aside from Brent. He was my only hope. Suddenly, I heard a light tap on the other side of the door and someone calling my name.

"Cassie?"

I bolted up from the floor and got to my feet; the chain dragging across the floor like I was Marley's ghost.

"Are you okay?"

I recognized the voice. It was Brent.

"Brent, is that you? Help me, I'm chained up and locked in here."

"I'm sorry, Cassie." He sounded calm and collected. Like it was no big deal that I was locked up in there.

"Brent, what the fuck? Let me out of here," I pleaded.

"Why did you call Charlie, Cassie? Why didn't you call me?"

"What? I don't know, Brent. Let me out of here, please."

"All I've ever done was try to help you and protect you."

"Then let me out of here!"

"You still don't trust me."

"What am I supposed to think? You have me locked up in here."

"There you go again. It's not me that did this to you, Cassie."

I take a deep breath, trying to calm my frayed nerves.

"Please, just let me out and we can talk."

"It was Charlie, not me," Brent said.

"Okay, fine, then let me out. Now!"

"I can't. The door is locked and I don't have the key and

he'll be back soon. I have to go, before he catches me here and he kills us both."

"No, please, Brent, don't leave me here alone."

"I'm going to get help, just hang on."

"Call the police, then, please."

"Of course I will, but we're in the middle of nowhere, and I don't have a cell signal out here. So, I have to get closer to town so I can call 911. So, hang tight, Cassie. I'll be back with the cavalry."

"No, Brent, don't leave me here."

"Hang tight and stay strong!"

"Brent please, I'm begging. Get me out of here."

"I will. For once, trust me," Brent said, his voice trailing off as I heard him running off away from the container.

All I could do was to continue to yell for him to not leave me there all alone, but I was met with silence and the frigid embrace of the steel walls of my new prison.

I must have banged on that steel wall for over an hour. The balls of my fists were on fire from the pain of banging on steel over and over. My ankle was chafed and red from the restraint rubbing up against it as I paced like a caged animal and my throat was raw.

At first, I ignored the water bottles. But the surfaces of my mouth were lined with a thick, sticky film, making it uncomfortable to even open it or move my tongue. I felt desperately parched. I needed to moisten my mouth and alleviate the discomfort, so I caved and reached for one of the bottles. I opened it and took several huge gulps feeling instant relief. I drank the whole thing in a few gulps. I eyed the second bottle but held off, not knowing how long I would be trapped with just the two bottles of water. I was hoping Brent was telling me the truth and he was out there getting help. Why chain me up like this? Was Charlie some sadistic psycho? I tried to scream again, but the words came out all garbled and I felt my skin tingle. My head felt like it weighed a ton and my vision was blurry. I was feeling so fatigued. I felt myself slouching down onto the floor. What was happening to me? I felt myself fading away.

THIRTY-SIX
ROBIN

I SAW THE GREEN HIGHWAY SIGN WELCOMING ME TO Big Plaine, even though I knew I was very much unwelcomed by Brent, Cassie, and the police chief.

I was about fifteen miles from town when Strand called me to let me know that Brent had unleashed his lawyers to rein me in.

Strand said I wasn't welcome at his station, furious to learn I had access to their prisoners and case files without proper authorization. "What were you thinking interviewing Cassie Walsh in my jail cell without my permission?" Chief Strand had bemoaned to me on the phone.

As soon as I got off the phone with Strand, my lieutenant called me to dress me down for sticking my nose in on police matters more than a hundred miles from St. Paul.

Brent's lawyer was earning his keep. I hadn't even arrived in town and I had already been yelled at and ordered to stay far away from Brent and Cassie.

I didn't care about a muckety-muck lawyer trying to scare me by rattling my boss's cage. Been there, done that. I was finally making headway in Mikey's long-cold case, whereas I doubted Chief Strand was doing much more than offering media-friendly remarks to mark the fifteenth anniversary of Mikey's disappearance.

But I did love my job, so I had to tread lightly from now on. Charlie's message sounded too important for me not to come down. Chief Strand and Brent's lawyers couldn't keep me out of my hometown.

I wished I could get a hold of Charlie who had gone dark on me. I hated to do this, but I called Charlie's wife. She told me she was worried. Charlie had gone out to meet Cassie at the hotel in town, and she hadn't heard from him, so she had been trying to get a hold of him without any luck. I told her I would check things out.

I drove to the hotel but didn't see Brent or Charlie's car there. So, I drove to the Walshes' home. I didn't know why, it was a gut feeling that I needed to be there.

I tried Charlie once again on the phone, but all I got was the default automated voicemail message.

"Charlie, I just got into town. You're making me worried. Where are you? Please call me as soon as you get this."

I got out of the car. There was a For Sale sign out front of the Walshes' house. I rang the doorbell and knocked, but no one came to the door. I bent down to look through the space between the garage door and the asphalt. Looked like the car was in the garage. From the corner of my eye, I noticed a shadow moving by the window that looked down into the basement. It was subtle and quick, but I knew what I saw. Someone was down there. So, I went back to the door and gave it the good old cop hard knock.

"Brent, Cassie, it's Robin. Open up. I know you're in there. And I'm not leaving until you come to the door," I stood out there knocking like a Jehovah's Witness, when suddenly, I heard the blood-curdling screams coming from inside.

I was now pounding on the door. "Is everything okay in there? Open the door." The door remained closed, but the screaming from inside sounded like someone was being murdered. I called 911, identified myself as a police officer, and I told the dispatch to send police out there right away. I hung up the phone. As I looked at the door, I noticed that it was an old, thin door. Since I went there straight from work, I was wearing my Danner ankle boots. I should have waited for backup, but I couldn't stand out there while someone was being killed inside. It took three kicks, and the door shattered in its frame. I removed my Glock and went inside. I rushed toward the sound of the screaming which was coming from the kitchen. I proceeded carefully and as I stepped inside, I saw Cassie running up from the basement and she was covered in blood.

I didn't know how badly she was injured or who else was in the house, so I whisked her outside as Big Plaine patrol car was pulling up out front.

A FEW MINUTES LATER, a swarm of cops was on us like ants on ice cream. They grabbed Cassie away. Strand beelined towards me with a hard glare.

"What the hell, Robin? Not thirty minutes ago I told you to stay away from the Walshes and yet here you are."

"I was just trying to find Charlie. He sent me a text that I needed to get down here right away. I haven't been able to get a hold of him for hours. So, I called his wife. She told me he left to meet Cassie at her hotel because she needed help.

I didn't see him there, so I came out here. I heard screaming from inside, so I just reacted."

Strand eyed me suspiciously, but his hardened face softened a little. "Charlie didn't show up for his shift two hours ago. He hasn't called in sick or checked in with anyone," Strand said, sounding concerned about his missing officer.

One of Strand's officers who had gone inside the house to investigate came running out looking pale and shaken. "Chief! It's Charlie," she said, holding back tears.

Strand bolted toward the house. I followed him. He turned around and yelled at me. "You. Stay put out here." He turned to another of his officers. "If she tries to go inside the house, arrest her for obstruction."

"Yes, sir," the officer said, giving me a dirty look.

Standing in the front yard helpless was eating me up inside. But I had no choice but to obey Strand's orders. Not only did this Barney Fife-looking asshole seem eager to cuff a big city detective, but I didn't want to get into any more hot water with my bosses in St. Paul.

So, I bit the side of my cheek as I stood there with my arms crossed, wondering what the hell was going on.

The paramedics had whisked Cassie away. I did not know how badly she was injured, but the amount of blood suggested that it was bad. I headed out to the street to talk to the remaining paramedics. Strand's cop followed me. I could have laid him out flat in five seconds, but I ignored him.

I recognized one of the paramedics with the fire department. He was the younger brother of one of my high school friends.

"Hey, Thor, how badly injured was Cassie Walsh?"

"She's not," he replied.

I was confused. "But she was covered in blood."

"Wasn't her blood. We checked her thoroughly. She didn't have any wounds and wasn't bleeding."

"No shit," I said, turning my attention back to the house, wondering what the hell had Cassie gotten herself into now.

When Strand finally exited the house, I could tell by looking at him and the other officers who had been inside what was going on. It was a look I dreaded seeing on a cop at a crime scene.

I could tell from all the way in the back. A fellow officer was dead. "Oh, God. Charlie," I said under my breath.

As I STEPPED into the front lobby of the police station, I was immediately hit with the tension of a high-profile ongoing investigation. And in cop-land, it didn't get more high-profile and chaotic than when one of their own was killed.

Strand told me to wait in his office, so I did.

I sat there waiting for him as he instructed me to do. I felt like I was back in high school, in trouble, waiting for the principal.

The details were fuzzy because everything happened so fast. I saw Cassie running up the stairs from the basement with blood on her, I assumed she had been attacked and, for all I knew, her attacker was still down there.

So, I grabbed her, and we ran outside just as the local police arrived on the scene only to find out that she wasn't injured, but Charlie was found dead in the basement. Was that his blood on Cassie? I wondered.

Strand entered his office, snapping me from my thoughts. He looked haggard.

He sat down in his chair, leaned back in it as far as he could, and he sighed loudly as he looked up at the ceiling.

"What a shit show," he mumbled. "I thought I left that type of crap back in Milwaukee."

"What's going on, Chief? Whose blood was on Cassie?"

Strand leaned forward in his chair and sat straight, putting both elbows on his desk. His chin rested on his balled-up fists as if he needed to do that in order to prevent his head from rolling onto the floor.

"It was Charlie's blood."

I couldn't believe what I was hearing. My eyes watered up.

"How?" was all I could muster to say.

"That crazy bitch killed him," Strand seethed.

Strand's comment took me aback. He'd always been so professional. But I got it. He had just lost one of his officers and it looked like Cassie was their only suspect since I assumed by bitch he'd been referring to her. I'd been on the job long enough to know anyone was capable of murder. Anyone. But still. I found it hard to believe that Cassie killed Charlie. "Cassie killed Charlie?" I asked, to confirm I was understanding how things are playing out.

"Looks that way."

"How?"

"A knife. Multiple stab wounds."

I sat there dumbfounded.

"You said Charlie sent you a text to come to town?"

I nodded almost absentmindedly before clearing my throat and collecting myself.

"That's right. He said he had information about Mikey's case and Cassie. But I was working, so I couldn't get back to him. When I finally had time to call him back, I couldn't get a hold of him. My calls kept going straight to voicemail. My texts to him went unanswered."

"Why did you go to the Walsh house?" Strand asked.

"I told you. I called Charlie's wife. She told me Charlie had stepped out to meet up with Cassie about a case. When they weren't at the hotel, I went to the house to look for them."

"And you heard screams from inside?"

"Not right away. I was knocking on the front door for a minute. I went around toward the garage, and I saw movement from the basement through the well window. That's when I heard the screams. You know the rest. I called 911 and kicked down the door."

"Did Cassie say anything to you?"

"No. She seemed in shock. I tried questioning her, but the paramedics took her to the hospital."

Strand jotted down a few notes on a legal pad and he put his pen down.

"Where was Charlie's body found?" I asked.

Strand looked up from his legal pad. He was quiet for a moment, as if deciding what he was going to share with me.

"There is a root cellar down in the basement. His body was in there."

I felt sick to my stomach. I'd kept pushing Charlie to help me get to the bottom of what happened to Mikey. Now he was dead. I pushed Jane Walsh. She was dead too. Both died within feet of each other in that damned basement.

THIRTY-SEVEN
ROBIN

I wasn't part of the investigation, but I wasn't ready to leave town, so I spent the night at my parent's house.

Charlie's death brought back memories of my rookie year. Only fifteen months on the job when tragedy struck our department.

One of our brave officers, who had dedicated sixteen years to serving on the police force, was killed in the line of duty while responding to a domestic abuse call.

The loss sent shockwaves through our tight-knit law enforcement community and left an indelible mark on all of us who wore the badge. I didn't know that officer well, just in passing, but his death was a gut punch. Even though I wasn't a member of the Big Plaine Police Department, Charlie's death hurt me more.

Although I was older than he was, I grew up with him. He was my brother's best friend. Family members of missing children cling to any connection to their loved one. As Mikey's best friend, my parents treated Charlie like a son over the years.

The connection went both ways. Charlie would always check in on them, and when he became a cop, he promised to keep Mikey's cold case alive and told them he would do whatever he could to help solve it. And then he helped me work the case even though it put his career in danger with the police chief.

Now he was gone. I had the horrible task of telling my parents who took it hard.

The first twenty-four hours after his death were surreal. The entire town was in shock. Officers walking around with reddened eyes. The sound of whimpering permeated the small department.

The somber black band clung to their badges, a stark contrast to the gleaming metal beneath, serving as a silent testament to their loss. It was more than a piece of fabric; it was a weight, a shadow that hung over the entire department, a reminder of the peril they faced each day.

Making it even more surreal was that they were accusing Cassie of killing Charlie. And now there were rumors that their own officer, whom they called "Sweets" because he was such a sweetheart to everyone, might have been living a secret life that was the antithesis to that nickname.

I hung around the department trying to figure out what was going on. I wanted to talk to Cassie, but that would be a touchy subject with Strand.

I couldn't wash my hands from this and head back to St. Paul. I felt terrible doing this, since I knew how stressed out the chief was, but I could help him. His office, surrounded by windows, was in the back of the station to offer him a modicum of privacy. He had curtains he could draw if he needed privacy. To my surprise, the shades were up. I took a deep breath and tapped on his door. He looked up from his desk. He couldn't contain wincing as he saw me there, but he waved me in.

"How are you holding up, Chief?"

"As bad as you can imagine. Take a seat," Strand said.

"I've heard the rumblings about Charlie out there in the station. That he was a serial killer. It can't be true," I said as I sat down.

"I hope you're right, but from the evidence that's been collected, it's not looking good for Charlie," Strand said.

"I can help, Chief. I have years of experience as a detective. No offense to your department, but you have one detective and he's in way over his head in this type of case."

Strand nodded his head in agreement. "You're correct. My detective is in over his head, and my officers are overwhelmed. And you do have a lot more experience with this type of case. In the big city, no less. But you're too close to this personally."

I opened my mouth to retort, but he held his hand in the air to stop me before I could utter a word. "Besides," he continued. "I've already called the BCA. They're sending two agents from Mankato."

The BCA was the Minnesota Bureau of Criminal Apprehension which was a statewide criminal investigative bureau headquartered in Saint Paul with field offices throughout the state. The BCA provided expert forensic science and criminal investigation services for the entire state and assisted smaller law enforcement agencies like Big Plaine that didn't have the experience and resources for these types of investigations.

I wasn't surprised the chief asked for the BCA to take over the case. I would have done the same in his shoes. When those agents arrived in town, they would cut off my access there and send me back to St. Paul. My time was running out to find out what happened to Mikey.

"That is great, Chief. The BCA will do an excellent job," I said, trying to sound like I was happy about it. Strand looked at me side-eyed, knowing I was laying it on thick.

"What do you want, Detective?" he said after a moment of giving me that look.

I smiled, knowing he saw right through my bullshit. "Can I see Cassie?"

Strand leaned back in his chair, which groaned loudly, as if to think it over. At least he didn't shoot me down right off the bat.

"Her brother and his high-priced pit bull of a lawyer are all up my ass about Cassie. The lawyer is on his way down as we speak. Like Cassie deserves special treatment. She killed a cop for chrissakes," Strand said, sounding annoyed.

"Please, Chief. Between the BCA agents and the lawyer, my window here is just about closed."

Strand sat up in his chair. He looked over at the cork board outside of his office with flyers and notices tacked to it. The cork board had Mikey's missing poster tacked on there for fifteen years. I put up a fresh one every couple of years to keep it fresh in the mind of the officers out there versus looking at an old, tattered, and faded flyer.

I wasn't sure if the chief was looking at Mikey's poster, but he turned his attention back to me and said: "Off the record, Robin. Ten minutes." He looked away from me and back to the paperwork on his desk. I knew better than to push my luck and ask for more time.

"Thank you, Chief," I said and got up and left before he could change his mind.

THIRTY-EIGHT
ROBIN

AN OFFICER BROUGHT CASSIE TO THE INTERVIEW ROOM where I was waiting for her. Handcuffed in front, it was evident that their anger towards the suspected cop killer was diminishing as nasty whisperings about Charlie spread throughout the station.

The officer sat her down. On his way out, he reminded me I only had ten minutes.

The room was small and cold, with just a table and three chairs in it. The walls were a pale yellow, dull, and uninviting. There wasn't a grand one-way mirror like in the movies.

It looked just like a cramped conference room you might find in an office building in the suburbs.

Cassie's hair was disheveled, tears streaked her face, and she seemed to sag under the weight of the situation she was in. They had replaced her bloody clothing with a light blue set of scrubs that had the word INMATE emblazoned on the back.

Cassie looked at me, her hazel eyes wide with fear and

disbelief. "Robin?" she whispered. "What are you doing here?"

"I'm here to help," I replied.

She looked downtrodden, but she gave me an incredulous look after saying that I wanted to help her.

"Yeah, right," she said sarcastically. "What are you even doing here? You're not a cop in town or even in this county."

"I know. I asked Chief Strand to let me talk to you. He agreed, but he only gave me ten minutes. So, I'm sorry, but I'm going to be curt."

"What do you want?" Cassie's eyes began to well up with tears after asking that.

"I want to get to the bottom of this mess. What the hell happened with Charlie?"

"I didn't do it, Robin," she said. "I swear to you, I didn't kill Charlie," Cassie said, putting her handcuffed arms on the table as she began to nervously pick on the skin around a fingernail.

"I believe you, Cassie," I replied, reaching out to take her hand, which made her flinch. "But we need to find out the truth. We need to find out who really did this and why."

I was so sure that this whole mess tied back to Mikey somehow and I needed to find out how before the BCA agents or Brent's lawyer banned me from seeing her ever again.

"Have you heard what they're saying about Charlie?"

She gave me a half nod. "One of the inmates told me they overheard guards saying that Charlie was The Basher. So, they began snickering and calling me the *serial killer killer*," Cassie said, shaking her head.

"Do you believe Charlie was The Basher?"

"No. But. Well. I don't know. I think my brain is broken.

From the drinking and these horrible memories I'd tried to suppress for fifteen years. I just don't know. And I don't remember a thing about last night. Why can't I remember?"

"Your blood work came back. You were swimming in fentanyl. Just like you were the night of your DWI arrest," I explained.

"That wasn't me, Robin!" she screamed, sounding frustrated about the accusation. She steadied herself and added more calmly: "Look. I'm not a saint. I've done opiates in the past. I've done time. But in the last few years, alcohol has been my drug. I haven't taken fentanyl for years."

"There's no question, Cassie. It's in your body. A lot of it. I'm amazed you didn't OD."

"It can't be. Why can't I remember?"

"Actually, there are cases of individuals abusing fentanyl that have developed severe short-term memory loss."

I wasn't playing her; there were studies with imaging scans of patients who have abused these types of drugs, showing damage to the part of the brain associated with memory. Perhaps that's why Cassie couldn't remember what happened.

"That might be true, but I don't abuse fentanyl. I wouldn't even know where I would score fentanyl in Big Plaine, for chrissakes."

"Brent is a doctor. It would be easy for him to get his hands on fentanyl," I said.

Cassie shook her head. "Brent would never give me that. He wants me clean and sober. He wouldn't even give me alcohol, so forget something as powerful as that shit."

"Okay, then, tell me what you do remember?"

"We cleaned out the house. One of the crew members that Brent hired handed me a document pouch he found under Mother's mattress. She had a bunch of clippings about The Basher, which I thought was weird. And..." Cassie stopped, looking at me with shame.

I was running out of time. So, I leaned forward to get closer to her across the table between us. I once again grabbed her hands.

"You can tell me anything, Cassie, even if it has to do about Mikey. No matter how awful it might be. It's been fifteen years. I can handle anything. I just want the truth," I told her, meaning it.

Deep down in my gut, I knew Cassie knew what happened to Mikey. But I needed to be very careful about how I approached her about it. I glanced at my watch. I had five minutes left.

Cassie spoke up. "That's what I wanted. To have the truth finally out there, no matter what. That's why I called Charlie and asked him to meet me in my hotel room. He came right over. I told him what I was thinking. Then his body demeanor toward me changed. He tensed up. Oh my God," Cassie said, stopping for a moment.

"Please continue, Cassie. We're running out of time," I prodded her gently.

"Charlie stood up and said something like that's going to be a problem. Then, I blacked out. I woke up in a metal container. I was chained up. Brent was there outside of the container, but he couldn't open the locked door. He told me Charlie locked me up. He said we were some-where without cell signal, so Brent left to get help. Then I woke up in that cellar, covered in blood. Charlie lying down beside me, also covered in blood. He wasn't moving," Cassie said, her voice cracked as she fought back the tears.

"Then what happened?"

"That's all I remember. It's all just a black void. What is wrong with me? Why do I keep blacking out like that."

I had to keep pressing her about Mikey.

"What did you tell Charlie, Cassie? Was it about Mikey?" I asked.

Cassie looked at me with tears streaming down her face. I'd seen that look many times, interviewing suspects and witnesses. She was about to break. She was about to give up the truth. I looked at my watch. I had a minutes left.

THE POLICE OFFICER took Cassie away right at the ten-minute mark. He made sure I didn't get an extra second with Cassie. As I exited the room, Officer Crystal Rogers was standing there waiting for me.

"Chief wants to see you in his office. Right now," she said smugly.

"Okay," I said. I made my way towards his office, with Crystal following me. The escort annoyed me. Did she think I would run out the front door? But I let her do her thing. "You wanted to see me, Chief?"

"Yes, please take a seat. Thank you, Crystal," he said, as she turned around and walked away.

"So? What do you think of Cassie's story?" Strand asked me.

I grinned. That sly devil. Off the record, my ass. I knew there was a recording camera in the interview room. It was right there in the open, up in the corner of the ceiling that pointed down. I figured it was recording but thought maybe he had it shut off since this was supposed to be off the record. But not only was it recording, he had watched me question Cassie in real time.

"I don't think she was lying. But she has all these significant blackout gaps and she had enough fentanyl to bring a hardened street junkie to their knees," I said. "And that stuff does affect memory which might explain why she can't remember what happened."

I had seen the aftereffects of fentanyl abuse in the past few years of the opiate crisis taking over the country. Right where I worked in St. Paul to the infamous gritty open streets of San Francisco, to the poverty-stricken Appalachia mountains of Virginia, or right here in rural America's farm country, it made no difference. Opiate abuse thrived. Fentanyl would bring its abusers into an immediate trancelike state where they would freeze, hunched over, or on their knees, passed out like a stiffened zombie. Farmer, car mechanic, lawyer, or street hustler, the opiates did not discriminate in its devastation of people.

"Still. That's quite a tale she told with these convenient memory gaps to gloss over the worst of the crimes she seems to get into," Strand said.

He then cleared his throat. "You okay with what she said about your brother?"

Cassie had told me what had happened fifteen years ago to Mikey. I still hadn't had the time to process it. But I believed her. Why make that up after all this time of getting away with it?

"I believe that too. I've long suspected whatever happened to Mikey was at that house," I replied.

A loud ruckus coming from the station interrupted our conversation. The chief looked out his office window.

"What now?" Strand said as he got up from behind his desk and made his way towards the loud voices. I followed along and saw the man of the hour. The one person I was desperate to get into an interview room, Brent Walsh. And he had brought backup.

You could tell they were lawyers from a mile away even before introductions were made. Bruce Kindsvater was in his late forties. He seemed to be the one in charge. The other lawyer, Erika Sundberg, was in her early thirties. Both wore expensive-looking shiny suits.

Kindsvater was harping about Cassie's rights. Brent was standing behind his legal goons when we made eye contact.

"Oh, of course, there you are in the thick of it," Brent said, looking right at me, his voice dripping with contempt and disdain. I'd been called every name in the book in my career, but his delivery gave me chills. He turned to his attorney. "That's Robin Moretti Dawson, who's been harassing me and my family for months."

I knew he was upset with me for hounding his family. He had been very clear about it. The comment took me aback. And everyone stopped talking and looked back at me. I wanted to ask Brent about the metal container that he had somehow found with Cassie locked inside. Where was it? How did he find it? But Strand would have my head for putting all his cards on the table like that. So, I just stood there and took his vitriol, wishing I had Ant-Man powers so I could shrink down and run off.

Kindsvater glared at me. "We'll deal with you soon enough, Detective Moretti," he said, as if sizing me up. He then turned to Strand. "But first things first, Cassie Walsh is my client. No one talks to her without me or my associate present. And I'd like her out of here. Right now."

"She killed a cop," Strand said.

"So, you have charged her with murder?"

Strand didn't reply, but he crossed his arms around his chest and clenched his fists.

"I didn't think so," Kindsvater said, smugly.

THIRTY-NINE
CASSIE

I had been locked up in one place or another, just about every day since I set foot back in Big Plaine, including my DWI arrest, the shipping container, the basement, and now back in the town holding cell. I should have stayed in Las Vegas looking for a new job. Far away from here.

I had been sitting in this one-person holding cell for forty-eight hours. I thought that my mind would have cleared by now. But I'd been struggling with alcohol withdrawal symptoms and, as Robin had informed me, I was getting fentanyl out of my body as well, and to make matters worse, the fentanyl might be messing up my brain. Making me forget what happened between Brent, Charlie, and me. All I could remember were bits and pieces. The frustration about not remembering was overwhelming, given that my long-term freedom hinged on it.

I was feeling better, but I still had the worst headache of my life. It felt like the top of my head was being jackhammered and the inside was being tightened by a vice grip. The tremors had tempered down, and at least I was no longer hallucinating that Mother and Mikey were in my cell with me, egging me on to join them on the other side.

During the worst of my hallucinations, I saw Mother in the cell with me. "You'll feel better," she told me. "Just use your jumpsuit. Tie it tightly around your neck, then tie the other end to the door, and just lean forward, and join us on the other side. It's lovely here." She gave me the hanging sign with her right arm and her tongue lolling out to the side with a smirk. It seemed so real.

Focus on reality, I chided myself. I closed my eyes as my head kept hurting, but all I could see were slivers of fragments of what had happened.

I remembered Charlie in my hotel room. Then me in that metal box. And Brent. He was there. He said he was going to get help. Then I blacked out. I awoke on the floor next to Charlie's dead body in Mother's cellar. How was that even possible?

I didn't get time to process any of it. When I saw Charlie lying on the floor covered in blood, I ran upstairs like I had done fifteen years ago, but instead of running into Brent, I ran into Robin.

A police officer took me away and had paramedics check my wounds. It was only then that I realized I didn't have any wounds and that the blood on me wasn't mine.

"Fucking cop killer," someone hissed as I sat on the stretcher in back of a firefighter ambulance.

They think I killed Charlie? Since I didn't have any life-threatening wounds, the police handcuffed me and hauled me away to the police station.

When I saw Robin earlier today, at first, I felt that dread of the secret of Mikey I had kept from her all these years. But I was done with handling that way.

I knew Brent would be furious, but I felt exhausted

from the lie. So, I gave Robin what she wanted. The truth about what happened to Mikey down in my basement all those years ago. And it felt good. A release that eased the tension and anxiety I had been feeling. If I ended up in prison, so be it. I had already trapped myself in a self-imposed prison, where I made alcohol my bars, locking myself inside my studio apartment and drinking until I blacked out most nights.

I stopped short of telling Robin everything. Surprisingly, I felt I owed it to Brent not to blow up his perfect life by telling her that Mother had hidden Mikey's body in her freezer all this time and that Brent had gotten rid of it a few nights ago. I told her the version of what I had believed happened all this time, that I killed Mikey and that mother told Brent and I to leave and not come back until she texted us to come home. She never told us what she did with the body. And we never talked about it again.

I was still sorting all this out in my head when the cell door opened. A woman in a power suit stood there smiling at me. Next to her, Officer Crystal, the one that arrested me for the DWI and who had been so nasty to me. From the looks she gave me, she hated me even more now. I supposed she thought I killed Charlie, a fellow police officer, so the hatred was justified.

I didn't know the other woman, but she dressed and carried herself like a lawyer. She came into my cramped cell and Crystal slammed the door shut, leaving me alone with her.

I sat on a thin pad on the cement cot. She stood stiffly, seemingly not wanting to risk ruining her fancy suit.

"Hi, Cassie. My name is Erika Sundberg. And I'm your lawyer. Your brother hired our firm to represent you. How are you holding up, all things considered?"

"Fine, I guess." What else could I say to her? She knew what a deep mess I was in facing charges for DWI and resisting arrest. And now I was being called a cop killer. Oh, and I just confessed to a St. Paul Detective that I also killed her little brother fifteen years ago. How were things going for you, Erica? But I didn't say any of that. I just looked at her while trying to keep it together.

"My boss is with Brent right now, working on your release. He's one of the top partners at the firm. And a heck of a litigator. Don't you worry, you'll be out of here real soon. Don't talk to anyone without me or my boss present. Is that clear?"

"Yes."

"Have you talked to anyone in law enforcement since your arrest?"

I looked down at the cheap plastic sandals I was wearing courtesy of the Big Plaine city jail.

"Cassie? Have you talked to anyone else today?" Sundberg asked again.

Shit. Brent was going to hit the roof.

"I talked to Robin. But only for ten minutes."

"Detective Robin Moretti?" Sundberg said, unable to mask the concern that washed over her face.

I nodded. I could see a lump in her throat as she swallowed hard, taking that in.

"We'll need a complete breakdown of what you said to the detective."

I opened my mouth to tell her, but she stopped me. "Not right now. Wait until we get you out of here."

With that, she left but not before yet again reminding me to stop talking to anyone else, especially cops.

I sat there alone for a few more hours. Time crawled when you were locked up with nothing to do. Even in

prison, you get yard time, television time, educational cour-
ses, and books and magazines to read. I was in limbo in the
city jail, which was designed for the short-term. The time
between being arrested until you're charged and transferred
elsewhere. All I could do here was sit and dwell on my poor
life choices, consumed by self-pity and loathing. Thinking
that I should have listened to Mother about joining her.

The sound of the door being unlocked snapped me out
of those dark thoughts. I looked up and saw Crystal through
the small window on the cell door. She opened the door,
looking at me even angrier than before, if that was possible.

"Get up," she barked at me.

I did as told. "What's going on?"

"Congratulations. Your brother's money got you a get
out of jail free card. For killing a cop, no less. Impressive."

I said nothing, not wanting to make things worse.
Crystal grabbed me by the arm roughly and she dragged me
from the holding cells down to the outward processing room
where Ericka Sundberg was waiting for me with a wide
smile. Her teeth were perfect and white.

She greeted me warmly as she gently massaged my
back, like we'd known each other for years. Even though she
was my lawyer, just doing her job, being paid handsomely
by Brent, I was sure. I appreciated the gesture. A kind touch
felt wonderful after the last few days.

"Told you we would get you out of here quickly," Sundberg whispered as the clerk handled the paperwork to
release me.

It took about fifteen minutes to get through that stage.
Because my blood-soaked clothing was under evidence,
Sundberg handed me a plastic bag from Target. "Change
into these," she said with a smile. I went into a room to
change. I put on the new bra she bought, which was the

perfect size. Same with the long-sleeve black yoga shirt and pants. I was happy to get out of those jail-issued scrubs and thick socks that felt like I was walking around with steel scrubbing pads on my feet. I felt like a new person already. I thanked Sundberg for the clothing items. I wondered how she got my measurements perfectly. Did she size me up? Or was it written somewhere in my intake form? I shook my head. Who cares, dummy, I told myself. I just wanted to get the hell out of there as soon as possible, so I kept quiet as I went through the system until finally I was given the okay to leave.

THE MOMENT I stepped out into the daylight, the brightness overwhelmed me, forcing my eyes into a tight squint to adjust after two days locked up. But it wasn't just the sunlight, it was the rush of fresh air, so different from the stagnant atmosphere I'd been breathing in jail. For a fleeting second, I basked in the sweet relief of freedom.

But my relief was short-lived. As we made our way down the station steps, a jarring cacophony broke the serenity of my newfound freedom. My heart sank. A throng of reporters rushed toward me. They must have stationed themselves in front of the station, eagerly awaiting something to report back. When they saw me, they rushed in like pigs at a trough. The reporters flashed their cameras and thrust microphones into my face. That's when I realized that the case had spiraled into a media frenzy, a circus I hadn't expected, yet I was front and center. *I'd never be able to get a job now*, I thought, as Erica wrapped her arm around me, nudging me through the gauntlet.

"Don't say a word," Ericka said as she kept pushing me

through the belly of the beast while I was peppered with questions about Charlie's death and about The Basher. Ericka's firm hand on my back was my only anchor. We moved with purpose, silent in our pact to ignore the probing questions and blinding flashes. A sleek black Cadillac Escalade with dark tinted windows was waiting for us on the street, it was a sanctuary on wheels. Ericka guided me inside, and the moment the door closed, the clamor outside was reduced to a distant murmur. In the quiet embrace of the SUV, I let out a breath I didn't realize I'd been holding.

"Are you okay, Cass?"

The hairs on my arm stood. I wasn't expecting to see Brent in the backseat of the SUV that was driving me away from the madness.

Brent must have seen me tense up when I heard his voice. He gave me a smile. Erica seemed intrigued to watch our awkward interaction, more akin to meeting up with two acquaintances than siblings.

There was another man in the SUV. He shook my hand and introduced himself as Bruce Kindsvater.

"I'm a partner at Kindsvater and Rivers. You've already met Erica, our senior associate."

During the car ride, Kindsvater explained what was going on. The evidence was pointing towards self-defense. Charlie locked me up in his dungeon. Drugged me, then took me to Mother's basement to kill me, but I came out of the fentanyl stupor, and turned the tables on him. As odd as it sounded, it seemed... plausible. But I stopped myself from going there.

"I didn't kill Charlie," I protested.

I saw the lawyers and Brent exchange worried glances. Kindsvater softly pushed back at me as if I were a delicate flower in need of careful attention.

"Well, Ms. Walsh, from the evidence I've seen so far,

and from what my source in the BCA has told me, said there is little doubt that you stabbed Officer Bell when he attacked you. They're still doing DNA and other forensic testing, but what they've done so far points to that. And I'm sure it's unsettling to have taken a person's life. But you had no choice. My source said Charlie Bell was The Basher. A serial killer with twelve known victims so far. You were going to be number thirteen, but luckily for you, thirteen was your lucky number."

"What about that metal container? Brent you were there, right?" I was so confused.

"After the night of your DWI, I was worried about you, so I slipped a tracking device in your bag. I'm sorry, but that's how I found you out there. By the time I got a signal on my phone and called the police they went to the container out in the woods, but you were gone."

"How can I not remember any of this?" I asked. I felt so confused.

Kindsvater again talked to me like I was a toddler. "Please excuse me if I appear insensitive, but in my experience, being direct with my clients is the best way to represent them to the best of my abilities. You have a documented history of substance abuse. Alcohol and opiates. Including two intensive outpatient programs and one inpatient. Two were court mandated. Recently, you got arrested for a DWI. There was also fentanyl in your blood and urine samples taken by the police on the night of your DWI arrest and two nights ago, after you were arrested at your house. So, it's not that unfathomable you might have significant time and memory gaps. Especially after something as traumatic as what you went through with Charlie Bell."

Brent nodded in agreement as Kindsvater pontificated

in nice lawyerly-speak that I was such a fuckup. It made sense I couldn't remember killing someone. I had spent fifteen years believing I had killed Mikey, only for Brent to inform me that it wasn't me. It was Charlie. Only for the very next day to be told now I'd truly killed someone. Charlie Bell. My head was spinning. I wanted a drink, but after getting past the worst of the withdrawals locked up in jail, I didn't want to start up again. Especially with these blackouts I went through. Maybe Kindsvater was right. He's a third party to all this with access to actual evidence and a legal expert. He's bought into the narrative that Charlie attacked me, and I fought back and won. One thing was certain, though. I knew I didn't take fentanyl. I would remember at least going out somewhere to buy it when I was sober, and I hadn't. But I was tired and didn't want to argue with Brent and his lawyers right now. I looked out the window and noticed we were on highway 169. "Where are you taking me?"

"We booked you a lovely room at the Radisson in Bloomington," Erica said.

"The Twin Cities?" I said, surprised.

"We felt it best you don't stay in Big Plaine since Charlie was a police officer after all, and not everyone knows about his extra-curricular activities as a serial killer yet. As a bonus, you'll be closer to our offices in Minneapolis and only forty miles from Big Plaine."

"You know you could stay at my house, Cassie, but I didn't want to bring it up again. It's up to you," Brent said.

"Hotel is fine," I said curtly. "I can leave Big Plaine? I'm not breaking court orders or anything."

Kindsvater chuckled. "No, that's fine. You'd best not leave the state but leaving Big Plaine is fine. Besides, Erica alerted the police and the prosecutor's office down there. If they need to talk to you, they go through us."

"It's very important that you don't talk to anyone without me or Bruce present. Not a friend. Family members. Especially the police. Same with the media. If they figure out your phone number, they're going to hound you. Just tell them no comment and hang up. And please don't ever speak to Detective Robin Moretti again without us," Erica said.

"Especially her," Kindsvater said. "But don't worry. The ball is rolling on a restraining order. Soon she won't be able to get within fifty feet of you or your brother."

"I know she seemed harmless, like she was trying to help you, but she wasn't and she is not your friend, Cassie. You can't trust anyone outside this car, sis."

I looked at Brent, his words hung thick in the air. *Can I trust you?* I wondered. I looked around the luxurious SUV. The fine leather felt so soothing after two days of a cement bed with a thin pad. The two powerhouse attorneys in my corner. All paid for by Brent. Without him, I might still be confined to the cement bed, awaiting my court-appointed public defender lawyer.

Despite everything, Brent always looked out for me. If he really was the killer, he would have already killed me, since I was such a liability to his perfect life. Yet, he continued to help me. I looked at him and for the first time I didn't feel anger towards him. I fought back tears. "Thank you, Brent, for paying for all this," I said, waving my arms around the Escalade and toward the two lawyers clad in their thousand-dollar suits, wearing BVLGARI and Rolex watches. "And for getting me out of jail and having my back." Brent seemed surprised by my words. And I didn't blame him. I'd been nothing but a bitch to him all these years.

"You're welcome, Cass," he said, sounding touched.

"So, what's next?" I asked the lawyers.

"Get some rest. The Mall of America is near the hotel if you need some downtime. In a couple of days, we'll meet at my office in the IDS building. By then, I'll know more about the case against you and our defense strategy so we can figure out how to get all this behind you," Kindsvater said.

"It's terrible. My understanding is that you just buried your mom and haven't even been able to grieve her with all this happening to you," Erica said.

The sentiment was noble, but I couldn't bring myself to explain our messed up relationship to her. Brent jumped all over that. "Yes. It's been horrible. The Big Plaine police and their serial killer officer haven't allowed us to properly grieve our mother. When this is all done, and Cassie is off the hook, I want to sue the whole fucking town."

Kindsvater smiled. "One case at a time, Brent."

I just looked out the window. I just wanted this night-mare to be over. As I kept repeating the same thing to myself over and over: *you will not drink.*

FORTY-ONE
CASSIE

THE LEGAL PROCESS WAS SLOW. THAT'S NOT A SHOCK TO anyone who has had the misfortune to go through it, especially on the criminal side of things.

I came to Minnesota for Mother's funeral and planned to go back to Las Vegas in a few days. That was two months ago.

Not that I had anything pressing waiting for me back in Las Vegas. I didn't have a job. And I lived in a dump compared to the nice place I was staying in. But I was in this bizarre state of legal limbo.

Bruce Kindsvater called me yesterday with good news. The BCA had reported that my killing of Charlie Bell had been in self-defense. The DA finally agreed and made it official. They wouldn't be pressing charges. Kindsvater then made a deal with the city of Big Plaine. If the police were to dismiss my DWI and resisting arrest charges, we wouldn't sue them for violating my privacy by leaking information about me to Robin Moretti and for one of their police officers being The Basher serial killer, who had drugged me, kidnapped me, and tried to kill me.

Eager to move on from that embarrassment, they agreed. And just like that, I was scot-free. I could see now how rich people get away with a lot more than regular people when they can afford lawyers like Bruce Kindsvater.

I was just relieved. I felt an enormous burden had been lifted from me. I could finally move on with my life. After a week in a hotel in the Twin Cities, I moved into one of Brent's and Jillian's investment properties in Minneapolis. They would usually rent it out on one of the different short-term rental websites. They took it off the market so I could stay there while the legal system slowly did its thing.

At the start, the arrangement felt awkward, but I had never felt closer to Brent in my entire life. And to my surprise, I found it felt nice, being around family again. For all my talk about not needing anyone, that was bullshit. Despite my social anxieties, we all depended on other people in our lives because human beings were not designed to navigate life alone all the time.

I felt stronger than I had in a long time. I hadn't had a drink in twenty-six days. It was likely more than a decade since I had gone that long without a drink. I even went out for a jog for the first time in two years. I almost puked and hacked out a lung after just a mile, but it was a start.

On the day the lawyers and Brent got me out of jail and drove up to a hotel in the Twin Cities, Brent and I had a long talk, once the lawyers were gone. I reassured him, that even though I told Robin about Mikey, I told her that I killed him after he tried to rape me. And that Mother sent us away while she got rid of the body. She never told us what she did with it and we never talked about it again. Brent was relieved. And he knew I was telling the truth since he didn't have the police at his door interrogating him about disposing of a body. His secret was safe. "I'll make sure you're set financially, Cassie," he had told me that day. Had he said that a few months ago, I would have told him off, that I didn't need his help. But the truth was that I felt close to him now, and I did need his help.

So, there were positive things that had come out of this mess. Although I wouldn't recommend getting kidnapped by a serial killer as an effective treatment program to kick booze, reconnect with family, and improve your finances. It hadn't been easy to stay sober. It wasn't a lie what they say in treatment that, as an alcoholic, you take it one day at a time.

Mother's estate had wrapped up rather quickly. I thought after all the press around my case and the fact that Mother took her life in the basement, it would spook away potential buyers. We priced the house to sell, and in this real estate market, an affordable home in good shape was too good to pass up.

The house sold quickly and last week Brent dropped off a cashier's check for $83,000. I told him he had already done so much for me, like losing rental income by having me in this house, and paying my very expensive lawyers, but he insisted I keep the entire amount from Mother's estate after legal fees and taxes. I knew to Brent that amount wasn't that much money, but for me, it made me tear up. I never had this much money at one time.

Even my relationship with Jillian had thawed some. And I enjoyed reconnecting with my two nephews. Being the weird, free-spirit aunt was a label I wore with pride.

Although I still had a difficult time wrapping my head around what happened because of my huge memory gaps, there was a mountain of evidence that painted a clear picture. I'd also been meeting with a hypnotist therapist that

Brent recommended, who had helped me uncover memories I had long ago buried.

BACK FIFTEEN YEARS ago in school, everyone knew Charlie had a crush on me. It turned out to be far more than a silly teenage crush. He had been obsessed with me. When I shot him down to be with his best friend, Mikey, he began to hate Mikey. That terrible day, when I was fooling around with Mikey in the basement, Charlie had been watching through the window. I caught him once, but he must have watched us the whole time. He must have seen my struggle with Mikey and my knocking him unconscious. When I ran upstairs, he climbed down into the basement from the window, picked up the dumbbell, and bludgeoned Mikey with it until his skull was crushed into oblivion. He was the one who killed Mikey, not Brent. Not me. A killing ritual that he continued to use as an adult when he became the serial killer known as The Basher.

Brent had led the police to the farmland that Charlie had inherited where he kept a shipping container that he used to abuse his victims, before killing them. He had me there. Why he took me back to the house, I'd never understand. Police theorized it had something to do with what had happened in that basement with Mikey. A coming full circle in Charlie's warped psychopathic head. Only he knew for sure, and he took that knowledge with him to the grave. Brent, worried for me, had hidden a tracking device in my bag. Creepy, sure, but at least he was able to find me in that shed and go get help. But Charlie must have arrived shortly after Brent to get help, and he took me to Mother's house while I was drugged out.

Brent finally came clean, like I did, on our involvement on that day. He came into the house and ran into me hysterical over knocking out Mikey. When he went down to the basement, he saw Mikey there with his head caved in and was horrified at what I had done. He only realized later that the basement window, which he always kept closed, was open. And he remembered seeing Charlie riding away in a rush on his bicycle from our house, but he thought little of it until years later.

Mother had told us we needed to keep what happened to Mikey in our basement to ourselves. And we did just that. Never talking about it for fifteen years and unknowingly, protecting Charlie's secret. We didn't tell the police about the body in the freezer so Brent didn't have to deal with legal ramifications for tampering with evidence and illegally getting rid of a cadaver.

That was what I had been realizing about myself recently. I'd always bottled up my emotions. It had always been Mother's way. Beating me with her leather strap on the back of the knees whenever I spoke up or tried to be true to myself. Locking me up in the cellar. By the time Mother told me to never talk about what happened to Mikey again, I did as she commanded.

For all these years, Brent and I thought I had killed Mikey. Then I put the blame on Brent. Mother must have come to the same conclusion when she read the articles about The Basher, and what she had seen was done to Mikey. Perhaps that's why she did what she did. The body in the freezer. Her estranged daughter was a drunk. Her son was a serial killer. It was too much. Only to learn Charlie had been the killer. When I told Charlie I was coming clean instead of keeping secrets about that day, he decided to make me vanish for good.

I also understood why Mother changed the way she treated me after that day. She never again beat me or locked me in the cellar. Not that she transformed into the loving, caring mother I wished I had. She became more distant. Cold and aloof. She saw Mikey's body and thought I did that, so she must have believed she raised a demon capable of doing that. Brent told me that was why he went along without calling the police. He too had seen the body and was certain the police wouldn't have believed I acted in self-defense after administering so many blows to the head.

With all this behind me, I was eager to move on with my life. I would go back to Las Vegas. But now that I had a bit of a financial cushion, I wasn't keen on going back to work in the restaurant and bar business and deal with The Strip. Too many temptations there to drink. I could buy a small condo somewhere cheap. Go back to school. Watching Bruce and Erica work and interacting with their paralegals made me think that could be a career move for me. Although as a former felon that did two years, and with the hoopla over the case with The Basher, a prestigious law firm would likely run as far away from as possible once they Googled my name. I had plenty of time to figure out my future.

My thoughts on that were interrupted when my phone rang. I recognized Erica's number. After picking up and exchanging brief *hellos* and *how are you,* she got into why she called me.

"I wanted to share this new report that just came in from the BCA forensic investigator. As you might know from the media, serial killers like to keep trophies from their victims. They found Charlie Bell's trophies. He liked to keep his victims' driver's licenses, including what the police believe was his first. Mikey Dawson's underage new driver's license was part of his collection. He also kept a bloody AC/DC shirt that was not only full of Mikey's DNA, but his family has confirmed that this was the shirt he wore the day he went missing. So, this proves law enforcement's suspicions that Charlie killed Mikey fifteen years ago. It's really over, Cassie," Erica said. She sounded excited to share this news with me, hoping it would alleviate my guilty feelings about what had happened. Little did Erica know that she wasn't delivering the good news she thought she was — quite the opposite. My blood ran cold, and I felt my knees buckling from what she had told me.

FORTY-TWO
CASSIE

I HUNG UP THE PHONE, THINKING ABOUT WHAT ERICA had told me. It made me feel nauseous.

What Erica and the police didn't know was that there was no way that Charlie had taken Mikey's ID and T-shirt fifteen years ago because I saw his body in the chest freezer two months ago still wearing that T-shirt. And Brent had pulled Mikey's velcro wallet from the body's jeans front pocket. That shirt, and that wallet with his id had been with Mikey in that freezer for all this time until Brent got rid of it all.

The only way Mikey's ID and bloody shirt ended up in a trophy box on Charlie's property was because Brent put them there in order to frame Charlie for not only The Basher's victims, but also Mikey. Why else would Brent frame Charlie? And me? He was the one who convinced me and Mother that I killed Mikey. He never mentioned Charlie until it was convenient for him years later. Brent was a doctor. He could get his hands on fentanyl. And he knew how to dole up the dose to keep me in the dark, my mind mush, while he molded it into memories that helped him.

I was living in a house he owned, using his lawyers, his therapist. Oh, God, he'd played me like the perfect fool and turned me into his alibi. No one even considered looking at him for all this. He even turned me away from my suspicions about him.

Stop it, Cassie, I said to myself. I always went to the darkest places when it came to my mother and brother.

But I couldn't shake that feeling. Could Brent have been behind the scenes, orchestrating all of this? Setting me and Charlie up to be his patsies while keeping his high-society doctor image intact. I looked around his house, suddenly feeling trapped. Like he was watching me, right now. He swore he was no longer tracking me with devices, but now, I wasn't so sure. I felt a chill coursing throughout my whole body.

Could he have really lulled me into this false sense of security?

My phone rang which made me flinch. It was Brent. Did he have my phone tapped? I needed to get out of there. I let the call go to voicemail as I went straight into the bedroom and I began to hurriedly pack my things. My phone pinged. A text message from Brent.

> Are you around?

> We should talk.

I ignored him. A few minutes later, he called again. Straight to voicemail. Twenty minutes later, I was on the road. I didn't know where I was going. I should've driven out west straight back to Las Vegas and put this damn state behind me for good. But I was surprised to find myself merging onto 169 heading south towards Big Plaine.

I CALLED ROBIN. She picked up. She didn't say hello, just started talking.

"Am I violating the restraining order you put out on me by taking your call?" She sounded cold and angry.

"Sorry. It was Brent and his lawyers' idea," I said, sounding pathetic.

"Well, they got you off smelling like roses. A hero no less. The brave victim who fought back and killed The Basher, saving countless future victims. And the cherry on top: Charlie was Mikey's killer too, solving that fifteen-year-old mystery and bringing closure to my family. Everything is nicely wrapped up. I'm surprised the mayor didn't give you the key to the city. Know what I got? Besides the restraining order? An official reprimand in my file at work," Robin said. Her voice was bitter and sarcastic.

"I shouldn't have called," I said.

"What the fuck do you want, Cassie?"

"I don't know. I panicked and took off. Next thing I knew, I'm driving down to Big Plaine, so I called you."

"Panicked? About what?"

I told her about Erica's call.

"I know that, Cassie. The BCA called me and my parents to let us know about that. It fits the perfect little narrative you and Brent have spun."

I remained quiet for a moment. Then finally I replied.

"No. That is a lie. What I told you was the truth. But there is more that I didn't tell you."

I took a deep breath, and I told Robin everything. The entire truth about what happened that day between Mikey and me. How Mother sent Brent and me away while she was supposed to get rid of the body. Then about the note

Mother left for us after she died letting us know to check the freezer and how we discovered his body inside, hidden in the freezer all this time.

"And you saw his body in the freezer? With your own two eyes?" Robin asked, sounding like she didn't believe me.

"I saw him, Robin. Still in that AC/DC T-shirt. And Brent pulled a wallet out of the body's pocket. It was Mikey's prized Scorpions rock band velcro wallet still tucked in his front pocket."

"Then what happened?"

"Brent said he would take care of it. Then he told me he got rid of all the evidence.

"Where?"

"I don't know. He didn't tell me, but I heard like a chainsaw from down in the basement."

"Oh, dear Lord," Robin said.

I stayed quiet as I drove. Robin then added, "It's too late now, Cassie."

"What do you mean?"

"Just what I said. It doesn't matter anymore. The ship to do the right thing sailed away from you long ago. They've closed The Basher and Mikey's case. Charlie is the evil boogeyman responsible for it all. That narrative wraps everything nice and tight with a pretty bow attached to it. Charlie was the one. And he is dead, which is what the top brass likes the best in these complex cases. No expensive, long trial. No pesky profession of innocence. He's dead and buried. Case closed. So, trust me, they're not going to reopen this mess of a case based on your word versus your brother and the truckload of evidence that backs Brent's version of events."

"I'm willing to tell them what I just told you. What I saw in that freezer."

"Forget it. Brent is a rich and well-respected doctor who hides behind a bevy of $500-an-hour lawyers. You're an addict with a criminal record. And they suspended me for a week without pay. It's over. Don't call me again."

Robin hung up on me.

I drove into Big Plaine at eight-ten p.m. The sun was just beginning to set. I had forgotten how late the sun was up in Minnesota during the spring. During summer sunset won't be until after nine p.m. There had been a constant but light spring shower for most of the day. But the rain had stopped for now.

I parked across the street from Mother's house. A placard declaring "Sold" hung from the Realtor's yard sign. The house was still empty. Its new owners wouldn't be moving in for another couple of weeks. I sat there for a while with the window down, enjoying the wet smell of spring after a rain shower. I could feel a cool breeze drifting inside. Despite everything, I felt calm and at peace.

If Robin, the police, and district attorney were willing to walk away from this believing Brent's narrative, then why shouldn't I?

Robin was right. They neatly wrapped up everything like they do at the end of a mystery novel. It was over. I needed to get as far away from here as possible.

I leaned my head back and closed my eyes just for a moment to enjoy the breeze before leaving Big Plaine forever when I felt a sharp pain in my neck. "Ouch, shit!" I said out loud as I bolted up in the car seat. My hand reflexively reached for the side of my neck, where I felt a lingering sting.

I looked out the car window, and I saw Brent leaning in. His left forearm casually rested on the door frame. A syringe in his right hand.

"You shouldn't have come down here, Cassie. I didn't want this for you," Brent said. I wanted to ask him what he was talking about. But I couldn't articulate what I was thinking. I opened my mouth to speak, but it was like chewing on glue. My vision began to blur, but I saw Brent dropping the syringe into a gym bag he had slung across his chest. He looked around. I tried to open the car door to run away, but my hands felt like silly putty and my eyelids were so heavy that I was struggling to keep them open.

I fell back into the car, and I sank into the seat, unable to resist. I couldn't move an inch. I felt myself floating away.

FORTY-THREE

CASSIE

The drumming sound of rain hitting the house gradually pulled me from the depths of unconsciousness. I blinked open my eyes, yet darkness enveloped me completely. There were no windows, no slivers of light— just the claustrophobic embrace of the basement. The air felt damp and musty against my skin.

For a moment, I lay still, disoriented. My heart began to thump louder in my chest as the fog of fentanyl slowly cleared, and a chilling realization dawned on me—I was back in the basement of my mother's house. The very place I had vowed never to return to. It seems no matter what, I was destined to die here. Cosmic justice, I supposed.

Panic surged through me as memories of the past flickered through my head like old film reels. I tried to move, but my limbs were stiff, my muscles ached as if I had been in the same position for hours. The air was damp and chilly. The coarse fabric of a blanket scratched against my skin, and I could feel the cold, hard floor beneath me.

Reaching out in the darkness, my hands trembling, I searched for something, anything that might tell me more about my situation. My fingers brushed against the dangling cord I knew would be there. Pulling on it, a single bare light bulb dangled in midair, chasing away the darkness and casting shadows against the cinderblock walls.

The sound of the rain seemed to grow louder, more insistent, as if urging me to fully awaken and confront the harsh reality of my situation. I strained to hear any other sound—a sign of movement upstairs, the creak of a floorboard that would indicate I wasn't alone in this dreadful place. But there was nothing, only the relentless patter of rain and my own ragged breathing.

Terror gripped me as I thought of Brent, his menacing presence outside the car window, a shadow that had loomed large over my life. I knew he was the reason I was back in the basement. My mind raced with questions and fears. Why had he taken me, again? If his plan was to kill me, why was I still alive? Or was this his plan all along, to bring me back to where our twisted family story had begun?

With effort, I slowly stood up and stepped out of the cellar. Brent was right there in front of the door, sitting on his portable toolbox, the same one he had used to dispose of Mikey's body.

"Hey, sis."

My body shook with tremors, but I was determined not to show my fear to Brent. I was done being a scared little mouse in his presence.

"I really did care about you, Cassie. I didn't want it to go down like this. I tried hard to fix everything, for the both of us," Brent said, his voice eerily calm. It felt surreal to hear him speak so calmly, even affectionately, while he exposed his darkest deeds. "All those years, pretending to be the protective big brother, and I meant it... in my own way."

"You were just trying to save your own skin," I spat out.

"That's true. Gosh, it's great that we're finally being honest with each other. It's just too bad we didn't do this years ago," Brent replied with a twisted sort of glee.

"You killed Mikey. Then you let me believe that I had killed him for fifteen fucking years," I said, my voice rising with anger that had been simmering inside me for far too long.

"It was convenient to let you believe that," Brent said matter-of-factly, as if he was discussing something as mundane as the weather. "And, don't forget, you're the one who set everything in motion, so don't act all innocent."

"Bullshit," I shot back fiercely.

"Come on now. You have to take some responsibility. After all, you weren't supposed to have boys in the house alone. You sure as hell weren't supposed to be in my room. Soiling my sheets with that idiot white trash punk. And you're the one who knocked him out, cold. That part impressed me," Brent said, his smile chilling me to the bone.

"But he was alive, Brent. Why did you have to kill him?" I demanded, needing to hear him say it, to confess his sinister motives.

He pursed his lips, giving me that aw-shucks face he had often used as a kid to wriggle out of trouble. "I'm just wired differently than most people. I had been fantasizing about killing someone since I was ten or eleven. I thought I would outgrow it. But the urge to kill only got stronger. I tried to satisfy it by going after rabbits, squirrels, neighborhood pets, but it wasn't enough. The fantasy was too strong. By the time I was seventeen, I knew that someday, I would live out my fantasy. I figured my time would come when I was away at college. But then you brought Mikey Dawson right to me. What was I supposed to do? Here was my chance. And I could blame you. I couldn't let this opportunity pass me by. So, I killed the little prick and made my fantasy come true. Then I managed to convince you and Mom to help get rid of the body and not call the police. I still can't believe Mom agreed to it, to be honest."

His words sent a cold shiver down my spine, the casual way he recounted his descent into madness chilled me to the core.

"And then you became The Basher."

"Guilty as charged. Although I didn't pick that stupid name. And it wouldn't be until years later. I thought I could stop after Mikey, but I couldn't. It's like you and drinking. You know you should stop, but you can't. It's the same for me, just that my addiction is different to yours," Brent's comparison made my stomach turn.

"You're a serial killer, Brent!" I exclaimed, the words tasting bitter in my mouth.

He simply shrugged. "Yeah. And a damn good one. Ted Bundy wouldn't last a week nowadays with cameras everywhere and DNA technology what it is. Yet, I was thriving. It just sucks. I couldn't scream it from the rooftops. And trust me, it hurts to give Charlie all the credit for my work. But it beats a life sentence in Stillwater."

His nonchalance about his horrific acts was unnerving, to say the least. His ability to remain under the radar, a dark reflection of his cunning and brutality which he began honing that day, fifteen years ago.

"And Mom... you killed our own mother, didn't you?"

"Like you care. You hated her."

"I didn't want her dead. Brutally murdered. No way did I ever wish that on her."

"Well, if it makes you feel any better, I spiked her vodka with fentanyl, just like I spiked your booze and those water bottles you drank in the shed. Mom didn't know what hit her. I was gentle."

"Why would you kill her after she kept your secret for fifteen years?"

"Uh, uh, I must correct you, sis... our secret," he said, his grin broadening in a way that made my skin crawl. "Like you, she started falling apart on me. Always staring at those stupid missing child flyers of Mikey. And she started looking at me differently. Like I was some monster, not her golden son. So, I checked her computer and saw she had been obsessing over The Basher killings. I knew then that she had figured it out. So, I had no choice. Eventually, she was going to tell someone. That was it. She had to go. It was a mercy kill, really. I put her out of her misery. You know that, Cassie. She never recovered after Dad died. It fried her brain. The way she treated us. It was horrific child abuse."

His words, cold and calculating, sent a final shiver of fear and revulsion through me. His justifications were monstrous, his actions unforgivable. And he just couldn't stop manipulating me.

"Did she even have Parkinson's?"

"Nope."

I couldn't believe what I was hearing.

"Come on, Cass. The way she would beat you and lock you in that cellar. You should thank me."

"Fuck you."

"Ouch. After all I've done for you, that's the thanks I get? And here I thought we had turned a corner. We were getting much closer these last few weeks. I had fooled everyone. The Big Plaine PD, the BCA, the district attorney, you. It was over. Then that stupid bitch, Erica, called you. You were almost out the door back to Las Vegas. I told Bruce and Erica all communication from law enforcement had to go through me. You were too mentally unstable. But Erica went behind my back. She thought she was helping you. All she did was seal your fate."

Since he hadn't killed me after knocking me out in the car, I had hoped maybe he wouldn't go through with it, but now the chilling realization of his plans made me tremble.

"Please, Brent, you don't have to do this. I'll go back to Vegas. You'll never hear from me again. Just like we planned. I kept my mouth shut about Mikey for fifteen years. You can trust me to keep quiet about all this."

"I wish I could, Cassie, but you already blabbed to Robin. You just can't let things go."

"I didn't!" I lied.

Brent laughed. "Such a liar. You think I would let you out of my sight willy-nilly? Especially after that stunt you pulled when I was busy disposing of the body, and you were stupid enough to drink and drive and get arrested. Ever since that night, I've been tracking your every move. I have GPS trackers and listening devices hidden in your purse, backpack, in the car you're driving, and my house that you're staying in. You might as well be living in the Big Brother house on live television and I'm always watching and listening. How do you think I always knew when to find you? Right before you did something stupid that could bring me down. It's how I found you tonight."

A wave of nausea washed over me as I realized the extent of his surveillance and control over me.

"What happened to Charlie?"

"I heard your pathetic confession to him. He already suspected me, so I knew I had to stop him. I spiked your water, just like I did with the water bottles in the shed. I was in the room next door the whole time listening and watching. Once the drugs started to kick in for you. I knocked on the door with my trusty syringe in hand. Charlie didn't know what hit him. Nice and easy. After that, it was just setting up the stage to frame Charlie and make you look like a hero. And it worked. But you just had to keep pushing it."

"Brent, please."

"Spare me the bullshit. I heard you call Robin and tell her about the body in the freezer. And about the T-shirt and the ID I planted. What were you thinking?"

"I'm sorry, Brent, but you heard her. She blew me off and hung up. She's done with all this. You don't have to worry about her or me."

"I wish I could, but it's too late. You signed both your death certificates the moment you told Robin about our family secrets."

"Brent, please. I'm your sister. You could have killed me long ago, but you didn't because you love me."

"It's true, Cassie. It's so hard to fit into this world when you're like me. I have to fake and mimic emotions expected from me. But the sibling bond we shared was real. It's silly. After what you did to Mikey, I thought maybe you were wired like me. We share the same DNA, so why couldn't it be possible? I thought maybe we could be a team. Like Buono and Bianchi, but that was just a fantasy. So, you're right, I don't want to kill you. It's probably why I kept dragging my feet. I should have followed my gut about you long ago."

"I'm your sister."

"Between you and me, it's an easy choice. Me. I have no qualms doing what I needed to. I just wanted to be straight with you. To know the truth. It feels good to tell someone about my true self."

"Brent, please..." I continued to beg, but he interrupted me.

"Don't worry, just like Mom, I won't let you suffer."

Brent got up, and he removed a syringe from his coat pocket. "You'll just go back to sleep, but this time, I won't let you wake up. Bye, sis," he said, sounding like a doctor getting ready to put a patient under for surgery.

As Brent got close, I reached into my pocket and grabbed the Narcan spray Charlie had given me, emptying it into Brent's face. He shrieked and jumped back. "What the hell is that?" he asked, shaking as he wiped his face. He looked at what I was holding.

He laughed out loud. "You're full of surprises. But hate to tell you, Narcan doesn't affect you if you don't have drugs in your system. You should have armed yourself with pepper spray or a gun, not Narcan."

He was right, I didn't know that, but it did buy me a few precious seconds and created enough space between us for me to lunge at him with all my might. Using my shoulder and the top of my head as a battering ram and catching him off guard.

I shoved him hard like I had been trained with pugil sticks in the army onto the large toolkit behind him, which made him trip and fall over it and onto the floor. I heard him yelp as he hit the floor. I dashed out of the utility room as fast as I could toward the basement stairs.

I reached the bottom step, feeling a surge of adrenaline. I was going to make it upstairs, then run outside into the rain toward freedom, and I wouldn't stop running until I reached the police station.

I was halfway up the stairs when I felt his hand clamping onto my ankle, causing me to fall hard onto the wooden steps. Pain flared in my knees and wrists as I landed hard.

Then I felt the dreadful sensation of being dragged back

down the stairs back into that damned basement. I tried to kick him, but he wouldn't let go, so I screamed, hoping someone outside would hear me as he continued to drag me from my ankles on my stomach across the hard, cold floor back into the utility room.

I watched in horror as the staircase got further away from my outstretched hands. He was much stronger than me, and he forcefully dragged me back into the utility room. He threw me in with such force that I felt my shoulder radiate with pain as it slammed into the concrete wall, and the side of my head smashed into the laundry standpipe where our mother's washing machine had once been attached.

I cried out from the pain. "Brent, please stop."

He stood over me, breathing heavily. The look on his face was one I didn't recognize in him. I wasn't looking at my brother. It was a monster. And I suspected it was the last thing the victims of The Basher, and our mother, saw. The face of evil. I screamed for help, my voice piercing the dank air of the basement, but it was quickly muffled as Brent pressed duct tape firmly across my mouth. He moved methodically, wrapping more tape around my wrists and ankles, effectively immobilizing me. Once he had me completely tied up, he paused to catch his breath.

"Nice try, Cassie. I'll give you that much. Forget me being nice with the shot. You're going to pay for that little show you just did," Brent said with a cold, harsh tone that made the hairs on the back of my neck stand up.

He then reached into his toolkit and removed a plastic bag, which he placed over my head, and then he wrapped duct tape around my neck to hold the plastic bag in place.

I could smell and taste the polyethylene as I desperately tried to breathe through my nose. I watched in horror through the bag over my head as Brent sat on his toolkit to watch me suffocate to death. His face was rapt in fascination.

As I gasped for air, I could hear him talking. "I've done this eighteen times now, and it never gets old. The facial expressions that people make when they know they're going to die is the part of this fantasy that I love the most."

Desperation clawed at me. Knowing my life was slipping away and seeing the twisted enjoyment in his eyes was terrifying. My mind raced for any possibility of escape as I writhed and twisted, trying to loosen the bonds, my fingers scraping at the tape, but it wouldn't budge.

I began to accept my fate. Cosmic justice once again rearing its head. I was destined to die in this basement and no one would know what became of me.

FORTY-FOUR
CASSIE

My breaths were shallow, panicked gasps inside the plastic bag that clung desperately to my face slowly siphoning my life from me. All the times I thought about ending my life, now I was desperately trying to save it. I didn't want to die.

I could feel the world around me fading as Brent stood over me, his face twisted into a grotesque smile of victory.

Each desperate attempt to draw air only pulled the plastic tighter against my nostrils, suffocating me little by little. My vision blurred, and my limbs felt heavy and distant, yet I could still hear the faint, ominous sounds of Brent's movements as he reached into his toolkit and removed a rubber mallet from it. He turned his attention back to me, eager to watch me suffocate to death. Then, what? Bash my head in with that mallet like Mikey and his many other victims. I kicked and fidgeted, flopping on the floor like a fish out of water.

I saw a shadow behind Brent and then heard someone yell: "Freeze!"

Brent turned towards the voice, raising the mallet over his head.

The room began to darken for me as I was about to pass out when suddenly a flash of light illuminated it and I heard the sound of a large boom echoing through the cinderblock, sounding like an M-80 firecracker had exploded in the utility room.

Brent flinched, his body jerked wildly as his hand went to his chest. I could see Robin standing there with her gun pointed at him and her eyes fixed on him. Brent gripped the mallet tighter.

"Drop it!" she commanded, her voice firm and steady.

Brent wasn't dropping the mallet. He breathed heavily, still facing Robin in a standoff as I was about to pass out.

Robin repeated her command, her tone now sharper, more urgent. "Drop it and get on your knees, now! My next shot will kill you!"

Brent seemed to snap from his trance. He looked back, and he smiled at me. "Never bring a mallet to a gunfight," he said with an odd cackle as he dropped the mallet. It bounced off the floor as he went down to his knees. His hands moving behind the back of his head in a show of surrender.

Robin stole a glance in my direction, her face horrified at seeing me struggling to breathe.

"Jesus Christ," she said.

As Robin moved in to cuff him, Brent's hand had slipped to the small of his back where he unsheathed a 6-inch sticking knife. I wanted to warn Robin, but couldn't and in one smooth motion he thrusted the blade deep into Robin's rib cage.

Robin staggered back, a pained cry escaping her lips as she clutched at the fresh wound on her side, her face contorting in agony. Brent leapt to his feet, knife raised high, ready to deliver a final blow to end her life.

In that moment of sheer terror and desperation, with my lungs screaming for air and my life hanging by a thread, instinct took over. I managed to gather all the strength I had left, and I kicked out at Brent's legs. My foot connected with the back of his knee, causing him to stagger for a moment.

That brief distraction was all Robin needed. Gasping through the pain, she regained her balance, her hands wrapped around the pistol, and I heard three more shots ring out loudly echoing off the walls.

Brent's body jerked back, a look of shock and disbelief on his face as he crumbled to the floor ending up on his back, the bloody knife landing near the mallet.

Silence fell, heavy and absolute, broken only by the sound of my labored breathing through the plastic bag and Robin wheezing from a collapsed lung.

She was bleeding heavily, but she dragged herself towards me. Her hands, slick with her own blood, trembled as she reached for the bag on my head. She wheezed loudly as she tore the plastic away from my face. I had duct tape on my mouth, but she ripped off the bag from my nose as I desperately sucked in air through my nostrils.

My wrists were taped in front of me, but my hands were free, so I desperately removed the tape from my mouth and began gasping as I sucked in even more precious air.

I looked up at Robin, her face pale and drawn with pain but alive with the fierce look of triumph and survival.

"Thank you," I choked out, tears streaming down my face as the reality of our escape from death settled around us.

Robin managed a wan smile, her breaths short and

pained. "We made it, Cassie. We made it," she whispered, her voice a brittle shadow of its former command.

I looked at Brent's body with trepidation, expecting him to sit up and lunge at me like they do in the movies, but he lay there with part of his skull blown off from Robin's head-shot. It seemed The Basher died with facial wounds similar to those of his many victims.

The nightmare was finally over.

———

THE LATE NIGHT's eerie silence in the aftermath of such violence was abruptly shattered by the wail of sirens and the flashing of red and blue lights that pierced the gloom of the basement. These lights pulsed like a strobe, illuminating the stark reality of what had happened down there.

Moments after the lights began their frantic dance, the sound of careful footsteps echoed down the staircase. The tread was heavy but measured, a stark contrast to the chaos of just minutes before. I could see the shapes of police officers as they descended, their figures haloed by the light from their flashlights. Leading the group were Crystal and Chief Strand, both with guns drawn, as they moved toward the utility room where we lay.

As they entered, Crystal's voice cut through the tension. "Holy shit!" The exclamation echoed off the walls, raw and startled, mirroring the shock in her eyes as she took in the scene—Brent's lifeless body, Robin and I battered but breathing. The torn plastic bag still taped around my neck.

Chief Strand's voice boomed in command, "Para-medics, now!" He then turned to Crystal, his words sharp and urgent, "Secure Brent."

Crystal glanced down at him. "He's dead. Half his head is gone," she said.

"I don't care, cuff the prick," Strand barked back, his gaze already shifting to assess Robin and me. His face softened for a fleeting moment, a brief flicker of relief at our survival before he was all business again.

Within seconds, paramedics burst into the room, their kits clattering with the urgency of their movements. They knelt beside Robin first, her injuries more apparent, their hands moving with efficient speed to assess her condition. One of them turned to me, his eyes kind but professional. "It's going to be okay," he told me as he cut away at the duct tape from my wrists and legs and he began to assess my injuries.

One paramedic checked on Brent, ready to render aid to a monster. "Mark this one DOA," he said before turning his attention back to us.

As the paramedics worked, the basement transformed from a place of near-death to a site of recovery. The urgency of the first responders filled the space with a flurry of activity, each movement and command pulling us further from the brink.

The reality of rescue grounded me back to the moment, the past horrors starting to recede like a tide going out as my adrenaline dumped. Relief seeped through the cracks of fear and pain for the first time in a very long time.

FORTY-FIVE
CASSIE
SIX MONTHS LATER

I HADN'T SEEN ROBIN SINCE I LEFT MINNESOTA. SHE was flying out to San Diego for a law enforcement conference, but she stopped by in Santa Fe, New Mexico, to spend the day visiting me.

I'd moved out there three months before. Bought a cute house, my first, with a breathtaking view of the Atalaya Mountains. After years of big-city living and after what happened back in Minnesota, I needed a change of pace. Slower living like some call it. I had been to New Mexico before for rehab and loved the state's chill vibe, stunning views, fresh air, and the low cost of living compared to Las Vegas and just about all of California.

The direct aftermath of what happened had been chaotic. I had to go through the whole process of being questioned and investigated, all over again. Different law enforcement agencies asked me the same questions about what happened starting back fifteen years ago with Mikey Dawson, over and over again.

Despite feeling exhausted, I persevered by smiling and sharing my story with cops from Big Plaine, agents from the

BCA, and even the FBI. Eventually, they cleared me of any wrongdoing including the death of Charlie Bell concluding Brent had killed him, and had framed me for it. Just like he had framed Charlie for his crimes as The Basher.

After all those investigations wrapped up, I was finally set free to move on with my life amongst the headlines that the real Basher was finally dead.

Robin went through the internal affairs wringer again but came out smelling like roses this time. Despite telling me off over the phone and hanging up on me, she reconsidered. She figured Brent might try to tidy things up further, starting by making sure that I vanished forever. Lucky for me, she showed up just in time. The BCA deemed Robin shooting Brent a clean shooting. The knife wound to her side missed the intercostal artery which passes between the necks of the first and second ribs and the pleura by mere centimeters, which saved her life.

Dealing with a second wave of media frenzy was just as bad as the first one, but eventually, they once again moved on to something new, leaving me alone. The only positive of the media exposure was being able to restore Charlie's name after Brent had framed him for his crimes. Big Plaine, especially the police department, could finally mourn one of their fallen heroes, whose name Brent had tarnished by making it seem like Charlie was The Basher. Charlie's family had insisted that he had bought the container and put it in the woods to turning it into a hunting and fishing shed. Brent planted evidence of his crimes as The Basher to make it seem like it was the nefarious lair of a serial killer. It's why he locked me up there before moving me to the basement. He wanted me to see it, to be locked in there, manipulating me into corroborating the storyline he was fabricating in order to frame Charlie.

I picked Robin up at the airport. It was great seeing her again, although when we were together, a lot of awful memories would come rushing back. I took her back to my place so she could see it.

"Your place is amazing," Robin said.

"Thanks, I really like it here."

"I kinda thought you would have moved back to Minnesota."

I shook my head. "Too many bad memories and I can no longer handle those freezing winters after a decade plus out west."

Honestly, beyond the notorious Minnesota winter weather, there was nothing left for me to get me to move back to my home state. The new owners of Mother's house finally could move in after everything that went down there. With Mother and Brent gone, I didn't have family left either. Jillian stopped talking to me. Like it was my fault her perfect doctor husband turned out to be a demented serial killer. I felt bad for my nephews. To them, Brent was just Dad. Not only did they lose their father, but when they got older, they would have to deal with the stigma that their father was The Basher. Hopefully, someday, Jillian would come around and she'd allow me to have a relationship with my nephews. But for now, I wasn't pushing it. I was giving her space to deal with the trauma of her high-society world blowing up on her. She not only lost her husband, but his high income. I had heard through the grapevine that she was putting their mansion on Lake Minnetonka up for sale.

"How are you doing with everything? To the world, Brent was The Basher, but he was your brother, after all," Robin asked.

"I'm actually good. I guess after years of mind games and what he put me through while pretending to be the nice brother. Let's just say I'm sleeping well at night."

"Good. I'm glad to hear that."

"How are you doing? You know. The shooting," I said, dancing around the fact that she had killed Brent.

"I'm okay. First time I had to use my gun in the line of duty, and it was a doozy. But I got some post-shooting therapy to deal with all that. I'll be fine." She reached into her purse and pulled out her cell phone. "I wanted to show you something," Robin said, changing the subject. She scrolled through her phone and handed it to me. "He's finally home, where he belongs."

I looked at the photograph. A headstone bore the inscription:

MICHAEL "MIKEY" DAWSON. FOREVER IN OUR HEARTS. FINALLY, AT HOME, FINALLY AT PEACE.

I felt the tears welling up in my eyes. The BCA was able to recover most of Mikey's remains from several lakes. And his family finally knew what happened to him, and now they had a gravesite where they could visit him.

I felt a great deal of guilt for not speaking up about what happened to Mikey for fifteen years. Robin had forgiven me, and we were now close, but her mother could not. "You should have said something," she had told me the one time I saw her after Brent was killed. "Even an anonymous note would have been nice, so we didn't spend fifteen years in the dark." It hurt, but I understood her anger towards me. I was such a coward.

After a couple hours catching up at my place, we went out for dinner at my favorite Mexican restaurant in Santa

Fe. Another reason I couldn't move back to Minnesota, they're lacking in good Mexican food places compared to back west.

We talked about our plans for the future while indulging in sizzling fajitas, tortillas, and chips dipped in gooey cheesy sauce. After our meal, we headed out to the airport so Robin could catch her flight.

AFTER DROPPING Robin off at the airport, I drove home. Robin was kind enough not to drink alcohol in front of me during dinner. But eating out was a struggle because it made me want to drink. An ice cold margarita to wash down my fajitas seemed blissful. I could feel my mouth dry up thinking about it.

As I drove home, I desperately wanted a drink, so I made a detour, finding the urge overwhelming. I pulled into a lot and parked in front of a nondescript, single-story building. I squeezed the steering wheel and exhaled deeply, hoping the urge would pass. But it didn't, so I got out of the car, licking my dried lips as I went inside.

I walked into a room filled with friendly faces and the familiar smell of strong coffee and sugary pastries. I took one of the empty chairs that had been arranged in a circle. When they got to me, I stood up and announced to the group: "Hi, my name is Cassie W. And I'm an alcoholic. It's been 168 days since I last had a drink."

THANK YOU FOR READING

If you enjoyed this book and want to stay updated on my latest releases, get exclusive insights, and receive sneak peeks, join my newsletter!

Simply sign up at www.alanpetersen.com/signup.

I hope the book was as thrilling for you to read as it was for me to write. Stories like this thrive on the feedback and support of readers like you.

If you enjoyed it, please consider leaving a rating and a review on Amazon. Your feedback helps me reach new readers.

Keep the pages turning!

Alan

ABOUT THE AUTHOR

Alan Petersen was born in Costa Rica and raised in both Costa Rica and Venezuela. He moved to Minnesota for college, where he met and married his college sweetheart. They now live in San Francisco, California, atop one of the city's famously steep streets, along with their feisty Chihuahua.

You can visit him online at his website: www. AlanPetersen.com

You can also tune into his podcast, "Meet the Thriller Author," where Alan interviews writers in the Mystery, Suspense, and Thriller genres. Notable guests include Dean Koontz, Lee Child, Freida McFadden, Walter Mosley, and many others. Discover these insightful conversations at ThrillerAuthors.com.

Connect with Alan...

ALSO BY ALAN PETERSEN

The Elijah Shaw-Alexandra Needham Crime Thriller Series

Gringo Gulch

The Past Never Dies

Always There

Under A Crimson Moon

The Pete Maddox Thriller Series

The Asset

She's Gone

Odd Jobs

Made in the USA
Las Vegas, NV
17 January 2025

16411684R00163